BELL, BOOK
& CANDLEMAS

ALSO BY JENNIFER DAVID HESSE

MIDSUMMER NIGHT'S MISCHIEF

BELL, BOOK & CANDLEMAS

JENNIFER
DAVID
HESSE

KENSINGTON PUBLISHING CORP.
http://www.kensingtonbooks.com

KENSINGTON BOOKS are published by

Kensington Publishing Corp.
119 West 40th Street
New York, NY 10018

All Kensington Titles, Imprints, and Distributed Lines are available at special quantity discounts for bulk purchases for sales promotions, premiums, fund-raising, and educational or institutional use. Special book excerpts or customized printings can also be created to fit specific needs. For details, write or phone the office of the Kensington special sales manager: Kensington Publishing Corp., 119 West 40th Street, New York, NY 10018, attn: Special Sales Department, Phone: 1-800-221-2647.

Kensington and the K logo Reg. U.S. Pat & TM Off.

ISBN-13: 978-1-4967-0494-8
ISBN-10: 1-4967-0494-0
First Kensington Mass Market Edition: January 2017

eISBN-13: 978-1-4967-0495-5
eISBN-10: 1-4967-0495-9
First Kensington Electronic Edition: January 2017

10 9 8 7 6 5 4 3 2 1

Printed in the United States of America

*For Grandpa Vic, whose sense of humor
and zest for life will be with me always.*

Chapter 1

The energy in the air was palpable. I could almost see it sparkling around the charred remains of the old bonfire. As I walked the perimeter of the stone-encircled clearing, I remembered the night I had learned about this place six months ago. My friend Farrah and I had stumbled upon a festive solstice celebration. We happened to be lost in the woods at the time, and Farrah kind of freaked out at the unexpected sight of a Pagan moon dance in the middle of the forest.

What Farrah didn't know was that her best friend—yours truly—was a Pagan, too. A Solitary Wiccan, to be precise. Farrah, my BFF since law school, would freak out all over again if she found out. I was sure of it.

Who would have thought? Sweet, levelheaded Keli Milanni: staid attorney, disciplined athlete, borderline yuppie. And witch.

We watched from the shadows that night a few months ago. Since then, I started coming back here on early weekend mornings, weather permitting.

It was a small, secluded glade, off the beaten track. I was able to access it through the open grounds of Briar Creek Cabins, which were nestled inside Shawnee National Forest about ten miles outside of town. Lucky for me, I always found it to be quiet and empty. Perfect for my own private nature-loving rituals.

Inhaling the crisp, woodsy air, I lifted my chin and closed my eyes. A light breeze rustled the bare branches above me, where watchful birds ruffled their feathers. The pure, familiar whistle of a cardinal called out like an old friend, and I opened my eyes in time to catch a glimpse of bright red flit through the trees. I didn't know why cardinals sang all year long. All I knew was it made me happy.

Smiling, I traced a circle in the earth four times, pausing to bow in reverence at each direction. When I faced east, I raised my arms to the sky in a literal sun salutation. I breathed deeply. Rooting my feet to the earth, I envisioned myself as one of the trees that surrounded me. I murmured a prayer of devotion and thanksgiving for Mother Earth.

Then I closed my eyes, my body humming, the earth and the air humming around me. For a few moments I let it fill me up, energize me. When I opened my eyes, the world shimmered around me in an aura of golden light. I exhaled, then slowly re-traced my steps around the circle to close the ritual.

Feeling light and peaceful, I walked over to the denim knapsack I had left next to an ancient white oak. I took out a small empty jar and used it to scoop some snow from the base of the tree. I would use it later, when it was time to say good-bye to winter. It wouldn't be long now before the earth showed signs of the life stirring beneath its surface. Candlemas was less than two weeks away.

After securely tucking the jar into a pocket in the knapsack, I took a swig from my water bottle. Then I grabbed a handful of candied almonds to munch as I wandered around the woods. Each time I came here, I explored a little more, being careful not to venture too far afield. It was easy to get lost in the thick forest.

I definitely felt a connection to this place. And more than a spiritual connection; I felt a familial one as well. I had a feeling my elusive Aunt Josephine's commune had been somewhere around here, once upon a time.

Aunt Josephine, my mom's older sister, was the black sheep of her Nebraskan family. When she was sixteen or seventeen, she ran off with a guy—"a long-haired Bohemian poet," according to the stories—who was a few years older than Josie. Her parents were livid. Josie left them a note but didn't contact them again for months. Apparently, she and her man were headed to a music festival out East somewhere but somehow wound up here in Southern Illinois instead. They made a home for some time, maybe a year or two. The next postcard Josie sent was from Florida, and the one after that was from New Orleans. Then the postcards stopped for a number of years, until out of the blue came one from another state. A few more years, yet another state. And so on.

. I had received some of the postcards myself, on my tenth, twentieth, and, most recently, my thirtieth birthday. It was nice to know she thought of me, even kept track of me—like a kindly fairy godmother, if only from afar. My aunt always intrigued me, even though I had never met her. Her story was part of the reason I chose to come to Edindale for law school, and then stayed here to live.

Lost in these daydreams, I almost dismissed the snap of a twig some ten yards off. At first, I assumed the nearby rustling I'd heard was a squirrel. Now I wasn't so sure. Senses on alert, I looked around, squinting through the thick stand of trees and shrubbery. In my meandering, I hadn't bothered to stay on a trail. Now I realized I was only a few feet away from a winding dirt path. And there was someone coming down it, toward me.

I ran to the nearest big tree and hid behind its massive trunk. While I wasn't skyclad—it was way too cold for nudity, not that I would remove my clothes outdoors anyway—I wasn't exactly dressed for company. In my faux fur moccasins and white velvet hooded cloak, I would certainly raise an eyebrow.

Cringing behind the tree, I stood as still as possible, though I did gently lift the silver pentagram hanging on a chain around my neck and drop it into my dress. Just in case.

As the sound of shuffling footsteps drew nearer, I rested my forehead against the tree and silently begged the Goddess to shield me in invisibility. I didn't dare peek around. If someone was to see me like this, I'd die of mortification. *Why did I have to leave this darn cloak on?* I was getting too complacent out here; I should never have been so bold.

After several quiet minutes, I realized the person must be gone. Breathing a sigh of relief, I tiptoed out of my hiding place and ventured over to the path. At first, it appeared deserted. I let my eyes follow the trail as it snaked through the woods, crossed a creek, and then disappeared around a bend. I was about to scurry back to my knapsack when something caught my eye in the distance. A blob of bright purple rose from the ground, then bobbed into the trees.

I shook my head and squinted. *What in the world?*

Without thinking, I followed the trail a few feet, trying to catch a glimpse of the purple thing again. Sure enough, there it was, flashing in and out among the brown trees. After a moment, it dawned on me what it was, and I had to clap my hand over my mouth to stifle a laugh.

It was just the hiker. He or she must have been bending over, and then stood up. The vivid purple was the person's jacket.

Here I thought I was dressed strangely.

The person was far enough away that I didn't worry about getting caught anymore. I couldn't even make out the color of their hair or any other features in the camouflage of the trees. Just that crazy purple coat, waving like a banner in a parade. As I watched, it moved farther away. Suddenly, it appeared to drop straight to the ground. Cocking my head, I waited a moment. Surely, it would reappear any time now.

When the purple jacket failed to materialize,

I clenched my jaw. Had the person fallen? Was he or she hurt?

I ran down the trail toward the spot where the blur had dropped out of sight. As I got closer, I realized the person must have left the path. Whereas the trail veered left, the purple jacket had been weaving among the trees to the right.

I crisscrossed the area for several minutes, even calling out twice. I was sure this was the spot I had last seen a flash of purple. But there was no one there.

Whoever it was had completely disappeared.

Two days later, I had pretty much forgotten my little Saturday morning adventure in the woods. It occurred to me that the purple-clad hiker had probably spotted me—a suspicious, fur-footed woman in a ghostly-white riding hood—and disappeared on purpose. Who could blame them? I would have to be more discreet next time.

As I dressed for work Monday morning, I selected the polar opposite of my Goddess-worship garb: a tailored navy business suit with a straight knee-length skirt and matching blue pumps. The shoes were stylish, but comfy enough for walking—which was important, as I liked to walk to the office every chance I got. With the recent trend of mild temperatures, most of the snow had melted away. All I needed was my trench coat and shoulder bag, and I was ready for the day.

It was only a few blocks to the downtown four-story office building that housed Olsen, Sykes, and Rafferty, LLP. On the way, I strolled through well-kept residential neighborhoods, cut across a rambling public park, and passed various shops and offices until I reached Courthouse Square. In the center of the square, set off on all sides by an open grassy space lined with a smattering of benches, was the courthouse, an impressive, one-hundred-plus-year-old limestone structure fashioned in the Beaux Arts style. Complete with arched entryways, two-story Doric columns, and a center dome with a clock tower, the Edin County Courthouse was a historical landmark and local treasure. It was also the place I routinely filed legal documents and represented clients at court hearings.

Today, however, I didn't even glance at the iconic building. My attention was focused across the street where I noticed a crowd gathering toward the end of the block. Curious, I turned left at the intersection, instead of continuing down the avenue to my office, and wandered over to see what was going on. As I approached the throng, I noticed two police cars double-parked along the curb.

Maybe someone broke into the art gallery? Or the store selling designer handbags? I recalled hearing that the handbag store had been robbed about a month ago or so.

My heart sank as I realized it was the shop between the gallery and the handbag store that was cordoned off by yellow crime scene tape. Squeezing my way through a group of onlookers, I finally glimpsed the cause of all the staring and chatter around me. Two jagged gashes marred the storefront window of Moonstone Treasures, one on each side of the front door. Worse, though, was the angry black scrawl spray painted above the hole in the window. It was a single word in all caps, like a shouted accusation:

WITCH.

I froze at the sight, eyes widening. Then I quickly scanned the area for Mila Douglas, the shop's owner, and exhaled in relief when I saw her. She seemed to be okay, if a little vulnerable, standing there hugging her slender arms. Already a petite woman, Mila appeared fragile in her ballet flats, lavender skinny pants, and black turtleneck sweater. Her cropped raven shag was pulled back from her face with a girlish headband. She and her young assistant, Catrina, were speaking to a police officer near the entrance of the store. While Catrina gesticulated excitedly, speaking quickly and pointing to the officer's notepad, Mila cast a worried eye at the shards of broken glass strewn in front of her store.

Part gift shop, part psychic boutique, Moonstone Treasures was usually a welcoming place. It was a delightful destination that attracted both tourists and townies. Come in for an artsy greeting card, stay for a fun palm reading. Plus, they had an impressive collection of esoteric books and tools. As for me, I had been coming here on the sly ever since the shop opened four years ago, as soon as I discovered it carried Wiccan supplies. I couldn't believe someone would vandalize Moonstone.

"I always knew that place was bad news."

I swung around to find the source of the snide comment. A middle-aged couple walked past me, the plump woman shaking her salt-and-pepper curls self-righteously, the tall, pinched-face man staring pointedly at the storefront, his eyes glistening with great interest. My eyebrows narrowed as I watched them stalk away. I had half a mind to rush after them to defend Mila.

Before I could do anything, I felt a tap on my shoulder. When I turned, a flash went off in my face. *What the—?* Blinking, I took a step back and thrust my palm outward to block any further snapshots. As my vision cleared, the camera lowered and I recognized the smiling, dark-eyed photographer.

"Sorry about that," he said. "I forgot the flash was on."

"Wes! What are you doing here?"

"Working." He raised the camera hanging from the strap around his neck and pointed to the press ID clipped to the pocket of his wool peacoat. I noticed his usual scruffy jawline now sported a goatee, while his unruly dark hair peeked out from the edges of a gray knit cap.

I squinted at the ID. "You work for the *Edindale Gazette*?"

He nodded. "Around four months now."

Four months. About the length of time since he'd last called me. I shook my head, conflicted. On one hand, there was no denying the excited flutter I felt every time I found myself within arms' reach of Wesley Callahan. There was definite chemistry here, and I was 99.9 percent sure Wes experienced it, too. Since we first met last summer, I felt a growing connection between us. At a minimum, we always had fun together. So, what was the problem?

I thought back to our last date. After dinner and a play, we had stopped in at the Loose Rock, a fun nightclub owned by a mutual friend of ours. It was over drinks that the conversation had turned to my best bud, Farrah, and her puppy dog of a boyfriend, Jake. Jake wanted to get married, while Farrah made it clear she wasn't ready to settle down.

"Good ol' Jake. He seems to have unlimited patience," I had commented, idly swirling the stirrer in my cocktail.

"Well, Farrah's got nothing to apologize for," Wes had said. "There's nothing wrong with dating around. People have multiple friends, right? I mean, until you're married or engaged, dating around makes the most sense."

I stopped stirring my drink and eyed Wes carefully. "Um, yeah. Of course. I guess. As long as both parties are honest about it."

Wes took a drink and gazed around the room, evidently not feeling a need to respond. I wasn't ready to let the conversation go just yet.

"Anyway, Farrah and Jake *are* exclusive when they're together. They've had their breakup phases in the past, but not lately. Farrah doesn't necessarily want to see other people. She just doesn't want to be a wife right now. She likes her independence."

"Farrah's cool," Wes said. "She knows what she wants, and she's true to herself. Jake should stop pushing the issue, before he ends up pushing her away."

Hmm. I didn't say anything more on the subject, but Wes's comments had rubbed me the wrong way. He had met Farrah, through me, only a few weeks prior, yet he talked like he knew her better than I did.

Or maybe he wasn't really talking about Farrah. Maybe he was talking about himself.

The rest of the date was pleasant enough, but we were both ready to call it a night after finishing our drinks. When Wes dropped me off at my town house, he kissed me good night and said he'd call me.

A week passed—the longest we'd gone without at least speaking on the phone. So, I shot him a text, asking if he wanted to meet for happy hour when I got off work. He replied that he was tied up and would get back to me later. "Later" never arrived.

Yet, now, months later, standing on the street in the midst of the crowd around Moonstone Treasures, Wes grinned at me like he always did, as if nothing had changed. His eyes flicked over my figure, and he playfully tugged on the lapel of my jacket.

"Look at you, all conservative corporate businesswoman. You look really nice."

I allowed a small smile in return. "Thanks. I need to get to work, but I wondered about all this commotion."

"Just a teenager's prank, probably."

"How could this happen with a police station right down the street?"

Wes shrugged. "It's pretty dead around here between last call at the bars and those predawn hours when some poor saps have to get up and make the doughnuts. It probably happened shortly after the three A.M. shift change when the on-duty cops were all at roll call."

"That doesn't give me a lot of confidence in our police force," I commented.

"Right," Wes said, with a wry grin. "Especially when they still haven't made an arrest in any of those break-ins that happened a few weeks ago."

I gazed down the street, trying to recall what I had read about those earlier burglaries.

"Anyway," Wes continued, "this is different. From what I heard, there was no cash in the store, and nothing appears to be missing. There's just some damaged merchandise—and, of course, the lovely graffiti." He inclined his head toward the front of the shop, where the police officer was now shooing the spectators away. There was no sign of Mila and Catrina. They had probably gone in to start cleaning up.

I would have liked to go help, but that would seem too strange. After all, why should I have any special interest in a New Age gift shop? Why would I be friendly enough with the "psychic" shopkeeper to help clean her store?

Why indeed?

As I said good-bye to Wes and headed to my office, I couldn't shake a feeling of uneasiness about the whole scene.

Chapter 2

After checking messages, reviewing my calendar, and planning my agenda for the day, I grabbed a notebook and pen and walked down the hall to the corner office suite of Beverly Olsen, senior partner. Having just returned from a two-week cruise, Beverly called a special meeting of all the lawyers—three partners and five associates in all—to bring her up to speed on everyone's projects.

I entered Beverly's lounge—a spacious area outfitted like a sitting room with upholstered seating, fresh flowers on side tables, and snacks on the coffee table—and joined the other attorneys in welcoming Beverly back from her vacation. She stood in front of the decorative fireplace, looking radiant and relaxed even in a power suit. Her salon-styled auburn hair was streaked with artful golden highlights, and her smiling face was softly suntanned.

As we chatted, I noticed something new on the mantel behind her. Seeing my stare, she turned around and picked up the item, which appeared to be a long curved animal horn mounted on a wooden base. With a sparkle in her eye, she held up the brownish black piece in two hands for all to see. "What do you think?"

I struggled to keep a neutral face. "Um, is that a souvenir from your trip?"

She shook her head. "This was a belated Christmas gift from Edgar. I saw him at a party he hosted last night."

We all knew who Edgar was: Edgar Harrison, prominent businessman and top client at our firm. Among other ventures, he owned a riverboat casino, a hotel, and a number of properties around town. He was also a longtime family friend of Beverly's.

"It's marvelous, isn't it?" Beverly went on.

"Where did it come from?" I asked. "I mean, is it a rhino horn?"

"What's the matter, Ms. Milanni? Does the objet d'art offend you as a vegan?"

Offend me as a vegan? No, it offends me as a human being.

I looked over at the source of the smarmy voice: Crenshaw Davenport III, fellow associate and perpetual thorn in my side. From his perfectly pressed pants and perfectly trimmed beard, to his perfect little side-part, he was a perfect pain in my butt. Last summer, a couple of incidents led me to believe he harbored a crush on me. As obnoxious as he was, I wasn't so sure anymore.

With everyone looking expectantly at me, I shrugged one shoulder. "I was just thinking it might be illegal. I'm pretty sure rhinos are endangered."

Beverly scoffed. "Oh, I highly doubt Edgar would

have something illegal, at least not knowingly. To be safe, why don't you do some research, Keli? Prepare a memo on wildlife import law."

I nodded, but Beverly had already turned to re-place the unpleasant thing. Everyone found seats and we began the meeting, leaving me to stew inwardly about this new homework—an assignment I would somehow have to fit in around my normal billable hours. *Terrific.*

After the other partners updated Beverly on their cases, it was my turn for the spotlight. That is, it would have been my turn by virtue of my seat next to the last person who had spoken. Wasn't it common courtesy to take turns, going around a room in order? Apparently, Crenshaw didn't think so. I had barely opened my mouth when his amplified voice filled the air.

"Beverly, you will be happy to know that, whereas you had sunny skies, I produced rain, as it were. In your absence, I picked up a new client."

Well done, brownnoser. I sat back in my seat and listened to Crenshaw's oratory for the next ten minutes, doing my best to appear interested. As he finally appeared to wind down, I readied myself to jump in next. Crenshaw was still talking when there was a tap at the door. Julie, our young receptionist, poked her head in and scanned the room above her trendy horn-rimmed eyeglasses. Her eyes fell on me.

"Keli, could you come here a minute, please?"

"What is it?" I asked.

"There's someone here to see you. Could you please come up front?"

I frowned. "I don't have any appointments this morning. Tell them I'm in a meeting, and they're welcome to wait or come back later."

"Um, I really think you should come now. She's making the other clients uncomfortable."

"She?"

The sound of Beverly's impatient throat-clearing spurred me to hop out of my seat. "Excuse me," I said, nodding at the inquisitive group of lawyers staring at me. I followed Julie to the lobby and stopped short when I saw who she was talking about.

With balled fists and flashing eyes, Catrina, the store clerk from Moonstone Treasures, paced like a tiger in front of Julie's walnut reception desk. I could almost see the energy crackling around her. She seemed oblivious to the gray-haired couple shrinking into the far corner of the brown leather sofa. They were clearly repulsed at the inch-wide wooden rings stretching the tissue of Catrina's earlobes. Or maybe it was the shaved half of her punk hairstyle that bothered them. On second thought, it might have been her ripped sweatshirt featuring the words "Heterosexually Challenged."

"Trina!" I said. "What's up? Is everything okay?"

"Catrina," she said automatically. "And, no, everything's not okay. Somebody is viciously attacking Mila, and it has to stop."

I glanced at the gray-haired couple, offering them a reassuring smile, and ushered Catrina back to my office. I had known Catrina for a few months, since meeting her and her girlfriend, Andi, at Mila's shop. My first impression was that Catrina was intensely feminist, sweet and likeable. She went by

"Trina" then and wore her dishwater blond hair in barrettes. Somewhere along the way, she began to change her image, becoming edgier and more hard core. I wasn't sure if she was still with Andi.

"Have a seat," I said, shutting my office door. "Is Mila okay? I saw the store this morning, so I know what happened."

"You don't know the half of it," she said. "Someone has been harassing Mila, threatening her, trying to drive her out of business. And it's somebody who obviously hates Wiccans. That's why they're targeting Mila. That makes this a hate crime!"

Whoa. Catrina was talking a mile a minute. Before I could think of a response, she continued.

"You should see the notes Mila received! Full of anti-Wiccan bigotry and fundamentalist bullshit. It's getting worse and worse. First it was private, but now it's public. The police are worthless, and Mila's at her wits' end. Keli, Mila needs you. Moonstone needs you. The whole Wiccan community needs you. You have to help!"

I opened my mouth but couldn't seem to form any words. As Catrina's intense gaze bore a hole through me, I finally found my voice. "Catrina, I'm not sure how I can help."

That set her off again.

"This is not only property damage and harassment we're talking about here— it's a violation of our constitutional rights! Mila needs legal representation. She needs justice. We also need to raise awareness about this, about the fact that witches are still being persecuted even in this day and age."

I chewed my lip and looked at Catrina. I was

conflicted. What she was saying was pretty disturbing, and I really was concerned about Mila. Mila had been like a big sister to me, or at least a hip aunt, always there to listen and offer helpful advice. With Farrah, I could gossip endlessly about men, but with Mila I could obsess over the love spell I'd cast shortly before I met Wes. Farrah and I could gab about music and books and politics. But with Mila, I could discuss symbolic dreams, signs from the Goddess, lunar phases, and herbal magic.

On the other hand, I was inwardly recoiling at Catrina's suggestion about raising public awareness. For one thing, my firm intentionally avoided controversy and politics. Discretion is what most clients expected of us.

Then there was also the small matter of protecting my secret Wiccan identity.

The phone on my desk rang, reminding me I had real clients to see that day. I let the call go to voicemail and took a deep breath before speaking.

"Catrina, I hear what you're saying, and I would like to help. Really, I would. But, this is a criminal matter. You should just let the police conduct their investigation. Besides, until the perpetrator is identified, we have no one to sue."

Catrina looked as if she wanted to keep arguing, but then thought better of it. She nodded. "I'll come back tomorrow."

Not if I can help it. I needed to speak to Mila. I wondered if she even knew her employee had come to me. Maybe Mila could keep Catrina from showing up at my office again. I couldn't have the girl frightening clients and drawing unwanted attention to myself.

As it happened, the day flew by, giving me no chance to skip out. After working straight through lunch, I looked up to see that it was now dinner-time. I stood up from my desk, stretched, and shut off my computer. After grabbing my purse, I flicked off my light and headed down the hall—only to run smack-dab into Crenshaw, who was trying to pull on his suit coat and pocket his keys at the same time, all while looking over his shoulder toward Beverly's office.

"Oh, pardon me!" he exclaimed.

Startled, I could only laugh.

"I must run," he said. "A thousand apologies."

I stared as Crenshaw hurried away. Smelling rose perfume, I turned to see Pammy Sullivan waft out of her office next. With smooth ash-blond waves, raspberry-red lips, and classic white pearls, Pammy today resembled a plus-size Grace Kelly, circa 1980. I smiled at her as she walked up to me.

"Oh, Keli. I'm glad I ran into you. After you left the meeting this morning, we talked about the Groundhog Festival. We're sponsoring a float in the parade, and I'm collecting donations. It's less than two weeks away, so if you can bring in your contribution tomorrow that would be great."

"Sure, no problem. Gosh, is it really less than two weeks away? I'm supposed to be doing the 10K, and I don't feel a bit ready."

Pammy waved away my concern. "Oh, I'm sure

you have nothing to worry about. You're in such great shape. Did you hear Rhett Shelby is performing at the festival?"

"Who?"

"Rhett Shelby, the big country music star?"

I shook my head. I had a hard time keeping up with popular music trends, country or otherwise. My tastes ran to the more indie and eclectic.

"This festival is the first big event since Tish Holiday took over as the city's tourism director. It seems like she really knows how to draw a crowd."

"Mmm." Pammy's chatter was wearing me out. My mind had gone back to the 10K I had committed to running with Farrah. When was I going to find time to train? Over the summer, when we signed up, I had no problem hitting the trail just about every evening. Then work picked up, especially when I was forced to take on half the caseload of a former associate who had abruptly left the job. But that was another story.

After saying good night to Pammy, I walked out into the cool, dark evening and headed toward Mila's shop. It wasn't yet 7:00 P.M., so the shop should have been open. By the light of the street lamps, I saw that the windows had been repaired and the graffiti removed, but the sign on the door said CLOSED. Cupping my hands around my eyes, I peered through the glass to see if perhaps there was a light on in the back room. All appeared dark.

For the heck of it, I walked around the side of the building to the narrow alley, where I knew Mila usually parked. There were a couple parking spots next to the steel door that served as Moonstone's delivery entrance. The spaces were empty.

Standing by the Dumpster, I tried to decide what to do next. I had only ever interacted with Mila at her shop. I didn't know her phone number or her home address. It seemed strange, now that I thought about it.

I returned to the front of the shop to take one last look before walking home. Whoever Mila hired to do the repairs had done a good job. There was no trace of the earlier destruction. I sighed, remembering Catrina's tirade, and turned to cross the street, when a glint of something in the gutter caught my eye. On the boulevard near the curb, the slush was littered and dirty—likely from the morning crowd. Leaning over to pick up the shiny object that was pressed into the slush, I discovered it was the broken face of a small clock. The metal arrow-shaped hands were bent, but the whole face was intact. I flipped it over and realized it must have popped out of some sort of casing, leaving the clockworks behind.

Turning back to the dark shop, I wondered if the clock had been among the damaged merchandise Wes had mentioned. I slipped the piece in my coat pocket, promising myself to ask Mila. That is, if I could ever seem to catch up to her.

Chapter 3

A friend in need is a friend indeed. A friend in need is a friend indeed. . . .

All evening, the saying kept going through my head. On my way home from work, I had passed an older gentleman in a baggy suit feeding pigeons from a bench by the courthouse. He had smiled happily, muttering to his feathered friends. The words that caught my attention naturally made me think of Mila. What kind of friend was I, not to check in on her earlier today?

After a late supper of spinach salad and spiced quinoa with chickpeas, I curled up on the couch with my laptop and pulled up the website for Moonstone Treasures. On the "Contact" page, I sent Mila a message asking her to give me a ring. That done, I browsed on the Internet until I found myself on the homepage of the *Edindale Gazette*, searching for photos by Wesley Callahan.

Why had he stopped calling me? Was he really not into me? I began to question whether I had been mistaken about the signals I'd picked up from the man. We'd always had a great time together. The attraction was unmistakable. Wasn't it?

The buzz of my cell phone made me jump. I reached over to grab it from an end table. It was an unfamiliar local number, but somehow I still knew who it was.

"Hello? Mila?"

"Hi, Keli. I hope it's not too late."

"Not at all. I'm glad you got my e-mail."

"Catrina set it up so that she gets alerts every time there's a message sent through the Moonstone website. She's here now, so she gave me your number."

Catrina. Of course. So much for circumventing the punky little pit bull.

"Mila, are you okay? I just wanted to check in on you, and see if . . . if there's anything you need." I hesitated slightly, careful not to offer something I couldn't deliver.

"I'm fine, just fine. Circle is here. We just finished our meeting. My husband is out of town this week—construction job near St. Louis. I convinced him there was no need to come home. So, the ladies stayed late tonight. They didn't think I should be alone. It's so silly. We just finished, and—" She faltered, as if aware she was beginning to babble.

"Mila, if you're not too tired, I'd like to stop by. Where do you live?"

She gave me her address without any argument, in spite of the late hour. By the time I threw on my coat and drove the ten blocks to her house, it was after 10:30.

Mila lived in a well-kept subdivision on the edge

of town, bordering a patch of privately owned woods. I parked on the street in front of her red-brick bungalow and walked up the lighted path to her front door. No sooner had I pressed the door-bell than the door swung open. Catrina ushered me inside, eyes flashing excitedly. The dishwater-blond hair on the unshaven half of her head stuck out as if she'd been twisting it worriedly.

"You've made the right decision," she said. "I knew I could count on you."

"Oh, I didn't—"

There was no point arguing. Catrina had turned her back, motioning me to follow her through the foyer and into the living room. When I walked through the arched entryway into the cozy, candle-lit space, I saw Mila sitting on a cushy green sofa next to a young redheaded woman I was surprised to see. I recognized her from my visit to the English department at South Central Illinois University last summer. Both women looked up and smiled at me, and Mila patted the seat next to her.

"Professor Eisenberry," I said, as I walked over to join them. "I didn't know you were in Mila's . . . group." As a Solitary Wiccan, I wasn't entirely comfortable with the idea of joining a coven. Mila had tried several times to coax me into attending a gathering of the sisterhood she called "Magic Circle." Now it seemed she almost had her wish, though the meeting was over and everyone else had left.

"Call me Max," the professor said warmly. "Small world, isn't it? I think it's so excellent that you're taking an interest in Mila's situation. I told everyone in Circle how you caught a thief and recovered that stolen Shakespeare Folio last year."

I sighed and looked closely at Mila. Her features were drawn and the worry was evident behind her brave smile. She squeezed my hand. "I guess I need to work on my protection charms, huh?"

Just like that, my hesitation fell away. I switched into investigator mode.

"Mila, who do you think vandalized your shop?"

She shook her head and shrugged her shoulders. Catrina, perched on a love seat adjacent to the sofa, reached for a small sheaf of papers on the coffee table. "It was whoever left these notes," she said, waving the papers in front of her before handing them to me.

There were half a dozen sheets of standard 8 x 10 printer paper, creased in the middle as if they had been folded in half. At first glance, they all seemed to say the same thing: "Close the shop, witch." The words were handwritten, apparently with a Sharpie, in large, neat letters in the center of each sheet of paper.

"Where did you find these?" I asked. "And when?"

"Various places," said Mila. "Once every few days for the past couple weeks or so. A few times, I found the notes on the floor of the shop, just inside the front door. A couple times there was one under the windshield wipers of my car. Today there was one in my mailbox." She glanced at the front door and shuddered. Max patted Mila's arm, then reached forward to pour hot tea from a carafe on the coffee table. I accepted a cup and inhaled the earthy scent of chamomile.

Looking at the papers again, I noticed there was something written in smaller letters beneath some of the messages. Squinting in the candlelight, I held a sheet up in front of me. "Is this a Bible reference?" I asked.

"You bet," said Catrina. "Turn over the page. I looked it up on the Internet."

I flipped the top sheet over and saw some writing in pencil. "You wrote this?" I said, looking at Catrina.

"Yeah, read it. It's totally creepy."

I frowned, as much from the notes as from the fact that Catrina had tampered with the evidence. But as I read her slanted handwriting, I had to agree with her about the creep factor:

Micah 5:11-12—I will tear down your walls and demolish your defenses. I will destroy your witchcraft and you will no longer cast spells.

I turned over a second sheet and read:

Deuteronomy 18:10, 12—Let no one be found among you who sacrifices their son or daughter in the fire, who practices divination or sorcery, interprets omens, engages in witchcraft . . . For all that do these things are an abomination unto the Lord: and because of these abominations the Lord thy God doth drive them out from before thee.

A couple other notes had different citations. I read one out loud. "'MM, Pt. I, Q. XVII.' What does that mean?"

"Catrina figured it out," said Mila.

Catrina bounced in her seat. "Yeah," she said. "It refers to the *Malleus Maleficarum*."

"'The Malleus' what?"

"Maleficarum. Haven't you heard of it? It was the definitive witch-hunter handbook in medieval Europe. It basically propagated the notion that witchcraft is evil. It sparked the hysteria that led to the loss of a lot of innocent blood. Especially that of women."

"Oh, yeah. I do recall reading about that before." I turned the paper over and read Catrina's writing again:

> *The Malleus Maleficarum, Part I, Question XVII.*
> *So heinous are the crimes of witches that they even*
> *exceed the sins and the fall of the bad Angels; and*
> *if this is true as to their guilt, how should it not*
> *also be true of their punishments in hell?*

I found myself shivering as I looked at Mila with renewed sympathy. The chosen quotations sounded like threats and certainly lent credence to Catrina's theory that the vandalism was a hate crime.

Catrina read my thoughts. "You see? We've got a witch-hater on the loose. A cowardly, mean, bigoted witch-hater. This is just like burning a cross on an African American's front yard, or painting a swastika on a Jewish person's home!"

"Well . . . " I couldn't quite match Catrina's fervor, but I was becoming increasingly alarmed about the situation. I turned to Mila. "Did you show these notes to the police?"

"No." Mila looked down at her hands. "Frankly, I

didn't expect it to go this far. I thought I could handle it on my own."

I looked at the notes again and wondered what I would have done in Mila's position. Unlike me, Mila was open about her Wiccan faith. But she was still a businesswoman. I could understand how she wouldn't want to drum up any negative publicity.

"Okay," I said. "So, who do you think is doing this? Has anyone ever said something to you in person? Or have you heard of anyone speaking out against the shop?"

Mila shook her head. "Not lately. When I first started the business years ago, there was a letter to the editor opposing the shop on moral grounds. At the time, there was nothing in the city ordinances to prevent the shop from opening. Moonstone Treasures is primarily a retail shop, with the tarot and palm readings offered as 'entertainment.' Later, the zoning code was changed to restrict fortune-telling even further, but that didn't affect me."

Max perked up, slapping her knee. "Oh! There was also that church group that made a big deal about Halloween a couple years ago. They spoke out against the shop, too, didn't they? I remember there was a church-lady type trying to get people to sign a petition."

Catrina crossed her arms. "I only moved here last year, but I do remember a guy like that last Samhain. He was like a reverend, or a brother, or something. He handed out flyers in front of the shop, spewing nonsense, calling Halloween 'the devil's holiday.' I can't believe I forgot about that!"

"Nothing ever came of it," said Mila.

"There's been nothing more recently?" I pressed. "Maybe just before or around the time the notes began?"

Mila shook her head again, while Max propped her chin in her hand and scrunched her face in thought. Catrina stood up and paced around the living room. Mila's cat, a velvety gray Chartreux, sauntered into the room, investigated my feet, then jumped into Mila's lap.

"This is Drishti," Mila told me. "You're not allergic, are you?"

"No," I said. "She's a beauty."

We fell silent again, and I stared at the dancing flame of a pillar candle in the center of the coffee table and considered the threatening notes. It sure seemed as if someone was bent on hurting Mila, at least emotionally. And perhaps financially.

"No one else has come out and directly asked you to close up and leave?" I asked.

"Not unless you count Yvette Prime," said Mila.

"Yvette Prime, the real estate agent?"

"Mm-hmm. She stops by now and then, maybe every other month or so, asking if I'm interested in selling. She says she has a client who wants to buy the shop. I once asked her who the client is, but she wouldn't say."

"When was the last time she came by?"

"Oh, several weeks ago, I think. Before the notes started."

Max stifled a yawn and tugged thoughtfully on a frizzy lock of copper hair. "Yvette Prime doesn't seem the type to leave creepy anonymous notes."

"What about that cruise director lady?" Catrina piped up.

"Tourism director," Mila corrected.

"You mean Tish Holiday?" said Max.

"Yeah," said Catrina, on her feet again. "She banned Mila from the Groundhog Festival. I'd call that an enemy action."

"She didn't ban me—"

"She refused to let Moonstone have a table at the courthouse luncheon!"

"Well, I missed the deadline. At least, that's what she told me. . . . "

Max stood up and stretched. "Steve's going to be wondering what happened to me. He's great with Janie, but she's teething again."

"Oh, go on home!" said Mila, moving Drishti off her lap so she could stand next to Max. "I'm just fine. Thank you so much for staying late, but get on home now."

Catrina gathered the teacups and took the tray to the kitchen, while Max said her good-byes and left. Standing in the front hall, Mila told me I could leave, too.

"But, first," she said, "I have something for you."

She turned to a small bookcase and retrieved something from a ceramic bowl.

"It's amethyst," she said, handing me a beautiful deep purple crystal.

"It's lovely," I said, holding the crystal up to the light. "But why?"

"I know how busy you've been at work," Mila said. "Amethyst is good for relieving stress, as well as for clearing the mind."

"This is so thoughtful," I said, carefully slipping the crystal into an inner pocket of my purse.

Mila squeezed my hand. "It was sweet of you to come over so late and help with this . . . craziness." She smiled, but the smile dropped away as worry crept into her eyes again. "It's just the weirdest thing. And, unfortunately, I'm afraid it's going to get worse before it gets better."

"What do you mean?"

"I've been consulting the tarot. No matter which way you look at it, it's clear there's more darkness yet to come. Darkness, chaos, and loss."

When I returned home from Mila's house, it was almost midnight. I knew I should go to bed, but my mind was too preoccupied to sleep. I stood at the sliding glass doors overlooking my backyard and stared up at the waxing gibbous moon. The swollen lunar curve, only a few days from being full, called to mind the final stages of pregnancy. The moon was like a mother about to give birth.

This made me think of the upcoming Pagan holiday, Candlemas. It was also known as "Imbolc," meaning "in the belly" or "ewe's milk." It might still feel like the dead of winter, but change was on its way. That made this a good time to think about what I wanted to grow in my own life. An image of Wes flashed before my mind's eye.

I knew exactly what I wanted.

Come to think of it, there was no need to wait for Candlemas. I walked over to a kitchen drawer and withdrew a package of white birthday candles and a book of matches. From a corner cabinet, I grabbed a bottle of grapeseed oil and a clay bowl. Then I sat down at my kitchen table, centered myself, and took a deep breath. I opened the bottle of oil, dabbed some on my finger, and rubbed it along the side of the candle—from the bottom up to the center and then from the top down to the center. In this way, I charged the candle with my own psychic energy.

I liked using birthday candles for quick, simple rituals. They were specially made for wishing. As I prepared to strike a match, I thought about my desire: to reconnect with Wes—to rekindle our romance.

A scratch at the window made me jump. The wind howled, and I realized it was only a tree branch scraping across the windowpane. I let out a breath and laughed. I would have to call someone to come out and trim the tree.

Turning my attention back to the small candle, I once again thought about my intention. Now, though, instead of seeing Wes, I visualized Mila's worried face. Maybe it was the adrenaline surge from being startled, but I suddenly realized there was something more pressing right now than my love life.

Mila had said darkness was coming. If I could help counteract it, even a little bit, that's what I wanted to do.

I lit the candle and held it up in front of me. As I stared at the fluttering flame, I visualized Mila wrapped in a protective cloak of white light. I held this wish as the candle burned down. When the fire neared my fingertips, I placed the candle in the clay bowl and let it burn itself out. I followed the last wisp of smoke until it disappeared in the air before me.

Blessed be.

Chapter 4

The next morning, I arrived at my office building extra early so I could get in a full day's work and still leave in time to go for a run with Farrah. Of course, I wasn't alone. Crenshaw stood in the downstairs lobby conversing with a nice-looking couple in their upper forties dressed in matching fur-trimmed parkas and expensive-looking leather boots. As I walked toward the elevators, I could tell Crenshaw was purposefully avoiding my eyes. However, the couple turned my way with bright smiles, leaving him no choice but to acknowledge my presence.

"Good morning," the man said, his eyes twinkling. "You must be another lawyer to get here this early."

"Good morning," I said and returned his smile.

With a telltale twitch of the eye, Crenshaw nodded his head at me. "Keli," he said. "This is Danielle and Marco Thomison. Mr. and Mrs. Thomison, this is my colleague, Ms. Keli Milanni."

"How do you do," the couple said in unison.

They laughed. Danielle flashed pretty dimples and tilted her head. "We—"

"Were just heading out to get coffee," Crenshaw interrupted. "I'll see you later, Keli."

With that, he steered the couple toward the exit, leaving me to shake my head once again at his strangeness. Crenshaw needed some serious work on his social skills.

Upstairs, the reception area was dark, but I could hear a few other attorneys quietly churning away at their caseloads behind closed doors. Like me, they wanted to impress the partners and clock in as many billable hours as humanly possible in a twenty-four-hour period.

After making myself some ginger tea, I sat down at my computer and stared out the window at the office buildings across the street. I couldn't stop thinking about Mila's problem.

Based on the Bible references, the harassment certainly seemed to be motivated by someone's misguided religious views, along with a warped sense of right and wrong. Dark threats and vandalism didn't strike me as being very Christian-like. I may have left the church of my upbringing long ago, but I still knew Jesus was all about forgiveness and tolerance. Whoever was trying to scare Mila was definitely not representing a peaceful and loving God.

Turning to my computer, I clicked open a browser and typed "Edindale Gazette archives." Mila had mentioned there was a letter to the editor opposing her shop when she first opened up. From earlier conversations, I recalled her saying she had purposely started her business venture around the

Wiccan sabbat Ostara, which coincides with the spring equinox and represents growth, prosperity, and all things new.

It didn't take me long to find all the old editions of the paper for the month of March from four years earlier. But I soon figured out that the archives didn't include the opinion pages. *Drat.* I would have to go to the library or the newspaper office and look through each paper by hand.

Or else . . . I could seek assistance from someone who just happened to work for the newspaper.

Before I could change my mind, I grabbed my phone and dialed Wes's number. He picked up after the second ring.

"Keli Milanni! What's up?"

"Hey, Wes. I have a favor to ask. I need to locate a physical copy of a newspaper from a few years ago."

I explained what I was looking for and crossed my fingers. "Is that something you can do?"

"Sure, I think so. When do you need it?"

"Well, the sooner the better. Any chance you can find it this morning and meet me for lunch or coffee later today?"

"Uh, hang on."

Tapping my fingernails on my desk, I tried to ignore my rapidly beating heart as I waited for Wes's response. After about a minute, he came back on.

"All right, sorry about that. I have an assignment I was supposed to do later this morning, but I just pushed it up. I can meet you at noon. How about that vegan bakery you like, the one with the café?"

"Perfect," I said, grinning in spite of myself. "See you then."

I hung up feeling a familiar rush of anticipation at the prospect of seeing Wes. It was just like him to suggest the vegan bakery. He wasn't a vegetarian, yet he always remembered my dietary preferences. Even better, he didn't make a big deal out of it.

The rest of the morning flew by as I fielded phone calls, drafted letters, and negotiated a settlement agreement. When I looked up and realized it was five minutes before 12:00, I grabbed my jacket, darted out of the office, and half ran the three blocks to the Good Karma Bakery. As I approached the entrance, the beep of a car horn caused me to look over my shoulder.

"Hey!" yelled the driver, a bright-eyed blonde with a wide, ready smile. She pulled over to the curb and waved me over. I grinned at my best friend and jogged over to her.

"What are you doing, Farrah? Stopping traffic?"

"Don't I always?" she said, wrinkling her nose at me. "I'm heading to an expo at the Harrison Hotel. I saw you galloping down the sidewalk and had to stop you. You run funny in heels."

"You would, too, lady! Especially if you were late for a lunch date with a certain 'rock star,'" I said, using the nickname we used for Wes.

"Oh! Well, why didn't you say so? Carry on, groupie. Just be sure to change your shoes before our run tonight."

"Right," I said, shaking my head. "See you tonight."

I entered the café and immediately spotted Wes sitting at a table in the back—and looking particularly fine in a new flannel shirt over a crisp white T-shirt and dark blue jeans.

Flushed and a little breathless, I slipped into the seat across from him and smiled apologetically. "Sorry I'm late."

The corners of his mouth quirked up in amusement. "If you know what you want, I'll go order for us," he said. "I know your time is tight."

"Oh! Okay, sure. I'll have the mushroom panini. They make their own cashew cheese here. It's really good."

While Wes was at the counter placing our orders, I stole a glance at my reflection in the compact from my purse. My mascara was slightly smudged and my hair was trying to escape from the French twist that had looked a lot more polished five hours ago, but there wasn't much I could do about it now. I sighed and took a sip of water as I watched Wes carry our food to the table and take his seat.

"So, how have you been, Keli? Have you made partner yet?"

I frowned slightly. "I've been pretty busy. I don't think anyone's going to make partner until the firm hires some more associates. And that's not going to happen for at least a few more months yet, when there's a new crop of law school graduates in May."

Wes nodded, chewing on his sandwich and waiting for me to continue.

"Um, congratulations on your new job. How are you liking it?" I asked.

"It's good. It pays the bills. I mean, when I'm taking pictures for the paper, I don't get to be as creative as I'd like to be. But it's still a good fit for me. I can still 'make art' on my own time." Wes gave me a brief crooked grin, then fell silent again.

I was starting to feel awkward about imposing upon him. There was definitely a strange, dense energy between us. As I nibbled on my lunch, I found myself looking around the room, wishing there was a candle I could light and wondering if there were any way I could subtly cast an air-clearing spell.

"I have that paper you wanted," Wes said, interrupting my thoughts. He reached into a scuffed leather satchel and pulled out a rolled-up newspaper, which he set on the table.

"Great, thanks. I thought about looking for it at the public library, but I figured you could probably access it faster. I hope it wasn't too much trouble. I didn't want to bother you."

Raising one eyebrow, Wes shook his head slowly. "You're not bothering me. You're kind of mystifying me, though."

"What?"

"Nothing, never mind." Wes took another bite, polishing off his sandwich, and then took a swig of soda. "I'm sure you need to get back to the office," he said, pushing back his chair. "Time is money, right?"

"Hang on," I said. Irritation bubbled over, drowning out any remaining qualms. "What is going on? What did you mean when you said I mystify you? Why are you acting like this?"

Wes sat back down and shrugged. "I don't know what to say. I thought you didn't want to see me anymore, and then you called and invited me out. And then, I don't know . . . I'm getting mixed signals from you."

My mouth dropped open, and I quickly closed it. "You thought I didn't want to see you? You're the one who failed to return my calls!"

Wes scoffed. "Not so. I left you, like, three or four messages, and you never called me back. I can take a hint."

"You left me messages? When?"

"I don't know, last fall. A few weeks after our last date, I guess."

"Wait a minute," I said, the light suddenly dawning. "The last I heard from you was a text, saying you'd call me later. Then, nothing. But . . . there were a few days when my cell phone was acting weird. I had to take it in to the dealer and have them reinstall the operating system. I lost a bunch of data. . . . " I trailed off, feeling like a fool.

Wes closed his eyes and let out an audible breath. Then he opened his eyes and gazed at me with a sheepish grin. "I should have called again. I'm sorry."

"No, I should have called you. I was so busy at work that time sort of got away from me. It never occurred to me that I missed your calls."

I gave Wes an apologetic look and wondered if there was any way we could pick back up where we left off a couple months ago. I also began to realize how the misunderstanding had happened. I had first met Wes shortly after casting a love spell. Ever since then, I had had these nagging doubts about the authenticity of our relationship. As a result, I had started to let him take the lead more and more, leaving it up to him to call me. That was why I didn't call him.

"Come on," Wes said. He squeezed my shoulder gently and gathered our trays. "I'll walk you back to your office. I'm going that way anyway."

I pulled on my jacket and followed Wes toward the exit. Before leaving, he stopped at the counter and purchased a ready-made sandwich, a bag of potato chips, and a bottle of water, which he stuffed in a brown paper sack. Leave it to Wes to be thinking ahead to his dinner.

"So, you really thought I was blowing you off?" I asked, as we strolled down the sidewalk. The warmth from our heated exchange—not to mention our close proximity—kept the chilly air at bay.

"Well, yeah. I thought maybe you'd started seeing someone else. Like another lawyer. I thought maybe you'd grown tired of slummin' with a struggling artist."

Before I could respond, Wes grabbed my hand and led me toward the town square next to the courthouse. "This'll just take a second," he said, as we approached the bench where the elderly man in a baggy suit sat surrounded by pigeons pecking at crusts of bread. The pigeons scattered as we drew near, but they soon crept back.

"Hello, Charlie," said Wes. "Nice day today, huh?"

Charlie looked up at Wes and beamed, revealing the gaps where his front teeth used to be. Deep wrinkles creased his yellowed skin, but his eyes shone brightly. "It's a beautiful day in the neighborhood, a beautiful day for a neighbor," he chirped.

"Beautiful day, beautiful neighborhood. Beautiful day, beautiful neighbor."

Wes nodded and handed Charlie the bag of food from the bakery. "Yes, it is," he agreed.

Charlie's bony fingers crinkled the top of the bag, but he didn't open it. His eyes fell upon me then, and his gums worked soundlessly until he began his chant again. "It's a beautiful day for a neighbor. A beautiful day for a beauty."

Grinning, Wes put his arm around my shoulders. "She is a beauty, isn't she, Charlie? You've got a good eye there."

I smiled at Charlie and felt beyond moved at Wes's thoughtfulness. It suddenly hit me how much I had missed him. It felt so good to have the air cleared between us. This lunch date had turned out so much better than I could have imagined. After bidding the old man a good day, we continued down the sidewalk hand in hand.

"How did you meet Charlie?" I asked, after we had crossed the street.

"I was experimenting with street photography a few weeks ago, especially around the square. Charlie kept showing up in my pictures, so I decided to get to know him. He's a real sweet guy."

As we neared Moonstone Treasures, I paused, thinking of Mila.

"Wes, I'm going to stop in here before I go back to the office. I'll call you later, okay?"

"Promise?" Wes said, the corner of his mouth twitching playfully.

"Cross my heart."

* * *

The sound of delicate chimes followed me into the shop, but when the jingling died away it was unusually quiet. Normally, Mila would have classical or world music playing softly in the background. The air was thick with the scent of a cloying herbal incense. Coughing and squinting to protect my eyes, I walked through the shop until I found Mila in the book section of her store. She held a ceramic dish in one hand, while using the back of her other hand to waft the aromatic smoke toward the edges of the room.

"That's a little strong, don't you think?" I asked, blinking back tears.

Mila looked at me and dropped her hand. "Is it? I'm sorry. I'll prop the door open for a few minutes. Let me just find Drishti first, so she doesn't escape."

I glanced around the shop looking for Mila's cat. Maybe she was upstairs hiding among the flowing dresses, capes, and other clothing for sale. "You don't usually bring her to work, do you?"

"Not usually," said Mila, putting the incense in a cabinet behind the register. "But I feel safer when she's near. Can I get you some tea or water?"

"No, thanks," I said, joining her by the counter. "I just wanted to see how you're doing. The shop looks good. You'd never guess there was a break-in here."

"Not unless you know where to look." Mila pointed to a small crack on the top of a glass display case. "I bagged up all the damaged merchandise and cast a spell to contain its dark energy. I don't want to throw it out until this person is caught."

I noted the circles under Mila's eyes and felt a pang of sympathy. "Nothing was stolen, right?"

"Actually," said Mila, "there is one thing I couldn't find. A small mantel clock made of mahogany and brass. There was a little poem about the circle of life etched around the face of the clock."

"Oh!" I suddenly remembered. "I think I found part of that clock on the ground outside, on my way home from work yesterday. It's in the pocket of my other coat."

Mila frowned. "I guess they didn't want the piece for its beauty then. That must be what they threw to break the window."

I turned and looked at the repaired storefront window and thought for a moment. "You mean the window was broken from the inside? Then how did the vandal get in?"

"The police said they either picked the lock or had a key. The doorknob was so old and scratched up, it was impossible to tell. I always meant to change the lock after I bought this place, but I never got around to it. Until yesterday, of course. So, it's possible there were other keys—"

A sharp scream from the back room interrupted Mila. We both jumped, looking at one another in alarm. Together, we rushed through the gauzy purple curtain, past the round table where Mila gave private psychic readings, and into the storage half of the back room. Catrina was standing by the open back door. She held a sheet of white paper by the tips of her fingers like a used tissue.

"Catrina, what is it?" said Mila breathlessly. "Are you okay?"

"It's another creepy note," said Catrina, through gritted teeth. "It says, 'Witch be gone' above another Bible reference."

"Why did you scream?" I asked, looking around the room. Nothing seemed to be out of place. Metal shelves lined the long wall, holding neatly stacked boxes of inventory. In the nearest corner to my left, two tall filing cabinets flanked a built-in desk on which sat a computer and some papers. To my right, a pair of Japanese folding screens separated the unadorned storeroom from the warmly decorated divination area.

"It freaked me out," said Catrina. "I had just taken out the trash, and when I returned, it was right there on the floor in front of me, as if it had materialized out of nowhere."

Mila dropped into the office chair by her computer desk. Out of the corner of my eye, I saw a blur of gray cross the floor, and then Drishti sprang into Mila's lap. Wordlessly, Mila began stroking her cat.

I turned back to Catrina, who handed me the paper. "I'll look up the Bible verse," she said, pulling a phone out of her back pocket.

As I scrutinized the sheet of paper, I saw there was a piece of dusty Scotch tape along the top edge.

"This must have been taped to the back door," I said. "It probably blew into the room when you went outside." Even as I said it, I realized this theory didn't make sense. The door opened outward, toward the alley. If the note was taped to the door outside, it should have fallen outside, not inside.

"Let me see those numbers again," said Catrina, taking the paper from me. She glanced at the note and then read from her phone: "'Revelation 21:8: But cowards, unbelievers, the corrupt, murderers, the immoral, those who practice witchcraft, idol worshipers, and all liars—their fate is in the fiery lake of burning sulfur. This is the second death.'"

For a moment, none of us said anything. Then Mila sighed. Addressing her cat, she spoke quietly. "I don't know who's doing this, Drishti. Whoever they are, their ill will is going to come right back to them. By the Rule of Three, that which they are giving shall return to them threefold. And, when the time is right, I will do everything in my power to make sure it does."

Chapter 5

As soon as I returned to my office, I called Farrah to cancel our after-work run. I apologized profusely and promised I'd make it up to her. I blamed it on my heavy workload—which was partly true. Mostly, though, I needed to do something to help Mila.

I pulled out the old newspaper Wes had retrieved for me and opened to the opinion page. It didn't take long to find the letter I was looking for. Written in the lofty language of a dogmatist, the letter condemned all psychics as "agents of the Devil" and repeatedly referred to Mila as an "avowed witch." The letter urged city officials to deny her application for a business license. It was signed by Reverend Nathanial "Natty" Schmidt of the First Church of the New Believers, over on Hickory Street.

For the next several minutes, I perused the Internet for everything I could find out about Reverend Natty. Apparently, he was a native of Edindale and a college dropout who had started his own church about twenty years ago as an offshoot of another

Evangelical church he felt was becoming too modern. As such, his "New Believers" denomination took a more literalist approach to biblical interpretation—and they weren't shy about vocalizing their position. As I soon learned, Reverend Natty was a regular contributor to the opinion page of the *Edindale Gazette*, railing against everything from women's rights and gay marriage to *Star Wars* and Harry Potter.

In spite of—or perhaps because of—his extremism, Reverend Natty seemed to have attracted quite a following. According to the church website, more than two hundred congregants counted themselves as members of the First Church of the New Believers. In fairness, it appeared their work wasn't all about opposition. As proponents of abstention, they were particularly welcoming of recovering alcoholics.

I was so engrossed in my reading I didn't hear the tap on my door until it was accompanied by a shrill birdlike whistle. I jerked my head up to see Julie standing there with an expression of amused sympathy.

"Your client's in the waiting room," she said.

"Oh! Thank you, Julie," I said, glancing at the clock on my computer. "Please bring her in."

I switched off my computer screen and cleared off the small round table in the corner of my office. I was dragging a second chair to the table when Julie ushered in my client, a tired-looking young woman wearing slacks and a nice sweater.

"How are you, Alisha? Did Julie offer you something to drink?"

"Fine, and yes," said Alisha, holding up a plastic

bottle of water. "I'm just eager to get this over with so I can move on with my life."

"Of course," I said, grabbing a file folder from my desk. "This shouldn't take long. I have good news for you. They've agreed to our terms."

As we took our seats, I flipped open to a clean page in a yellow legal pad and made a note of the time. Then I handed Alisha a copy of the custody agreement I had negotiated with her soon-to-be-ex-husband's attorney. I proceeded to go over every provision, making sure she understood all of the terms, and answered all her questions as we went. In less than an hour, we had finished, and she signed and initialed all the appropriate spaces.

Sitting back in her chair, Alisha exhaled. "You know," she said, "the thing that bugs me most is that I can't just pick up and move now. I mean, I'm glad we have joint custody; I know this is for the best. I just hate that I'm kind of stuck here now."

I looked at her in surprise. "I thought you were happy here," I said. "I thought Edindale was a good place to raise children. The schools here are supposed to be really good, right?" Hoping to have children myself one day, I paid attention to such things.

"Well, yeah," Alisha agreed. "But, I'm worried crime is on the rise. There have been all those burglaries that the police can't seem to solve. And there was all the ruckus with that occult bookstore, or whatever it is." She made air quotes when she mentioned the "occult bookstore" and shook her head in disgust.

I said something vaguely reassuring to Alisha, as

I walked her out of my office. Inside, I lamented the fact that Mila was the one getting a bad rap just for being the victim of a crime. I could hardly wait for the end of the day, so I could do some investigating and, hopefully, shed some light on Mila's problem.

It was nearly 8:00 P.M. when I steered my silver-blue Ford Fusion into a street-side parking space in front of the First Church of the New Believers. After cutting the engine, I pulled up the collar on my long wool coat and peered over at the white clapboard building. To me, it looked more like a quaint old house with a steeple than a vibrant church large enough to hold two hundred congregants.

Stepping out of my car and into the cold air, I gazed at the dark church. The only light came from a basement window on the west side of the building. From what I had read on the church's website, I knew there was an Alcoholics Anonymous meeting from 7:00 to 8:00. My plan was to strike up a conversation with someone in charge as soon as the meeting let out.

With a flutter in my stomach, I walked up the sidewalk, wishing Farrah were with me. *I should have asked her to come along!* As a legal software saleswoman, she was a much better schmoozer than I could ever pretend to be.

As soon as the door opened and a young man came out, I slipped inside and walked downstairs, following the sound of cheerful voices. Before long, I found myself in a bright wood-paneled room with folding chairs arranged in a circle on the linoleum floor. In the back of the room, an old green card table held a coffee urn and several packages of store-bought cookies.

Luckily, I didn't recognize any of the attendees chatting over coffee or leaving the meeting. But the tall man shaking hands at the doorway looked vaguely familiar. Spotting me, he immediately pasted on a practiced smile and waved me over.

"I'm afraid you've just missed the meeting," he said good-naturedly. "Welcome. I'm Natty Schmidt, pastor, preacher, and founder of New Believers. Most folks call me Reverend Natty, but it's not a requirement." He flashed a toothy grin.

I offered my hand, and he grasped it with both of his. His penetrating eyes made me feel uncomfortable, but I managed a small smile.

"Hi, I'm Keli. I'm actually here to pick up some information for a friend," I said, not caring if he thought the information was actually for myself. "Do you need to sign up for these meetings?"

"Not at all," the pastor replied. "We're more than happy to have folks just show up. We understand that oftentimes it's a last-minute decision." He shifted his gaze and waved at someone over my shoulder. As he said good-bye to a middle-aged woman with gray hair, I suddenly remembered where I had seen the pastor before. He was one of the people who had passed by me in front of Mila's shop. His companion had made a nasty remark about the shop being bad news.

He turned back to me and looked directly into my eyes. "Listen, I would love to chat with you if you have the time. Won't you have some coffee?"

Gladly, I thought. I nodded and followed him to the table with the coffee and cookies. I helped myself to a cup and sat down on a cold metal chair. Reverend Natty sat across from me and pushed the package of cookies across the table. Like a magician performing a trick, he produced a small bundle of pamphlets.

"These brochures describe a number of our programs, besides this one. Where do you attend church, dear?"

I took a sip of the coffee, politely ignoring its bitterness. "I was raised Catholic," I answered truthfully. "But I don't attend any church right now. I guess you could say I'm something of a seeker. I'm interested in learning more about the beliefs of the, er, New Believers."

The pastor's eyes lit up. For the next several minutes, he walked me through the history of the church, highlighting its many social programs and emphasizing the number of souls that had been saved within its doors. Several times, he quoted scripture to convince me of the divine rightness of his vision for the church. He only briefly touched upon some of their social mores, including the religion's ban on the consumption of alcohol. Apparently, Reverend Natty had been lobbying government officials unsuccessfully for years to turn Edindale into a dry city.

Finally, I was able to steer the conversation to what I was really after. "I understand you've also spoken out against metaphysical practices such as palmistry and tarot reading. Is there really any harm in those things? Aren't they usually done just for fun?"

I noted with interest the way Reverend Natty's nostrils flared. He sat up straighter in his chair and leaned forward. "Actually, those things can be quite dangerous. And it's especially dangerous because young people think it's all fun and games."

I raised my eyebrows and let him continue.

"Only God knows the future. Anyone else who claims to have such power is either a charlatan or worse."

"Worse?"

Reverend Natty lowered his voice. "Now, I don't want to scare you, but it's a fact that some people are weak and succumb to the seductions of Satan. There are people today who call themselves witches and claim to cast spells, which is clearly an abomination against the Lord."

My heart started thudding, and I struggled to remain calm. Squeezing my hands tightly together under the table, I managed to speak in an even tone. "Is that so?"

"Oh, yes, the Bible is clear on this."

Biting my tongue, I nodded my head to encourage him to go on. I had to find out—was Reverend Natty fanatical enough to vandalize Mila's shop?

"We even have sinful witches right here in Edindale," he said. "One of them was branded as such just yesterday."

"You mean the graffiti on that gift shop, Moonstone Treasures? I, uh, noticed that on my way into work yesterday."

"That's right," said Reverend Natty. "I saw it too. I was on my way to have breakfast with a congregant. We were going to discuss our visiting ministry program."

"Oh?"

"Yes. Once a month we spread the New Believers' message in other towns around the country. In fact, I think there's a pamphlet about that in this stack I gave you."

Clearly Reverend Natty was intent on spreading his beliefs as far and wide as possible. I pondered this tidbit after I thanked him and walked back to my car. The question was, were all his church members as zealous as he was? Or was he the lone crusader? More importantly, how far would he go to eliminate what he undoubtedly viewed as an "abomination" in his town?

I shuddered at the thought.

Chapter 6

On my way home from the First Church of the New Believers, I stopped off at my favorite Thai restaurant for takeout. It was after 9:00 by the time I got home with my vegetable fried rice and tofu, and I ate from the white carton with relish as I opened my mail and checked messages on my phone. Then I called Wes. He sounded pleased when he answered.

"Hey," he said. "I was wondering if I'd hear from you tonight."

I smiled. "I did promise I'd call, right?"

"That you did. So, did you have a productive afternoon? Was that old newspaper any help?"

I hesitated. I forgot to think of an explanation for needing the paper. "Uh, yeah. It did."

"Oh, I get it. Say no more. Attorney-client privilege, right?"

"Something like that. Thanks again for bringing me the paper. If not for our lunch meeting, who knows when we would've cleared up our little . . . misunderstanding."

Wes chuckled. "I know. Crazy stuff. So . . . when can I see you again?"

"Well, I have plans with Farrah tomorrow evening. How about Thursday?"

"Perfect."

After hanging up with Wes, I changed into yoga pants and a comfy blue sweatshirt, then took my laptop over to the couch. I needed to research wildlife import law for the special memo Beverly had assigned to me.

First, I looked up rhino horns and opened a page created by a wildlife conservation group. My hand flew to my mouth as a grotesque image filled the screen—a mutilated rhinoceros whose horn had been hacked off.

"Oh, jeez," I muttered, scrolling through similar distressing photos.

Quickly, I switched to a database of federal statutes and delved into the legalities of import/export law, jotting notes on a pad of paper as I went. As I suspected, some species of rhinoceros were on the endangered list. It was against the law to buy or sell rhino horns—or anything made out of them. However, it wasn't illegal simply to own a rhino horn if it had been acquired prior to the enactment of the law. Hopefully, Edgar's piece was an antique.

Still, I thought, yawning, *having one on display is pretty tasteless.* I'd have to add some facts to the memo to win Beverly over to my point of view.

I continued to read about the plight of the poor rhinos. In many parts of Asia, people coveted rhino horns, believing they contained powerful medicinal properties. Wanted as not only an aphrodisiac, but also as a cure for a host of ailments—including cancer, of all things—rhino horns were worth more than their weight in gold. This, of course, led to rampant poaching and a dangerous illegal trade.

Belief is a powerful force, I thought sleepily, as I closed my laptop. *Those gullible people might as well ingest their own fingernails. They're made from the same stuff as rhino horns.*

Pulling an afghan over my legs, I leaned back to lay my head on the arm of the couch. I would get up and go to bed pretty soon. I just needed to rest my eyes for a minute.

The sound of my cell phone jarred me awake. Fumbling in the darkness, I reached over and grabbed it from the coffee table.

"Hello?" I croaked.

"Keli, you need to get over here right now."

Rubbing my eyes, I pulled the phone away to squint at the unfamiliar number. I also noted the time—3:30 A.M.

"Who is this?"

"It's Catrina. Sorry I woke you, but we need you at the shop. There's been a fire."

"What?" I sat up on the couch and shook the fog from my brain.

"Please," she said. "The fire department has already been here and left. I want you to see what's left before we clean it up."

Alarm coursed through my veins. "What do you mean 'what's left'? Was the shop destroyed?"

"No, that's not what I meant. Please just come here as fast as you can."

Catrina hung up, leaving me staring at my phone in disbelief. *Terrific.* After a quick trip to the bathroom, I pulled on a coat, a scarf, and some boots and quietly slipped out of my town house. The last thing I needed was to awaken my curious neighbors.

The streets were empty as I drove the few short blocks to Moonstone Treasures. Stepping out of the car, I could see my breath by the light of the corner street lamp. Light flurries swirled in the air before me. I jogged up to the front of the shop and tapped on the door. After a few seconds, Catrina opened the door and ushered me inside.

"You said there was a fire," I said, taking in the quiet, shadowy shop. A light from the back room cast a soft glow that reached the center of the store. From what I could tell, nothing appeared to be disturbed.

"Come on," said Catrina, pulling back the purple curtain. As soon as I entered the back room, I detected the faint acrid smell of lingering smoke, along with a strange mixture of other odors. The floor was littered with assorted containers, bottles, boxes, and candles. It appeared as if someone had ransacked the place. In the middle of it all stood Mila with her eyes closed and her arms outstretched, intoning some words I couldn't make out. She appeared even thinner than usual, in an open black cloak over a white nightgown. Her feet were bare.

I didn't want to interrupt Mila in the middle of

her spell, so I turned to Catrina and spoke in a whisper. "Where was the fire?"

Catrina, who looked incongruous herself in combat boots and an army jacket over Hello Kitty pajamas, led me to the back door. She opened it, revealing a mess of white foam over a pile of candles and charred books.

I gave Catrina a questioning look.

"Check it out," she said, pointing. "Someone spray painted a crude pentagram on the ground and arranged candles in a circle around it. In the center of the star, they had themselves a little book burning. From what I can tell, the books aren't connected except that they all have black covers."

I stared at the heap of damaged books and felt frustration rise within me. Catrina had woken me up to see this? I thought the place was going to be up in flames, the way she had sounded on the phone. She had me really worried. *Enough with the melodrama already!*

I took a deep breath. "Was there a note?"

Catrina shook her head. "Not that we've found."

"Well, what did the police say? Is this still a crime scene, or what?"

"They asked some questions and took some pictures. They said it appeared to be a prank," Catrina said scornfully. "They didn't seem to realize the significance of the pentagram. This is clearly another hate crime."

I rubbed my temples. *Why did this girl always give me a headache?*

"Let's clean it up," I said. "Do you have a snow shovel we can use?"

Catrina disappeared inside. I stuck my hands in my pockets to keep warm and looked up and down the dark alley. There was nothing to see besides garbage bins and darkened back doors. At one end of the alley, a neighboring building had a shed attached to its back door, effectively blocking the view of the street beyond.

I shuddered. *Mila should install a spotlight out here,* I thought, trying not to imagine what other unsavory crimes could easily take place in the secluded alleyway.

Catrina returned with a shovel, a broom, and a box of trash bags. For the next few minutes, we worked silently to clear away the debris. As we did, I counted nine pillar candles and five paperback books. All of the books had pages ripped out, presumably to help fuel the fire. Catrina was right that there didn't appear to be any particular significance to the chosen books other than the color of the covers. There were a couple of guides to witchcraft, a book of spells, a memoir, and a young adult novel.

Still, while the books were random, the whole setup itself appeared to have been done with careful deliberation. I doubted the perpetrator would have been careless enough to leave fingerprints. Even if the person had, the foam from the firefighter's extinguisher probably would have obliterated any prints.

As I tied up a garbage bag, a thought occurred to me. "How did you and Mila find out about the fire?"

"Someone was driving by and saw it, so they called

nine-one-one. A police officer called Mila, and she called me. It didn't take the firefighters very long to put out the fire. Luckily, it was outside instead of inside the store. Which is kind of weird, since they made a mess of the place inside."

When we went back in, Mila was cleaning up her divination parlor. She had already put away the bottles and containers and was sweeping up spilled herbs and bits of broken candles. She smiled faintly when she saw me.

"Catrina called you before I could tell her not to," she said, with a note of apology in her voice. "I can make you some tea, if you'd like, but I'm sure you'd rather just go back home."

I followed Mila through the curtain into the main part of the shop. I started to ask her how she was holding up, when I was distracted by headlights that momentarily shone through the front window. I walked over to the window and peered outside. Mila and Catrina joined me, and we watched as a small car pulled into the parking space nearest the alley. A slender young woman wearing a trench coat got out of the car and took a few tentative steps toward the alley. Her shoulder-length honey-colored hair gleamed under the streetlight.

"Who is that?" I asked.

"Looks like Sheana Starwalt. She's a reporter at the *Edindale Gazette*," Catrina answered.

Uh-oh. The last thing I wanted was to see my name in the paper in connection with Moonstone Treasures. I also wondered if Wes knew this reporter. *What would he think if he found out I was here?*

Mila hugged her arms across her chest. "I assume she heard about the fire on a police scanner. The vulture."

Feeling a twinge of panic, I turned to Mila and lightly squeezed her arm. "I'm gonna get going now, but I'll stop by tomorrow." With a curt nod to Catrina, I opened the door and ran to my car, wrapping my scarf around my face as I went.

As I started the engine and shifted into reverse, I spared a glance toward the sidewalk. The reporter, who was now heading toward the entrance to Moonstone Treasures, turned my way at the sound of my car. I hurriedly looked away and hit the gas.

When my alarm clock rang at 6:00 A.M., I groaned and rolled over. My body was so tired, I considered calling in sick—which was something I hadn't done once in all of my six years with the firm.

But no. There was too much to do.

After forcing myself out of bed, I took a bracing shower; applied makeup, to at least give me the appearance of being more awake; and then dressed in one of my favorite power suits. I went to the kitchen and concocted an energy-boosting smoothie consisting of almond milk, bananas, kale, and frozen berries, as well as an assortment of powders—macca root for vitality, flax seed for longevity, cayenne for heat, and guarana for a caffeine kick. As I prepared the smoothie, I muttered an improvised spell:

"Oh Blessed Shakti, Mother bright
Hear my plea and bring your might
I'll work by day and sleep by night
Rest at dark and wake at light
Give me strength that I may fight
By your grace, I'll be all right."

By the time I walked into the reception area of Olsen, Sykes, and Rafferty at five minutes before 9, I had a spring in my step and a grin on my face. My spell had worked wonders. The only thing I didn't know was how long it would last.

"Well, you seem awfully chipper," said Pammy, by way of greeting. She was standing next to Crenshaw, who was leaning his elbows on Julie's desk. He turned to me and raised one eyebrow.

"Morning, Keli," said Julie, looking up from her computer. "Did you hear what happened last night? It was on the *Gazette*'s website this morning."

I froze in my tracks, unable to think of a reply. *Is she talking about the fire at Moonstone Treasures?*

"There was yet another burglary," said Pammy. "This time it was Gigi's Bar and Grill."

"Do you know the place, Ms. Milanni?" asked Crenshaw, with a sly smirk. "They have wonderfully juicy steaks."

Another jab at my veganism. Every chance he gets. I gave Crenshaw a weak smile that was more like a grimace and turned to Pammy and Julie. "How many does that make now? Do the police think it's all the same burglar?"

"The police aren't saying much at all," said Julie.

"Just that their investigation is 'ongoing.' This is the fifth burglary in three months."

"At least it's always businesses," said Pammy soberly. "If these were residential break-ins I don't think I could sleep at night."

Crenshaw straightened and began stroking his beard. I sensed he was about to pontificate, so I quickly excused myself. I didn't think my energy spell was strong enough to withstand one of Crenshaw's speeches.

As soon as I settled in at my desk, I dialed the number for Moonstone Treasures. Mila answered on the second ring.

"Hi, Mila. It's Keli. How are things this morning?"

"Everything seems more or less normal," she said. "So far."

I could tell from Mila's voice she was holding something back.

"What did that reporter want last night? I hope she didn't keep you up much later than it already was," I asked.

"She didn't stay long," Mila said. "I raised a psychic shield as soon as I sensed her aura. I didn't like her insinuations."

"Why? What did she say?"

"It was her questions. She asked me if one of my spells or 'curses' had gone wrong, thus causing the fire. She asked if I performed rituals in the shop. And she asked me what 'brand of magic' I practiced, and if it could be considered 'black magic.'"

"Well, she's definitely angling for a story," I said. "What did Catrina say?"

"Oh, I sent Catrina to the back room before the reporter even came inside. I know Catrina thinks publicity is important, but I'm not so sure I agree."

You and me both, sister.

"Did you tell the reporter about the threatening notes you've been receiving?"

"No," said Mila. "I just wanted her to leave. But I did mention the vandalism, which, of course, she already knew about. She asked if I thought it was a dissatisfied customer who damaged the shop. Perhaps someone who bought a charm or potion that backfired."

"Sounds like she's seen one too many witchy movies," I said, trying to lighten the mood.

"She was trying to find a way to blame me, Keli. To make this all my fault." Mila paused, then continued in a quieter voice. "No matter what I do, I'm afraid it's my reputation that is going to suffer."

Unfortunately, I was thinking the same thing.

Chapter 7

With the early boost from my energy spell, I managed to fly through my morning tasks. I even worked through lunch, munching on a big salad I had brought from home as I prepared a client's divorce papers. However, by 1:00 my stamina started to wane. I stood up to stretch my legs and began pacing the length of my office.

My mind returned to Mila's problem. What was the culprit thinking? What was the point of using Mila's supplies to create a pseudo-magical arrangement? Was the person sending a message to Mila? Or was the message for the public, to show them how unsafe witchcraft was?

This made me think of Reverend Natty. It seemed clear he wanted to convince people of the "danger" of fortune-telling and other such practices. And the burning of books certainly seemed to be consistent with his approach of "ban and prohibit."

But why set the fire outside the shop instead of

inside? Unless, the culprit didn't really want to destroy the shop itself.

Mulling over the possibilities, I thought back to the night I went to Mila's house and reviewed the threatening notes with her, Max, and Catrina. I remembered asking who might want to drive Mila out of business, and she had mentioned a Realtor by the name of Yvette Prime.

I had recognized the name right away. I had encountered Ms. Prime several times over the years during real estate transactions. I'd also seen her name in the paper on occasion.

Sitting back down at my computer, I clicked open a browser and Googled "Edindale Realtor Yvette Prime." My Internet search didn't uncover much more than I already knew. Besides being a successful Realtor, Ms. Prime was an active community leader. She was a member of several professional organizations, including the chamber of commerce, the Illinois Association of Realtors, and the Edin County Association of African-American Entrepreneurs. She was also on the board of directors for the Edindale Historical Society and volunteered for Big Brothers Big Sisters.

Talk about upstanding.

Max was right. I couldn't picture Yvette Prime throwing rocks or wielding a spray-paint can in the dead of night.

But I did wonder who her client was who was so interested in Mila's property.

* * *

After another busy afternoon, I made a point of calling it a day at 5:00 P.M. Normally, Crenshaw would gloat anytime he caught me leaving the office before him. He liked to cultivate the appearance of burning the midnight oil, ever the dedicated worker intent on making partner first. In such moments, I would comfort myself with the knowledge that at least *I* had a life outside of work.

Today, however, Crenshaw once again left for the day just ahead of me. I expected him to say he was off to meet a client or attend a night meeting, but he just nodded at me distractedly and rushed to the elevator before the doors closed. He didn't bother to hold them for me.

Pursing my lips, I texted Farrah while I waited for the next elevator. As tired as I was, I still looked forward to seeing my best friend. She brought some balance to my life when I got too caught up in work.

A short time later, we met up at our usual spot near a fountain at Fieldstone Park. I had already changed into a tracksuit and running shoes. As often happened with the two of us, without planning it we found that we matched perfectly, today both of us wearing red sweats with a white side stripe, her high blond ponytail mirroring my high brunette one.

We took one look at each other and laughed.

"Are you ready to smash this 10K or what?" said Farrah.

"Girlfriend, I gotta say I'm not feeling this one.

I haven't run in weeks, and I did not sleep well last night."

"What are you talking about? This is nothing. You'll catch your second wind before you know it."

Farrah started jogging down the sidewalk, and I fell into step next to her.

"How was your lunch date yesterday? Did Wes come to his senses and realize what he's been missing?"

"Get this," I said. "Remember when my phone was all wonky?"

"Wait a minute," said Farrah. "Are you saying he called you, but you didn't know he called you?"

"Exactly. And he didn't know I didn't know. So, he thought I wasn't calling him back."

Farrah snorted. "There's something vaguely tragic about that. In a *Romeo and Juliet* sort of way."

"Ha! Tell me about it."

We chatted for a couple more minutes, then grew silent as we found our stride. At the edge of the park, we cut over to the rail trail, ran for a mile and a half, and then turned back. After logging three miles, we circled the park and started up the rail trail again. A quarter mile down the path, just before a street crossing, I began to slow down.

"Are you pooping out on me?"

Breathing heavily, I shook my head and held my side. "Just a little stitch. You go on if you want. This is a good start for me, but I've had it for now."

Farrah stuck out her lower lip, then shrugged. "I'll walk back with you. Tomorrow we'll go a little farther, and by next weekend you should be able to handle six miles. Right?"

"Sure," I said. But instead of turning back, I walked up to the small side street that intersected the trail. "This leads to Broadway, right?"

"Yeah, why?"

I headed down the side street, toward the well-lit avenue, where several shops and businesses were still open.

"There's a Realtor's office I'd like to stop by for a minute."

"Now? What, you're suddenly in the market for a new house?"

"Um, not really. There's just something I want to check out."

With Farrah at my heels, I wandered up to the storefront office space shared by a small group of local Realtors, including Yvette Prime. The sign on the door said CLOSED, but the place looked as if people might still be inside. I stood for a moment gazing absently at the glossy flyers showcasing the most desirable homes currently on the market. Maybe it wouldn't be such a stretch to act like a house hunter as an excuse to talk to Yvette.

"Ooh, check it out! The Cadwelle Mansion's open, and they're hosting a murder-mystery dinner!" Farrah said, peering over my shoulder.

"Huh?"

Farrah grabbed my arm and turned me toward a flyer next to all the real estate ads. "You've heard of the Cadwelle Mansion, haven't you? That big, beautiful Queen Anne Victorian at the top of the hill on Archer Avenue? The place was empty for a long time, until some new owners bought it last year and began renovations to turn it into a B&B. Looks like they're open now, and they've got a murder-mystery dinner theater thingy happening there. How fun! We should totally go. This would be perfect for a double date."

I winced and shot Farrah a skeptical look. "Are you kidding? Isn't that kind of ghoulish, turning something as horrible as murder into entertainment?"

Farrah rolled her eyes and softly punched my arm. "Lighten up, Kel. You take everything so seriously!"

Before I could respond, the door opened and a tall young man stepped outside. I recognized him from a closing I'd handled not long ago.

"Hi, Brian."

He glanced over in surprise. "Oh, hello. I was just leaving, but we can go inside if you'd like. I stayed late to make some client calls, so I'd be happy to open back up."

"Oh, no, that's okay. We were passing by and just taking a look. Actually, I was hoping to speak with Yvette at some point. I assume she's not here now, is she?"

Brian looked disappointed but managed a rueful smile as he shook his head. "She's a busy woman. I'm going to have to reconsider sharing an office with her, seeing as how she's snatching up all the clients lately."

"Oh?"

"Well, the high-profile clients, anyway." He nodded to the flyer about the Cadwelle Mansion. "Yvette sold that one and is getting all kinds of attention for it. She's even being presented with a little award at the first performance this Friday. But, hey, more power to her, right?"

"I think this mystery theater idea is so neat," Farrah said.

"You know what?" said Brian, reaching into his coat pocket. "I actually have two tickets I can't use now. My wife's sister had a baby yesterday, so we're heading out of town this weekend. I need to give these away before I forget. You interested?"

"Yeah, totally! Thank you!" Farrah took the tickets. "I can get Jake to go with me."

After a few more pleasantries, we said good-bye to Brian and walked back toward the trail. I took a deep breath and turned to my friend.

"You know," I said, "maybe it would be fun if the two of us went after all. At least it would be something different, right?" I smiled weakly, and Farrah laughed.

"That's my girl."

Chapter 8

On Thursday evening, Wes and I caught up over enchiladas and margaritas. We sat across from one another in a red vinyl booth at Los Frijoles, one of Edindale's most popular Mexican restaurants. Over the din of salsa music and laughing patrons, we chatted about random topics—his trouble decorating his new apartment, my trouble finding space for all the houseplants I kept buying. We talked about our mutual friends, and I asked Wes about his family. I had first met them over the summer when they were my clients.

"My parents are in Clearwater, Florida, for a few weeks," he said. "They had enough of the winter already."

"Sounds lovely. How lucky for them."

"Yeah, no kidding. Rob has it pretty good, too. He's heading to Arizona this weekend. He's doing this gambling addict support program that involves lots of retreats and getaways."

"I'm glad he's finally getting help," I said, giving

Wes a sympathetic look. I knew he had been troubled by his brother's gambling problem for a long time.

He nodded. "Me too."

"I wish I could go someplace warm," I said. "I went to Nebraska over the holidays to see my family. I was treated to a snowstorm and below-freezing temps."

Wes chuckled. "I hope I get to meet your family sometime."

I smiled and wondered if this was an indication he wanted to take our relationship to a more serious level. Then again, that's what I had thought last fall when things were going so well . . . until he made that comment about dating around and then waited a few weeks to try calling me. It was so hard not knowing what was really going on in a guy's mind.

Maybe I should just stop obsessing and enjoy the moment.

Whether it was the buzz from the drinks or the rush from our fun date, I found myself in a great mood. I couldn't keep my eyes off Wes. In fact, I realized I was probably lucky someone else hadn't snatched him up during our little hiatus. Our twenty-something waitress couldn't keep her eyes off him either. She kept coming back to refill our basket of tortilla chips even though it wasn't empty. Finally, Wes handed it back to her.

"*No mas*," he said, with a grin. "*Gracias*, anyway."

She simpered and flipped her wedge-cut hair. I smirked.

We finished our dinner, and then Wes checked the time. "I think the SCIU observatory is open to the public tonight. Want to go?"

"Yeah! I haven't been there in ages."

When the waitress brought our check, Wes grabbed it and pulled out his wallet. I offered to split the bill, but he waved me away. "I've got it," he said. He placed a wad of cash on the table, then helped me on with my coat. The waitress shot Wes a yearning look as we headed to the exit.

Eat your heart out, honey.

The observatory was a few miles from the main campus, all the better to see the night sky. We parked in the nearly empty parking lot and entered the quiet brick building. A student wearing a skirt and a cardigan greeted us at the door.

"You just missed the last tour," she said. "But you can go on up and look around on your own. We close in ten minutes."

On our way up the metal steps to the upper level of the observatory, we passed a family of three on their way down. The little boy was raving about all the planets he had seen. When he spotted Wes and me, his eyes lit up. "You gotta look in the big telescope! There's a billion stars out there! I even saw the rings around Saturn!"

"Awesome!" Wes held out his hand to give the boy a high five.

"Thanks for the tip!" I told the boy before he left with his parents. I held on to Wes's arm as we continued up the steps. "What an adorable little stargazer."

"Smart too," said Wes. "Now I *really* want to look in the big telescope." He pulled away and jogged over to the center of the round room, where he took a peek through the giant instrument.

I couldn't stop grinning as I walked up behind him. "How well do you know your constellations?"

"Well, I know about the Big Dipper. There's a Little Dipper too, right?"

"Hmm. Those aren't really constellations. The Big Dipper is part of Ursa Major. The Little Dipper is part of Ursa Minor."

Wes looked up and made a face. "I knew that. I was just testing you."

I laughed. "Sure you were."

For the next several minutes, we marveled at all the dazzling objects in the Milky Way. I especially loved seeing the moon up close, which was full and luminous tonight. Like many women—and most Wiccans—I felt a special connection with the moon and its mysterious feminine energy. I almost mentioned this to Wes, but then I stopped myself. *What if he laughed at me?* As much as I longed to be open with him, I didn't want to risk messing with a good thing—especially so soon after rekindling our relationship.

"Five minutes til closing!" the student called up at us, so we made our way downstairs. Before leaving the building, we walked by an Astronomy Club exhibit on comets and meteors. I paused, gazing at the images of fiery balls shooting across the sky. They brought to mind the Bible verse Catrina had found in Mila's shop a couple days ago. What had it said? Something about a "fiery lake"?

I blinked as another thought sprang to mind. They'd found the reference to fire on Tuesday afternoon . . . and the fire outside Mila's shop was set on Tuesday night. Was that just a coincidence?

I tried to recall any details from the earlier notes. What was the last one Mila had discovered before someone broke the window in her shop? Wasn't there one that talked about "tearing down walls" and "demolishing defenses"? Could that threat have presaged the vandalism at Moonstone?

Wes put his hand on my waist and I jumped. "Whoa there. Where did you go? Outer space?"

I giggled shortly and buttoned up my coat. "Yeah, I guess so." I shook off my disturbing speculations. I was probably attaching too much meaning to the language of the Bible verses and other quotes. They were meant to be creepy, for sure. But not literal.

Right?

Fridays were normally a little slower, a little more casual around the office. The dress code was relaxed. Most meetings and court appearances had already taken place earlier in the week. Everyone was looking forward to the weekend.

For some reason, my Friday wasn't cooperating. My phone kept ringing off the hook, and people kept stopping by with problems they wanted me to solve right then and there. To top it off, Beverly managed to remind me about the memo I owed her, while also transferring one of her cases to me, all in the same breath.

So, when my cell phone rang and I saw that it was Catrina, I almost didn't answer. I had just left

Beverly's office and was finally going to run out and grab a late lunch. I stood in the lobby, hesitating, as my phone rang in my purse. Julie propped her hand on her chin and watched to see what I would do.

Ugh. What if something else had happened at Moonstone? I picked up.

"Hello?" I said.

"Keli, I was going to stop by your office, but Mila said I should call first. I can be there in two minutes. Is that okay?"

I gritted my teeth. "Sorry, Catrina. I'm all booked up this afternoon. What did you want to talk about?"

"We got another note. I found it mixed in with the mail. And talk about your hate mail! This one may be the worst yet."

I closed my eyes and sighed. Julie was still watching me from behind her reception desk. I wavered for a moment near the exit, then decided to go back to my office. Maybe I'd just have my lunch delivered today.

"Hang on," I said. "I want to get a pen and write this down."

Once in my office, I closed the door and set down my purse. "Okay. What did this one say?"

"The message in the middle of the paper said, 'Shutter your business.'"

"Is that it?"

"There was another reference to the *Malleus Maleficarum*."

"Did you look it up?"

"Of course. Are you ready for this? 'For the divine law in many places commands that witches are not only to be avoided, but also they are to be put to death, and it would not impose the extreme penalty of this kind if witches did not really and truly make a compact with devils in order to bring about real and true hurts and harms.'"

Chills crawled up and down my arms. This one did sound worse than the others. Although, they were all pretty bad. "Did Mila call the police?"

Catrina hesitated. "Uh, no. I don't think so."

"Let me talk to her. Please."

"She's with a client right now, giving a tarot reading."

"Catrina, tell Mila to call the police. You need to give them the note so they can figure out who's doing this and put a stop to it."

"I'll tell her," said Catrina. "How's it going on your end? Do you have any leads?"

I pressed my lips together. "I'm working on a couple of possible angles. I'll fill Mila in later. I gotta go now."

After the call with Catrina, I stared down at the sheet of paper where I'd jotted down the message she had read to me.

They are to be put to death. . . .

How much worse could it get?

Chapter 9

By the time I left work Friday evening, I was more than ready for a night out. In fact, I was actually looking forward to my mystery-dinner date with Farrah. She would often suggest some outlandish scheme or crazy adventure—at least, crazy by my standards. I would protest at first, then reluctantly agree. Of course, I would end up having fun after all. Thanks to Farrah, I had experienced rock climbing, spelunking, and nighttime horseback riding.

I should be able to handle a little murder-mystery skit.

To avoid showing up as accidental twins, I called Farrah before I got dressed. She told me she was wearing a baby blue sweater with a black skirt and tall boots, so I opted for a green V-neck sweater, pinstriped skinny pants, and ankle boots. But when she showed up at my doorstep, we still laughed out loud. We had each decided to wear our hair in two low, loose braids.

"I'll take mine out," I said.

"No, no," said Farrah, shaking her head. "Just

leave it—maybe we'll start a trend. Anyway, I don't want to miss the tour."

Fifteen minutes later, we had entered Edindale's historical district on the east side of town. The homes on Archer Avenue were all large and set back from the street. Cadwelle Mansion, a charming painted lady overlooking the Muddy Rock River, was all lit up like a showplace. As we parked on the street and walked up the long sidewalk leading to the front door, we noticed there was a vineyard adjacent to the mansion's wide lawn.

"That's a good sign," said Farrah approvingly.

I laughed and rang the doorbell. A uniformed maid opened the door and led us through the wide entryway to the parlor.

"I bet she's part of the show," Farrah whispered.

Like a handful of other guests, we had arrived thirty minutes before showtime to take advantage of the advertised sneak peek at the newly renovated bed-and-breakfast. The maid took our coats and told us to help ourselves to wine and hors d'oeuvres prior to the tour, which would begin shortly.

"This place is gorgeous, isn't it?" I said.

The spacious parlor featured plush overstuffed chairs and gleaming early twentieth-century side tables accented with artful flower arrangements. A baby grand piano took up one corner of the room, while an inviting fireplace crackled on the other side. The entire floor was covered in a large colorful Persian carpet.

About half a dozen people sipped wine and chatted quietly near the fireplace. I was pleased to see that Yvette Prime was among them. She was dressed modestly in stylish trousers and a red blazer over a black turtleneck. Her long gold necklace flashed in the lamplight.

In contrast to Yvette's unassuming appearance, her companion stood out like a pop star in a pantsuit. She was a tall, striking woman with short platinum blond hair and bright red lipstick.

Farrah picked up two glasses of white wine from the sideboard and handed one to me. I was trying to figure out a way to casually start a conversation with Yvette when the tall blonde's loud voice caused all heads to turn her way. Her boisterous manner drew the whole room into her circle.

Fine by me. Now I wouldn't have to pretend not to listen in. Farrah shot me an amused look and turned to stare curiously at the woman, too.

"Yvette, you were so right. This place is brilliant! I'm going to feature the B&B on the town's website and add the vineyard to our wine trail. And we have *got* to get this house on the historical registry. I'll do whatever I can to help move that along."

Farrah snapped her fingers and gave me a nudge. Turning her back to Yvette and the blonde, Farrah said, "Now I know who that woman is. It's Tish Holiday, the new Edindale tourism director. I saw her on the local morning show the other day promoting the Groundhog Festival."

I nodded to Farrah and looked back over at the pair. I recalled Catrina saying she thought Tish didn't like Mila for some reason. Now Tish and Yvette were huddled together, so I couldn't hear what Yvette was saying. Tish, however, didn't seem to have any volume control.

"I know!" she said to Yvette. "Do we have Barney Fife running the police department, or what? I told the mayor she needs to do something ASAP. Our downtown businesses are all feeling nervous."

Farrah elbowed me again. "They must be talking about the burglaries. Did you hear Gigi's Bar and Grill was the latest to be robbed?"

"Yeah," I said. "Tuesday night, right?"

Farrah bobbed her head. "I know the bartender. He told me the police questioned him and the other employees, because there was no evidence of a break-in. They implied it was an inside job. But, I have a theory. You know how—"

Farrah was interrupted by Tish's booming voice. "And here are our esteemed hosts now! Danielle, the place looks *marvelous*. Marco, you married a design genius."

I turned to see a familiar-looking couple enter the room. Smiling graciously, they shook hands with people as they made their way to the front of the small crowd. As they took their places in front of the fireplace, I remembered where I had met them before. They were the well-dressed couple who had been talking with Crenshaw in our office building earlier this week.

"Thank you all for coming," Marco said, clapping his hands together. "We are pleased as punch to have you here for our very first mystery dinner, as well as our first official tour of Cadwelle Mansion Bed and Breakfast. I'm Marco Thomison, and this is my lovely wife, Danielle. She's the smart one, so I'll let her start the tour."

Danielle gave a mock bow, then laughingly waved

away her husband's compliment. "Right. So, as some of you know, Marco and I moved here from San Francisco last fall. It was always our dream to open a bed-and-breakfast. It goes along perfectly with two of our passions—mine for cooking and Marco's for antiques. Well, we had been keeping our eye out for the perfect place—"

"San Francisco was too expensive," Marco interjected.

"And when we learned about this opportunity, we jumped on it," Danielle continued. "See, I had been to Edindale as a little girl, because my grandfather ran a candy store here. So, I already knew what a lovely town this is."

"Oh," said Marco, jumping in again. "Let's not forget the reason we saw the listing in the first place. None of this would have been possible if it weren't for the tireless efforts of the world's best real estate agent—and our new best friend—Ms. Yvette Prime."

The small crowd clapped, and Tish stepped forward. She was holding an engraved plaque, which she presented to Yvette for her "longstanding dedication and valuable contribution to the economic development of Edindale." Apparently, Yvette had sold a number of downtown business properties in addition to the B&B.

"Now, about the mansion," Marco said, gesturing for his wife to continue.

"Yes," said Danielle. "Cadwelle Mansion was built in 1901 by Orion Cadwelle. He was from a wealthy Chicago family, but he moved here and became the town druggist. He did quite well. He was a known philanthropist and a generous neighbor. He and his wife, Violet, often threw big parties in this mansion."

"And then came Prohibition," said Marco.

"Right," said Danielle. "In 1919, the government banned alcohol. But, of course, some folks found a way around that. There were rumors that Cadwelle became a bootlegger. And, as we'll see on the tour, there's an old-fashioned speakeasy in the basement."

"Sweet!" said Farrah, next to me.

"We'll start our tour upstairs," said Danielle. "You'll be able to see all the rooms that are available for nightly stays. Then we'll take the back stairs down to the kitchen and make our way to the basement. After that, we'll finish up in the dining room and get ready for the show."

As we moved along from room to room, I kept trying to catch Yvette's eye. At one point she saw me and gave me a brief smile. My plan to question her tonight was not panning out as I had hoped.

At least the tour was interesting. The speakeasy was especially intriguing. The shiny long wooden bar had been restored, and there were vintage pieces placed throughout the room, including an antique ivory chess set on a cocktail table and an upright candlestick telephone on one end of the bar. In a far corner of the basement, a pair of high-quality butterscotch-colored leather club chairs flanked a small glass-topped table.

In spite of the upscale touches, the room wasn't exactly comfortable. The bare walls were made of stone, and the air was cool and dank. The dim lighting gave it an eerie feeling.

"It looks like the bar is well stocked," remarked Farrah.

"That's right," said Marco, with a twinkle in his eye. "We plan to host private parties in here eventually."

"Yes, so keep us in mind!" said Danielle.

"You want to hear something funny?" said Marco, running his hand over the smooth bar top. "Yesterday, the doorbell rings, so I answer it and there's this preacher at the door. Says his name is Reverend Natty Smith, or Schmidt or something. Anyway, I invite him in, because I want to be neighborly, you know. I think he's out soliciting donations for charity or something. Well, come to find out, he's here about the vineyard. Said he heard we're opening a winery, and he wants us to make grape juice instead!"

"Yeah, like that would attract tourists," said Tish.

Marco laughed. "Some folks thought Prohibition was a good idea. And apparently some folks still do!"

I shook my head and chuckled with the rest of the group. It would seem that Reverend Natty could find a way to be against just about anything.

At the conclusion of the tour, we assembled in the dining room and looked around. From the shiny parquet flooring to the ornate brass chandelier, there was a lot to admire. The room was outfitted with four round cloth-covered tables arranged in a semicircle facing a wall of windows, which were covered in heavy emerald-green drapes. In front of the windows stood a podium, two microphone stands, and a small table of props.

Farrah moved toward one of the end dining tables, while Yvette and Tish headed toward a middle table. Quickly, I brushed past Farrah and grabbed a chair next to Yvette. Looking over at Farrah, I plastered on a bright smile, hoping she'd understand. She gave me a quizzical look and joined me at the table without saying anything.

As soon as we were seated, the four of us introduced ourselves. I reminded Yvette that we had met before.

"Oh, of course," she said. "Beverly and I go way back. Her firm has thrown business my way many times, and I've done the same."

Just then, two other guests joined our table. They were a young, fresh-faced couple dressed in slightly old-fashioned outfits—the young man in slacks and a striped dress shirt under a sweater vest and the girl in a cap-sleeved pink dress. When they introduced themselves as Kitty and Dale Valentine, it dawned on me that they must be part of the show.

But I wasn't really interested in the show. I was interested in finding out what Yvette and Tish thought about Mila's shop. I wanted to know just how badly Yvette's client wanted to buy it. And I wanted to know if Tish really had something against Mila, as Catrina had implied.

Ragtime music started playing softly in the background, and the maid entered the room pushing a drinks cart. I realized I didn't have much time. I took a deep breath and turned to Yvette and Tish.

"So," I began, in what I hoped was a casual tone. "Did everyone hear about the New Age shop that was vandalized a few days ago? It's right around the corner from my office. I walked by on my way to work the other day and saw that someone had spray-painted the word *Witch* on the front of the store."

Farrah stared at me suspiciously, while Yvette gave me a politely impassive look that probably hid her judgment of my awkward social skills.

But Tish took the bait.

"I saw that on my way to work, too. I about flipped my lid. I mean, of all things!"

"I know," I said. "It did seem outrageous."

"You know," she continued, "if I had been here when that shop went before the zoning board, I never would have let it be approved. It just doesn't fit with the character of this town."

"Oh. It doesn't?"

"This isn't Salem," she said sardonically. "Our visitors—at least, the kind of visitors I'm trying to draw—are looking for upscale relaxation. They come for the wineries and the antiques, not any weirdo, psychic nonsense."

I sensed a presence at my elbow, but I wanted to hear more from Tish. "Who do you suppose—"

"Well, well, what do we have here?" Tish interrupted, looking over my shoulder.

"Good evening, ladies and gentlemen," said a deep voice behind me. "My name is Woolworth Jenkins, house butler and humble servant. I will be your waiter this evening."

I turned around to look up at the waiter and nearly fell out of my seat.

There, holding a silver platter and looking like

a character straight out of *Downton Abbey,* was Crenshaw Davenport III.

Farrah clapped a hand over her mouth. I could only gape.

Crenshaw noticed me then and almost dropped the platter. He quickly recovered and gave me a small bow.

"For your first course," said Crenshaw the butler, "we have a tossed salad with toasted walnuts and homemade raspberry vinaigrette."

He set bowls of salad in front of each of us. Then he held up another small bowl. "Crumbled feta," he said smoothly. "For the nonvegans, of course."

After Crenshaw left the table, I met Farrah's eyes and let out a giggle.

"What is he doing here?" she hissed.

I just shook my head. I knew Crenshaw dabbled in acting ever since I found out he was in a Shakespeare-in-the-Park production of *A Midsummer Night's Dream* last June. He had played Bottom, the donkey. *So, this must be where he's been rushing off to after work. He's probably been going to rehearsal.*

As soon as our salads had been cleared away by two "maids," Crenshaw walked over to a microphone, which was now in a spotlight.

"Ladies and gentlemen," he began. "The year is 1921. The place, downtown Chicago. Picture, if you will, a high-class speakeasy—much like the one you saw in the lower level of this mansion. The place is hopping. Drinks are flowing, jazz is playing, flappers are dancing the Charleston. Then a stranger enters the room. He wears a black suit and a fedora, and he has trouble written all over his face . . . ."

As Crenshaw narrated, various characters took the stage, and I soon found myself caught up in the entertainment. For the next hour, the performers acted out scenes in between the courses of our meal. At one point, Farrah got in on the action when a character took her hostage. At another point, we were all startled when "Dale Valentine" was "shot" at our table.

When it was finally revealed that the maid was really a gangster and the show ended, several audience members walked over to the performance area to meet the actors, while other guests mingled or made their way to the exit. I noticed Yvette was talking to Danielle. I didn't see where Tish had gone.

"See how fun that was," said Farrah, giving me a gentle shove. "Aren't you glad you came?"

"Yes, of course." I gave her a grudging smile. "You were right, as usual."

"I'm going to remember you said that, you know," she said, gathering up her purse.

"Oh, I'm sure of it. Listen, I'm going to go find the powder room before we leave."

"Take your time," Farrah said. "I'm gonna go talk to that cute guy with the cigar."

Rolling my eyes, I left the dining room and followed a short hall to where I remembered seeing a bathroom during the evening's tour. The door was closed, so I lingered in the hall, admiring the décor as I waited. The attention to detail really was remarkable, I thought. Antique sconces hung on the wall on either side of a gilt-framed oval mirror. In a corner, near the doorway leading to the parlor, stood an ivory-trimmed pedestal table displaying an authentic-looking Grecian urn.

A sound at the end of the hall drew my attention. It was the click of the basement door, which was now swinging open. I watched as Tish emerged and slowly closed the door behind her. She glanced to her right, toward the kitchen entrance, then to her left. She let out a squeak when she saw me.

"Oh, my! You gave me a start," she said, fluttering her fingers to her chest.

"Sorry about that," I said. My eyes slid to the basement door behind her.

Tish lowered her voice. "I just had to have another peek at that speakeasy. I think it would be the perfect location for a party I'm planning."

I nodded and was about to ask her a question when the door to the powder room opened. An elderly woman stepped out and paused when she saw me. Smiling, she reached back into the room to flick the light switch on again. As I thanked her, I noticed Tish brush past me without a word.

What an odd woman, I thought.

I also realized that she was capable of being quiet after all.

Chapter 10

As I approached the dining room, Farrah walked through the doorway carrying my coat.

"Ready?" she asked. "I already thanked our hosts. Your buddy, Crenshaw, must have skipped out. I was going to tease him about being the butler, but I couldn't find him."

"Yeah, let's go," I said, putting on my coat. I didn't have the energy to do any more investigating tonight.

We stepped out into the cold night air and started walking to my car.

"Well," said Farrah, "are you going to tell me now, or am I going to have to pry it out of you?"

"What do you mean?" I said. Then I saw the look she gave me. "Oh, all right. I'm trying to figure out who vandalized Moonstone Treasures."

"Go on," said Farrah.

"The woman who owns the place is a nice lady, and I'd like to help her. Someone is harassing her. Besides the vandalism, she's been receiving threatening notes."

"And you think Yvette Prime has something to do with it?"

"Well, I don't know. Probably not. But she's been after Mila to sell the place, and she won't reveal who her client is. I thought maybe the client could be trying to drive Mila out of business."

I unlocked my car, and we climbed in and buckled up. I started the engine and cranked the heat.

"Sounds like a long shot," said Farrah. "Now, if you've got the itch to solve a mystery, you should take a look at all the burglaries that have been happening downtown."

"Oh, yeah, you said you had a theory," I said. "Let's hear it."

"Okay. There are two things, actually. The first is about the timing," said Farrah. "I think I've uncovered a pattern. There have been five burglaries so far. Two were near the end of November and two were at the end of December. Now we've had one at the end of January. If the pattern holds true, there will be another burglary in the next six days."

"Interesting," I said. We were just approaching the downtown business district, and I suddenly didn't feel like going home. "Do you want to stop off for a drink someplace and then tell me the rest of your theory?"

"Yes, ma'am," said Farrah. "The Loose will be too loud. How about if we go to Gigi's?"

"The scene of the crime," I said, grinning. "Sounds good to me."

As I drove four more blocks to Gigi's Bar and Grill and found street-side parking, Farrah and I reminisced about our first foray into detective work last summer. Now that I was on the other side of that stressful episode, I could appreciate the fun we had.

We were still laughing as we entered the dimly lit establishment. The dinner crowd had largely dispersed, so we didn't have to wait to be seated. As we crossed the wood-plank floor toward the back of the restaurant, I noticed the walls were covered in wood paneling and the tables were fashioned from a heavy scarred wood.

"I never realized how woody this place is," said Farrah, with a giggle.

"I know, right? At least the seats are vinyl," I said, sliding into the booth.

The waiter, a short man with a ready smile, appeared at our table with menus in hand.

"Cute pigtails, ladies. Here for dinner, or just drinks?"

"Just drinks," said Farrah, touching her braids. "I almost forgot about our matching hairstyle."

After we ordered our drinks—an Irish coffee for Farrah and a Black Russian for me—I asked Farrah to continue telling me her ideas about the burglaries.

"Check this out," said Farrah, pulling her iPad from her purse. "I made a list of all the places that were robbed and plotted them on a map of downtown Edindale."

"Wow," I said. "Slow day in software sales?"

"Very funny," said Farrah. "Do you notice anything about all these places?"

I looked at the list on Farrah's iPad:

1) *Harper's Drugstore*
2) *Elena's Boutique*
3) *Handbags and More*
4) *Junior's Electronics*
5) *Gigi's Bar and Grill*

"Hmm," I said. "They're all specialty shops? Well, except for the restaurant. I guess they're all private establishments that aren't part of a franchise or chain?"

"True," said Farrah. "They're also all pretty old. These businesses have been around for at least twenty years, and the buildings even longer. I have this booklet at home on Edindale history that a client gave to me a couple years ago. The chamber of commerce had it made to celebrate the new millennium. Anyway, it has all these cool black-and-white pictures of downtown Edindale—including some of the places on this list."

"So, what does that tell us?" I asked.

"Well, since there was no evidence of a forceful entry at any of these places, I think somebody has a key. Either that, or we have a master lock-picker on the loose."

"Huh." The waiter returned with our drinks, so I handed Farrah her iPad and sipped my cocktail as I considered what she had said. My mind drifted back to the vandalism at Moonstone Treasures. Apparently, there was no evidence of a break-in there either. *Could there be a connection between Mila's harasser and the burglaries?*

"There was merchandise stolen from all of these businesses, right?" I asked Farrah.

"Yep. I think one of the places had some cash stolen, too."

"What about from here?" I asked, tapping on the table.

"Bottles of liquor. According to Ted, the bartender I was telling you about, they lost more than a thousand dollars' worth of inventory."

"Jeez. We must be looking at a team of burglars, don't you think? One person couldn't very well cart off that many bottles by himself or herself."

Farrah shrugged. "Maybe a second person drove the getaway car."

I stirred the ice in my drink and took a second look at the map Farrah had made.

"None of these stores had security cameras?"

"No. Not cameras with very good coverage, anyway. That's what made me realize these are, by and large, older mom-and-pop stores. I also figure the thief or thieves are entering from alleys out back."

Remembering the dark alley behind Moonstone Treasures, I again wondered if the crimes could be related somehow. However, nothing was stolen from Mila's shop. And, as far as I knew, the burglary victims hadn't received any intimidating notes.

I was on the verge of telling Farrah about the notes, when she leaned forward, a gleam in her eye.

"I have a plan," Farrah whispered.

"Oh?" I said, my stomach tightening already.

"So far, the burglaries have always occurred early in the week, from Sunday to Wednesday. Maybe because there are too many people out on the other nights. Anyway, I figure the next chance for the burglar to strike will be this Sunday."

"And?" I said, not liking where this was going.

"And, I think you and I should take a walk Sunday night. We should patrol the downtown alleys and see what we can see."

"What? No way, Farrah! Are you kidding me?"

"Come on! Where's your sense of adventure?"

"It's with my sense of safety," I retorted.

"We'll be perfectly safe," Farrah said. "We'll wear black, so we'll be practically invisible. And we'll have our cell phones at the ready. We can alert the police the second we see anything going down."

"You're crazy, you know that?"

Farrah grinned and finished off her drink.

"Crazy like a fox," she said.

After all the drinks on Friday night, I decided to call a cab and leave my car at Gigi's Bar and Grill. Late Saturday morning I walked downtown to retrieve it and then met Farrah at Fieldstone Park. We went for a long run down the rail trail and back. She pestered me about "Operation Alley Cat" practically the whole way.

Farrah claimed she was only interested in helping out the town's small businesses. As proof, she gave me her booklet with the old photos of downtown Edindale. However, I suspected she was really just bored. I suggested she sign up for an adventure cruise instead. She only laughed.

By the end of the day, Farrah had finally given up her scheme. We watched an old movie at her house and made a homemade vegan pizza. Wes was out of town covering a college basketball game for work, so I knew I wouldn't see him. Around 9:00, I went home, took a hot bath, and turned in. Then I had a dream that convinced me to go along with Farrah's plan after all.

In my dream, I saw Mila's cat, Drishti, sauntering down a narrow dirt trail. I followed the beautiful gray cat, worried that she would become lost or hurt. It was dark outside and lightning flashed in the sky. Trees rose on either side of the trail as I walked faster and faster, and then ran, trying to catch up with Drishti, but I couldn't catch her. She slipped farther and farther away from me until she became a speck in the distance. Then she disappeared.

I woke up feeling a profound sense of guilt and shame. I had let Mila down.

As I brushed my teeth and dressed for the day, I couldn't help thinking there must be some connection between Mila's cat and Farrah's "Operation Alley Cat." I believed dreams were sometimes divine messages. Maybe wandering the streets at night wasn't such a bad idea after all.

Besides, I wasn't totally defenseless. I did have a protection spell or two up my sleeve.

When I called Farrah, she was stunned at my change of heart. She asked me why I had changed my mind, and I told her I would tell her some other time. She was cool with that.

I spent most of the day Sunday doing laundry, cleaning house, cooking some meals for the week, and trying not to think about what I had agreed to do that night. At one point I gave Wes a call, but he didn't pick up.

That evening, I did a sitting meditation for fifteen minutes to calm my mind and relax my body. Then I went to bed early and set my alarm for 1:00 A.M. Farrah and I had planned our little recon mission to coincide with the time we thought the break-ins must be taking place. When the alarm woke me, I rolled out of bed and immediately began preparations for a glamour spell.

First, I walked over to the table I normally used for an altar and dragged it to the middle of the room. On the left of the table, I placed symbols of the Goddess: a green candle and a silver chalice. On the right, I placed symbols of the God: a red candle and my ritual knife, or athame. In the center, I placed a round lighted make-up mirror.

When my altar was set, I ran downstairs to the kitchen to collect a clove of garlic. Then I stopped off in the den to find my sewing kit and gather a small square of black cloth and a spool of thread. After returning to my bedroom, I placed the garlic clove in the center of the cloth, tied the corners, and placed my makeshift amulet on the altar next to the mirror.

Next, I lit the candles and cast a protective circle around the altar by walking around it three times while drawing an invisible line with my athame. At each cardinal point, I invoked a deity associated with the corresponding element for each point: to the east, I called upon Aradia, a goddess of air; to the south, I called upon Horus, a fire god; to the west, I called upon Osiris, a god of water; and to the north, I called upon Demeter, a goddess of earth.

When invoking the gods and goddesses, I allowed my heart to fill with gratitude and love. As a Wiccan, I felt lucky to have access to all of history's deities. I knew they each represented different aspects of the archetypal God and Goddess and, as such, each carried a unique, magical energy. It was an empowering knowledge.

At last, I faced the altar, cupped my hands over the garlic clove amulet, and gazed into the mirror. Softly, I murmured the spell I had written the day before:

"I call now Morpheus, god of night,
Shapeshifter, gatekeeper, guardian of dreams.

Shield me, hide me, vanish from sight,
Concealed in darkness, I shan't be seen.

Cloaked in mist, bright moonbeam's light,
This charm I bear will all deceive."

As I stared at my reflection, I unfocused my vision until the edges of my face became blurry. I imagined I was becoming transparent like the Invisible Man of science fiction. After a moment, I took a deep breath and slowly blew it out. Then I extinguished the candles, closed the circle, and pocketed the amulet.

Farrah sent me a text when she arrived and told me she would stay in her car to wait for me. Quickly, I laced up my black sneakers and bounded silently down my front steps, then walked to her car. When I opened the front passenger door, she jolted in her seat.

"Jesus! How did you do that? I thought I was watching your front door, but I didn't see you coming."

"Good," I said, as I buckled my seat belt.

The spell had worked.

Chapter 11

The streets were desolate as we made our way downtown. A light fog limited visibility and added to the overall eerie feeling of the night.

It was about 3:00 A.M. when we parked in the municipal parking lot near the courthouse. Our strategy was to proceed on foot, up and down the alleys, keeping an eye out for any suspicious-looking vehicles.

"It's freezing out here," I whispered. "I can't believe we're doing this."

"Come on," said Farrah, ignoring my complaint. "Let's go this way and stick to the shadows."

I followed Farrah down the alley behind Harper's drugstore. We stuck close together. In our black pants, black coats, and black stocking caps, we really were nearly invisible. If we were to encounter any police officers, I was sure they would think we were the burglars. We walked for ten minutes, my thoughts wandering between how ridiculous we looked and how much I wanted answers.

Tires crunched against gravel up ahead.

"What do we do?" Farrah hissed.

Oh, great, I thought. *How could we not have a plan?*

I cast around for a hiding place and saw a large green Dumpster. "Let's hide over there!" I said.

We scurried over to the Dumpster and crouched on the ground. Clasping onto the garlic clove in my pocket, I listened intently as the car went slowly by. When it was past, we dared to peek out and peer down the alley. As the vehicle rounded the corner, we instantly recognized what it was. A police car.

"Well, it's good to know they're out patrolling, too," said Farrah.

"Yeah," I agreed. "Except what would we have said if they found us? I think we should call it a night."

"Oh, all right," said Farrah. "But let's go down another block, and then turn back. I don't want to run into that police car again."

At the end of the alley, we crossed the street and hurried down one more alley. Then we turned the corner and walked down the sidewalk toward the parking lot where we had left Farrah's car. When we reached Main Street, I looked over at Moonstone Treasures, expecting it to be dark.

I froze in my tracks. At first, I thought my eyes were playing tricks on me. Then I looked again and knew they weren't. I grabbed Farrah's arm.

"Look over there! There's a light on."

Farrah squinted. "You're right. Maybe it's a nightlight."

"I don't think so. Let's check it out."

Without waiting for Farrah, I ran over to the shop. By the time I reached the front door, the light had gone out. I peered in the window but couldn't see anything.

"What's going on?" asked Farrah, joining me at the door.

"The light's off now," I said. I tried turning the doorknob, but it was locked. "Let's check the back."

We ran down the block and around the corner to the alley. It was dark and empty, but when we reached the steel door leading to Moonstone Treasures my breath caught in my throat. The door was ajar.

Hesitating only a moment, I pulled open the door and stepped inside. Farrah was right on my heels.

I felt around for a light switch but couldn't find one. Stepping gingerly, I moved into the darkness and waved my hands above me, hoping to latch onto a cord. Then my toe caught on the edge of a rug, and I went stumbling into the room. I nearly fell again when Farrah ran into me from behind.

"Sorry," she whispered. "Hold on. I have a flashlight."

After a moment of fumbling in her purse, Farrah pulled out a penlight and switched it on. It cast a small beam, but at least we weren't in complete blackness anymore.

"I wonder if the vandal has been here again," I muttered, as I tried to look around in the dim light. Farrah was moving her flashlight so quickly, I couldn't focus on anything. I was about to tell her to hold it steady so we could find a light switch, when I heard her gasp beside me.

"Oh, my God!"

"What?" I turned around, trying to see what the beam of light had settled on.

"Oh, my God!" she repeated. "There's someone there!"

Adrenaline coursed through my veins as my body prepared to flee. Then I saw it.

"Oh, no," I said, rushing over to the lifeless form on the floor. "Farrah, bring the light over here!"

Farrah complied, but the flashlight trembled in her hand. When she managed to shine it on the pallid, immobile countenance of the body on the floor, she screamed and dropped the flashlight.

Dropping to my knees, I covered my face with both hands. Then I took a deep breath and reached out a tentative hand. I had to be sure.

His cheeks were stiff and ice cold. He was beyond any help I could provide.

In the darkness, Farrah crouched down next to me. She felt on the floor for the flashlight, and switched it on again.

"Do you know who it is?" she whispered.

"Yeah," I said, blinking back tears. "His name was Charlie."

Farrah paced the length of Moonstone Treasures, while I perched unsteadily on a tufted ottoman in the book section of the store. We had finally found an overhead light and had quickly surveyed the rest of the shop. Satisfied that we were alone, I pulled out my phone to call 911. I punched "9" and then hesitated.

"What should we say about why we were here?" I asked.

Farrah stopped pacing and looked at me. "You saw a light in the shop, remember?"

"No, I mean . . . this." I indicated my all-black beatnik attire. "Operation Alley Cat."

"Oh. Well . . . let's just say we were out for an early-morning run. We *are* training for a 10K after all. We have busy schedules, so we have to train when we can."

I sighed and nodded. "Okay."

After I made the call, I scrolled through my phone for Mila's number. She answered groggily after the fourth ring.

"Hello?"

"Mila, it's Keli. I'm so sorry to have to tell you this, but . . . a person has died at your shop."

I heard a shuffling sound through the phone and pictured Mila sitting up in bed. She was probably trying to decide if she was still dreaming.

"You probably didn't know him," I continued. "His name was Charlie. He was an older man who sometimes sat outside the courthouse feeding pigeons."

Mila found her voice. "He died at Moonstone?"

"Apparently so," I said.

Suddenly, sirens pierced the air and bright red and blue lights flashed outside the store window.

"The police just arrived," I said. "You'd better get here as soon as you can."

As I ended the call with Mila, Farrah came through the curtain from the back room. She gave me a knowing glance and patted her own phone, which she then slipped into her purse. Then she walked to the front door and let the police officers inside.

The next hour was a blur of activity. Police officers swarmed the area like worker ants, taping off the front and back entrances, snapping pictures, filling evidence bags, and asking questions. After Farrah and I gave our statements, we were told that we could leave and that we might be contacted for further questioning in the coming days. Instead of leaving, we lingered in the front of the store, trying to make sense of what had happened.

Shortly after the coroner arrived, Mila and her husband entered through the back door. As soon as I heard Mila's voice, I headed over to join her. I was distracted when I glanced through the front window and noticed a commotion near the yellow crime scene tape. Through the glare of the rotating police lights, I recognized the reporter, Sheana Starwalt. She was showing her press ID to the officer on the sidewalk.

I groaned. *Should I sneak out the back?* I didn't want to desert Mila, but I didn't want to speak to the reporter either.

Before I could make a decision, I spotted the tall, dark-haired photographer standing next to Sheana. With his unshaven jawline and rumpled jacket, he looked just as irresistible as the first time I'd laid eyes on him.

I opened the door to the shop at the same time the police officer was allowing Sheana and Wes around the yellow tape. The cops must have been done with their crime scene work. Wes's face registered surprise when he saw me, and then concern.

"Hey," he said, when he drew near. "What's going on? We heard there was police activity here. There was a death in the store?"

I swallowed the lump in my throat and nodded. "Wes," I said gently, "it was Charlie. I don't know how it happened, but—"

My voice broke and Wes enveloped me in a strong hug. We held one another for several seconds. When we pulled apart, I saw the tears in his eyes.

"I'm so sorry, Wes. I know how much you liked him." I reached for his hand and squeezed tightly. "I wish I had gotten here sooner. Then maybe—"

Just then, the shop door opened and two paramedics came out, maneuvering a gurney between them. A white sheet hid the body beneath it. Reluctantly, Wes lifted his camera and shot a photo as the body was loaded into the waiting ambulance.

I felt a tap on my elbow and turned around to see Farrah. "There's a reporter inside talking to the shop owner," she said quietly. "We should go now."

"Okay," I agreed, feeling a sad weight settle in. I caught Wes's eye and gave him a wave. Then Farrah and I quickly stole away.

Chapter 12

It was well after 6:00 A.M. when I finally flopped onto my bed, still fully clothed in black. As tired as I was, I really didn't want to close my eyes. Finding a dead body will have that effect on a person. I lay there for a while, my mind spinning like a top. The last threatening note had mentioned death. Now there had been a death at the shop. That couldn't be a coincidence.

When daylight began to break outside my bedroom window, I decided this might be the day to end my streak of perfect attendance at work. Then my cell phone rang. I ignored it, letting the call go to voicemail. Seconds later, it rang again. On the fourth call, I hauled myself out of bed and went straight to the shower. By the time I got out, toweled off, and threw on a robe, I had missed seven calls.

I sat on the edge of my bed and stared at my phone. *Had last night really happened?* It seemed surreal now. With a sigh, I dialed into voicemail before the phone could ring again.

Three of the calls were from Catrina and one was from Max Eisenberry, the professor I had met last summer who turned out to be a member of Mila's coven. Catrina begged me to call her, while Max simply said she'd like to stop by my office today. Two of the other messages were from my boss and our administrative assistant, each asking me to call her. The last message was from Sheana Starwalt. The reporter. *Terrific.*

The phone started ringing again. I recognized Catrina's number and promptly stuffed the phone in a dresser drawer. Then I pushed myself off the bed and headed toward the kitchen. When I was halfway there, the doorbell rang. I froze.

"Yoo-hoo! Rise and shine!" called Farrah.

I relaxed my shoulders and opened the door with relief.

"What are you doing here so early?" I asked.

"You and I have a lot to talk about," she said, walking past me. She carried two cups of coffee and a white paper sack from the Good Karma Bakery, which she placed on the small table in my breakfast nook. "Anyway, I have a sales meeting later today."

I joined Farrah at the table and gratefully inhaled the warm aroma of fresh coffee. I peeked in the bag. "Chocolate zucchini muffins?"

"Don't you know it," she said. She opened the lid on her cup of coffee and took a sip, regarding me closely. "Sleep much this morning?"

I made a face at her.

"Yeah, me neither." She reached into her large purse, pulled out her iPad, and touched the screen.

"We made the 'Breaking News' page on the *Edindale Gazette*," she said, handing me the iPad.

"Not a photo!"

"No, just our names," Farrah said.

I glanced at the article and grimaced when I saw the headline: DEATH AT PSYCHIC OCCULT SHOP.

Trying not to groan, I read the first paragraph aloud: "'Local psychic Mila Douglas didn't predict the tragedy at her occult bookstore last night, nor can she explain it. Charles Morris, eighty-one, was found dead in a private back room of the shop at four A.M. by local attorneys Keli Milanni and Farrah Anderson, who were passing by.'"

Farrah snorted. "Well, that much is true. We were passing by. Sort of."

I skimmed the rest of the article, reading snippets to myself: *The cause of death is under investigation. . . . The police have not ruled out foul play . . . . Ms. Douglas could not explain why Mr. Morris was in her shop. . . . Mr. Morris was a resident of St. Xavier House.*

I looked up at Farrah. "What's St. Xavier House?"

Farrah shrugged and fished her phone out of her purse. She typed in a query and read me the result. "'St. Xavier House provides both temporary shelter and permanent low-income housing for single-room occupants.' It's run by Our Lady of Mercy Catholic Church."

"Hmm." I fell silent and took a bite of chocolate muffin. *Why would someone want to kill Charlie?* He was harmless. I highly doubted he had any enemies. Maybe he was just a pawn, sacrificed for some bigger purpose, though I couldn't fathom what that might be. *Was the murderer the same person who was threatening Mila?*

Farrah cleared her throat. "I have a bit of information that didn't make the news."

"Oh?"

"When our ace reporter arrived, the body had already been covered up. She didn't see what I saw."

I gave Farrah a quizzical look, recalling that she had been in the back room while I was on the phone with Mila. She had also watched the police do their work. Had they found a threatening note? In the moments after we had found the light switch, I looked for one, but I didn't see any white sheets of paper lying around.

"Check it out," said Farrah, holding up her phone.

"Oh, Farrah!" I said, averting my eyes. "You took a picture of a dead body?"

"What, you're not squeamish, are you?" said Farrah. "This is really interesting. Take a look."

"Ugh," I said. "Give me your phone."

With a mental prayer to the Goddess for strength and fortitude, I took the phone and studied the picture. Farrah was right. There was something very interesting in the photo.

"What is that powdery stuff sprinkled all over him?" I asked. "I didn't notice it last night."

"The flash on my phone camera really brightened it up," Farrah said. "I think those are herbs and spices. I saw one of the investigators scrape some of it into a baggie. He even sniffed it, like in TV cop shows."

I frowned. "Come to think of it, I did smell something like cinnamon and patchouli in the back room,"

I said. "But Mila's shop always smells like that, so I didn't think anything of it."

Farrah gave me a strange look. "So, uh, how well do you know this Mila Douglas anyway?"

"Huh?" I said. "I don't know. I've been in her shop a few times. It's just around the corner from my office, you know."

"Mm-hmm," said Farrah.

"Why?"

"I heard one of the cops speculating last night. He said this might have been a ritual killing."

I put down the coffee cup I had been raising to my lips and shook my head. "Uh-uh. Mila didn't have anything to do with this, if that's what you're suggesting."

"Well, maybe one of her kooky customers did," said Farrah. She must have seen something in my expression, because she softened her tone. "Sorry. You were one of her customers. I get it. I'm not talking about people like you. I'm talking about those New Age freaky people who dabble in witchcraft or Satanism or whatever. That could be what we're dealing with here."

I rubbed my temples, not knowing what to say. It was hard to accept the fact that my best friend would think I was a freak if she knew I practiced Wicca. Not to mention the fact that she lumped Satanism in the same category as witchcraft.

"Look at this," Farrah said, oblivious to my inner turmoil. She touched her phone and pulled up another picture, which showed a different angle of the body. "See how his arms are crossed at the wrists, over his chest? That was purposeful. Someone arranged him that way."

I stared at the image, feeling a surge of sympathy for poor Charlie. He was wearing the same baggy suit he had been wearing when I last saw him on the bench. The suit was dirty and rumpled, with the collar all bunched up behind his neck. His thin hair was matted in the back and covered in black dirt. His appearance was anything but ceremonious.

Yet, the scented powders and crossed arms did call to mind an ancient Egyptian burial. Maybe someone was reenacting some sort of mystical ritual after all.

Someone pretty kooky.

Beverly had warned me to expect an onslaught when I arrived at the office. Of course, everyone had seen or read the news this morning. I tried to slip in quietly a few minutes after 9:00 A.M., but someone must have seen me enter the building. I was accosted the second I stepped foot into the law firm's lobby.

"I can't believe you came in today," said Julie, standing up behind her reception desk.

"Oh, Keli," said Pammy, coming up to me. "How are you holding up?"

Crenshaw stepped in front of Pammy. "What were you doing wandering the lonely streets in the wee hours of the morning?" he demanded.

"All right, people," said Beverly, rounding the

corner into the lobby. "Give her some room to breathe."

I smiled weakly at Beverly and hitched my purse on my shoulder. *Dang*, I thought ruefully. *I should have refreshed that invisibility spell.*

"Keli," Beverly said, in her no-nonsense manner. "To save yourself the trouble of multiple retellings, why don't we convene in my sitting room in five minutes? Better to let the facts squelch the speculation, I always say."

I had no choice but to agree. After dropping my coat and purse in my office, I rejoined the others and took a seat in a wingback chair near Beverly's fireplace.

"I'm afraid I don't have a lot to tell you," I began. Seeing their skepticism, I hurried to come up with something to satisfy their curiosity.

"Okay. My friend Farrah and I were out for an early-morning run when we saw a light on in Moonstone Treasures. We looked again, and the light was off. Because of the recent incidents there, we went to take a closer look and noticed the back door was open. We went in and found—"

Several colleagues interrupted me at once.

"You went in?!"

"Are you out of your mind?"

"Oh, Keli, that was dangerous."

I winced. "I know, I know. We assumed someone had just left, and we wanted to see if everything was okay. Anyway, we called the police right away."

I looked around at all the questioning faces and knew I had to give them something more.

"Um, in the brief time I saw the body, I couldn't tell how he had died. But it looked like he had been placed there. I don't think he just wandered in and died."

Beverly cleared her throat. "This stays in this room, but I can tell you what the coroner's report will say. It was blunt force trauma."

We all looked at Beverly, and she shrugged. "I know someone in the coroner's office."

"Poor Charlie," murmured Pammy, as she played with her wide tortoiseshell bracelet.

"Did you know him?" I asked, surprised.

"Not really," she said. "I saw him outside the court-house sometimes."

"Me too," said Randall, one of the junior partners. "He was a funny dude. Always talking in rhymes or little songs."

"I can't imagine why anyone would kill him," said Pammy. "He seemed peaceful, as far as I could tell."

Everyone was quiet for a moment, until Crenshaw broke the silence. "Three o'clock in the morning, Ms. Milanni? You take your exercise at three o'clock in the morning?"

I stood up and looked over at Crenshaw as I headed for the door.

"You don't?" I said.

Chapter 13

Work kept me occupied for most of the morning. Julie, bless her heart, screened my calls so I wouldn't be interrupted by any gossip seekers or journalists. At 11:30, she buzzed my desk phone.

"There's a Max Eisenberry on the line," Julie said. "She says she's a friend. Want me to take a message?"

"No, that's okay, Julie. You can put the call through. Thanks."

I closed the document I had been reading and swiveled in my chair to gaze out the window as I spoke on the phone to Max. She asked if she could join me for lunch.

"I'll tell you what," I said. "If you'd like to bring some food to my office, we can eat right here."

"Fine by me," Max said agreeably. "Anything you like at the Cozy Café?"

"A large bowl of vegetable soup would be marvelous," I said.

An hour later, Julie ushered Max into my office. As I cleared off the small round table in the corner,

Max unpacked the food and asked me how I was faring.

"I'm okay," I said, touched at her kindness. "How's Mila? Have you talked to her?"

"That's partly why I'm here," Max said. "I'm worried about her."

I nodded. "I'm sure she's more than upset. I can't imagine being targeted the way she has. And now a murder at her shop? That would be enough to give anyone a nervous breakdown."

Max unwrapped a slice of crusty Italian bread and furrowed her brow. It occurred to me once again that she looked too young to be a college professor—I had mistaken her for a student the first time I met her. Even so, she was sharp and self-assured. She shook her coppery-red curls.

"Mila's not going to have a nervous breakdown," she said. "At least, not anytime soon. She's incredibly strong. The problem is, she's so used to caring for others that she doesn't know how to let others care for her. She thinks she ought to be able to handle everything on her own."

I sipped my soup and glanced at the purple amethyst sitting on the desk next to my computer. It was true: Mila was not in the habit of asking for help—she was the one who was always offering assistance, or guidance, or gifts.

"I don't know if you know this," Max went on, "but Mila and her husband are not able to have children. So, perhaps to compensate, Mila has become like a mother to everyone—her friends, her customers. Even strangers."

"Which makes it all the more inconceivable that someone is trying to sabotage her business," I said.

"Yeah," Max agreed. "I have no idea what or who is behind this, but Mila can't face it alone. Yet, she canceled this week's Circle meeting. I'm afraid she's starting to withdraw, shoring up her energy for something big."

"What do you mean?" I asked.

Max hesitated, apparently reluctant to talk about Mila in this way. "Well, she's naturally turning to magic for a solution. That's all well and good, except I think we should be focusing on the practical issues here, like the police investigation. Do you have any contacts at the police station?"

"Not many. I do have a friend of a friend on the force," I said, thinking of Farrah's on-again, off-again boyfriend whose police officer pal had helped me last summer. "Is Mila being open with the police now? I know she didn't tell them about the threatening notes before."

"Yes," said Max. "Her husband convinced her to hand over the notes. I think she was hoping to use them in a banishing spell. But I'm worried Mila will be under suspicion because of the latest incidents. The fire was started with items from the shop. Now the death . . . These things implicate Mila."

I recalled the photos Farrah had taken. "Did Mila tell you about the dried herbs and powders on Charlie's body?" I asked.

Max nodded. "She said someone had grabbed a bunch of jars from a cabinet and scattered the contents, without any apparent rhyme or reason."

"So, it was just meant to appear magically motivated to the layperson?"

As I pondered the pseudoritualistic nature of the incidents, an image of Catrina popped in my mind. She was so zealous about raising awareness about the persecution of witches. Surely, she wouldn't have vandalized the shop and harassed her boss just to make a point . . . . Would she?

Not to mention commit a murder.

"Anyway," said Max, "the fact that Mila is just now producing the notes makes it look like she's trying to deflect attention from herself. Plus, there wasn't any note at the scene of the murder."

I pushed my bowl away and dabbed at my mouth with a napkin. "Speaking of the notes, there's something that's been bothering me." I told Max what I had noticed about the book references that had preceded each incident. "Mila needs to be extra careful. Maybe she should even invest in a security guard."

"I agree." Max bit her fingernail, then looked at me earnestly. "Keli, Mila told me you're private about your religion. And I respect that. But we could really use your help."

"If Mila is accused of anything," I began, "I'll refer her to the best criminal defense lawyer I know."

"Not that kind of help," Max said. "You have a keen mind and a knack for figuring things out. On top of that, you're intimately familiar with witchcraft. We need you to help find out who is behind these crimes. I'm afraid the police aren't working fast enough."

For a minute, I didn't say anything. I had already

been talking to people and trying to deduce who would want to drive Mila out of business. However there was more at stake now. It wasn't just vandalism and harassment we were talking about. It was the loss of a human life.

And that wasn't the only thing weighing on me. From the start, it was clear that Mila's unconventional religion was somehow at the center of it all.

Mila's religion was my religion, too.

My gaze returned to the amethyst as a cloud parted in the sky outside. A ray of sunshine streamed through the window at the exact spot I had placed the crystal, causing it to glint in the bright light. I took it as a sign.

"Okay," I said to Max. "I'll do it."

After Max left, I made a couple of phone calls and then told Julie I was going over to the courthouse. I needed to file divorce papers for one client and conduct a title search for another one. Since I had other errands to run after that, I let her know I would likely be out for the rest of the afternoon.

It felt good to get away from my desk. Part of me wanted to go straight home and crawl into bed, considering my lack of sleep the night before. Being outside in the fresh air perked me up, though. As I walked the short distance to the courthouse, I thought about Mila and wondered how she was doing. Looking over at Moonstone Treasures, I saw that the police tape was gone, but the store was closed.

Once inside the venerable old courthouse, I filed

my client's divorce papers with the county clerk, and then made my way down the wide marble stairs to the courthouse basement, where property records were stored. As I walked along the hallway toward the Office of the Recorder of Deeds, I heard a loud clang up ahead. A heavy steel door opened and was held ajar by a uniformed police officer. Another officer led a handcuffed prisoner through the doorway. They were coming from the county jail, which was connected to the courthouse by an underground tunnel.

I regarded the men as they walked down the hallway toward me. The prisoner, a scrawny kid with a buzz cut, stared at his laceless high-tops as they passed by. Dressed in a bright orange jumpsuit, he looked embarrassed and contrite.

As well he probably should, I thought.

This made me think of the person terrorizing Mila. So far, my only suspects were upstanding citizens who were all apparently very nice people. But what the culprit was doing was not nice at all. If caught, would that person feel embarrassment or remorse, like the kid who was on his way upstairs to face a judge? Would he or she feel shame?

I completed the title search for my client and left the courthouse with copies of the records stashed in my briefcase. I would take them into the office tomorrow. For now, I wanted to stop off at city hall and see if I could catch up with Tish Holiday.

As I approached the Edindale city hall building, a three-story limestone structure on the next block over from the courthouse, I was surprised at who I saw exiting the building. It was Reverend Natty, dressed in a long gray coat and wearing a matching gray fedora. He didn't seem to notice me as I passed him on the concrete steps.

I consulted the directory just inside the entrance and learned Tish's office was on the second floor. I took the stairs and paused at the top, not knowing which way to turn. Then I heard Tish's voice.

"You have got to be kidding me!" she said. "It's almost February, for crying out loud! How can we have rain in the forecast? Rain is not charming. Snow is charming. Not rain."

Following the sound of her voice, I reached her office and peeked my head in. She was standing behind a large wooden desk speaking into a headset. When she saw me, she motioned me inside and pointed at a leather chair in front of the desk. I sat down and mentally rehearsed my excuse for being there as I waited for her to finish her call.

"I know, I know," she said into a tiny microphone. "We're going for a Punxsutawney vibe here, not dreary London Town. . . . Listen, I gotta go. Ring me tomorrow, okay?"

She took off the headset and shook her head. Then she looked at me and snapped her fingers. "Keli, right? We met at the mystery dinner the other night."

"That's right," I said, wishing she would sit down. She continued to stand, tapping her long red nails on the desk in front of her. Her short white-blond hair was styled in thick high spikes, which made her seem even taller than she already was.

"What can I do for you? Please don't tell me you want to complain about all the town's new wineries or the beer tent we have planned at the Groundhog Festival. I've already had one of those today." She rolled her eyes to the ceiling.

"Oh, I take it you had a visit from Reverend Natty," I said. "I saw him leaving the building."

"You know him? The little bugger. He's been a thorn in my side ever since I took this position. But you gotta be nice to all the people, right?"

I managed a polite chuckle and nodded. "Yeah. So, I actually stopped by to talk about the courthouse luncheon this coming Saturday. My law office is sponsoring a float in the parade, and we were considering the luncheon as well. I was wondering if it's too late to participate. I think there was a deadline?"

"No, it's not too late," said Tish, grabbing a manila folder from her desk. "What's the name of your law firm?"

"Olsen, Sykes, and Rafferty," I said. "I'm just gathering information today. The partners have to vote on any final decisions."

"I have a price sheet here," Tish said, handing me a piece of paper. "The tables aren't cheap. Gotta keep out the riffraff."

I glanced up at her to see if she was serious.

She laughed. "Just kidding."

Somehow I doubted it. Tish didn't strike me as the most truthful person. Apparently, she had lied to Mila about missing a deadline to join the luncheon.

"Ahem," I said, folding the price sheet. "I guess you probably heard about the man found dead at Moonstone Treasures."

"I didn't see the news this morning, but I heard some people talking about it," Tish said. "How perfectly dreadful. I think the man was some kind of street person or something, wasn't he?"

"I'm not really sure," I said. "It seems odd that he ended up in that shop."

"I'll tell you one thing I know for sure," Tish said. "That shop's days are numbered. That fruity psychic lady should take a hint."

"It's a shame," I replied, in a measured tone. "It really is a lovely gift shop. It draws local customers as well as tourists."

"We can do better," Tish said dryly. "I have a vision for this town, and that shop doesn't fit it. I mean, save the fortune-telling for the carnival. I don't want it on my Main Street, you know?"

Yeah. I knew. Tish was loud and clear about her feelings for Moonstone Treasures. Now I also knew she would resort to dishonesty to dismiss the business. The question was, how much lower would she stoop?

Chapter 14

The B&B is connected to this somehow.

Those were my first thoughts upon waking Tuesday morning. After a fast shower, I dressed in a trim black pantsuit and twisted my hair into a low bun on the back of my neck. Then I threw some green veggies and an apple into my juicer and blended them into an energizing, vitamin-rich tonic. I carried the glass with me to the bathroom and sipped the juice as I applied makeup and put on my earrings. All the while, I pondered how curious it was that Tish, Yvette, and Reverend Natty had all visited the B&B. Was that just a coincidence? I needed to go back there and ask some questions, I decided.

It was a few minutes past 8:00 A.M. when I pulled up in front of Cadwelle Mansion. I figured I had time to do a little information gathering before going into work. Leaving my briefcase in the car, I walked up the long sidewalk and contemplated what fib I should tell this time. I rang the bell and Danielle answered, wearing a pretty apron over a navy blue sweater dress.

"Well, good morning!" she said cheerily.

"Hello," I said. "I'm sorry to bother you so early, but I think I may have lost an earring here on Friday evening. Did you happen to come across a small gold hoop?"

"Oh, I'm afraid not. We had a cleaning service come in the next day, and I'm sure they would have given me something like that. But I'll ask around. I'll check with the actors, too."

"Thanks," I said. "Um, would you mind if I took a look where I was sitting the other night?"

"Not at all!" said Danielle, opening the door wider. "In fact, why don't you stay for breakfast? We only have a couple of guests right now, and we have plenty of food. I have a quiche cooling on the stovetop as we speak."

"It smells lovely," I said, following Danielle into the foyer. "But, actually, I can't eat eggs." I didn't want to get into a discussion about my vegan diet, but I also didn't want to miss this opportunity to speak with the owner of the B&B.

"You have an allergy?" asked Danielle. "Not to worry. I also have freshly baked bread—made without eggs—and marmalade, as well as fresh fruit, bacon, and coffee."

"That sounds very nice. Thank you," I said. No need to correct her assumption that I was allergic to eggs. Plus, I could easily pass on the bacon without comment.

"Join us in the kitchen after you look in here," she said, opening the French doors to the dining room.

I strolled into the quiet room and gazed around.

It was neat and empty, with nothing out of the ordinary. I took a cursory look around the table I had occupied the other night, fulfilling my pretense of searching for a lost earring. Then I made my way to the large country-style kitchen, where I heard the sound of clinking silverware and friendly conversation.

"Have a seat right here," said Danielle when she spotted me in the doorway. She patted the back of the nearest wooden chair along the rectangular oak table. Marco sat at the head of the table. Seated at his right were a gray-haired couple wearing khakis and matching college sweatshirts. On Marco's left, much to my surprise, was Yvette Prime, looking very much the part of a real estate agent, in nice slacks and a blazer. Her black hair was brushed smooth and tied neatly in a short ponytail.

I sat down next to Yvette and smiled at the group. Everyone said good morning and began passing food my way. Danielle stood over me with a coffeepot, so I turned over the ceramic cup at my place setting.

"It was so kind of you to invite me for breakfast," I said, spreading orange marmalade on a thick slice of bread.

"The more the merrier," said Marco. "We were just talking about one of my favorite subjects: antiques. The Carlyles here were asking about the antique bureau in their room."

"You should see it," Mrs. Carlyle said to me. "It's a beautifully restored French provincial dresser, with intricately painted trim work."

"Like I said, Mrs. Carlyle," said Marco, "I'll give you a good price if you're interested."

"Marco's an antique dealer," Danielle explained, taking the seat adjacent to me.

Marco touched his chin and regarded Yvette, who was munching on a piece of bacon. "You too, Ms. Prime. You see anything here that fits in with your remodel, you let me know. Check out my online catalog, too."

"Oh, I will, Marco. Don't worry." Yvette turned to me and said, "I'm having my house painted this week. That's why I'm staying here."

I nodded and took a sip of coffee. *Interesting. I wonder how long she's been staying here.* I recalled Yvette's real estate colleague saying Yvette had become friends with the owners of the B&B.

"So," I said, addressing Marco, "I imagine you give lots of tours of the mansion, not only to showcase the B&B, but also to exhibit the furniture that's for sale."

"You bet," he said. "The other night was our first official tour, but I'll take folks through the house any chance I get."

"I'm sure there's quite a bit of interest," I said. "I remember you mentioning Reverend Natty stopped by the other day. Did he get a tour, too?"

"Ugh. That Reverend Natty," said Danielle, before Marco could answer.

Yvette smiled sympathetically at Danielle. "I'm afraid lots of locals feel that way about Reverend Natty. He's very outspoken and not very popular."

"Yeah," said Marco. "He wasn't too interested in

the antiques. But, he eagerly followed me through the house, talking about the evils of alcohol the whole time. He didn't think it was very funny when I offered him a shot of whiskey in the speakeasy downstairs."

Everyone laughed along with Marco, and I checked the time. I needed to get to the office. I still hadn't figured out a way to ask Yvette about her client who wanted to purchase Mila's shop. Apparently, I was going to have to pretend to be in the market for some real estate after all.

In spite of a full morning of client meetings and phone calls, I managed to take a break at 1:00 P.M. I left the office, telling Julie I was going to grab some lunch, and walked straight over to Moonstone Treasures. It was still closed, but there was a light on inside. I knocked on the door and peered through the window.

Mila opened the door and mustered up a smile. Her usually shiny dark hair hung limply around her face, and her skin appeared wan and tired. She beckoned me inside and locked the door behind me.

"Can I get you some water or tea?" she asked, fingering the pendant around her neck.

I shook my head. "No, thanks. How are you holding up, Mila? Is there anything I can do for you?"

For a moment, Mila didn't answer. "I'm doing fine," she finally said, avoiding my eyes. "But, there is one thing you can do for me."

"You name it," I said. "I'll do whatever I can."

"It's the back room," she said, gesturing toward the purple curtain. "I've been trying to cleanse the energy in there, but it's still so dark and dense. Would you mind giving me a hand?"

"Sure thing."

I followed Mila through the curtain and was immediately assaulted by smoky, thick incense. In the center of the storage area, Mila had created an altar using a long, narrow console table. Various objects adorned the table, including a chalice of water, a bowl of salt, and a bronze bell with a hand-carved wood handle. All around the room, candles burned in glass jars, which made me slightly worried about the risk for another fire.

Mila stood next to the altar, wringing her hands. "I think if you lend your voice to mine, and if we circle the room together, we'll have a bigger impact than when I did it alone."

"That sounds good," I said, trying not to inhale too deeply. "Can I make a suggestion first?"

"Of course," said Mila. She peered at me beneath her long bangs.

"Anytime I've wanted to banish negative energy and perform a cleansing, I've found that a physical cleansing amplifies the spell." I walked over to the back door and put my hand on the knob. "So I think we should air out the room first and give it a thorough cleaning, top to bottom. What do you think?"

Mila blinked, then nodded. "You're right. I did sweep the room with my ritual broom, but a more methodical cleaning is an excellent idea. We can chant a banishing spell as we go."

"Good," I said, turning the doorknob. Then I paused. "Is Drishti here?"

"She's hiding in the front room." Mila chuckled. "She doesn't like all this smelly incense either. It's good we're clearing the air."

With that, I opened the door and doused the incense, while Mila gathered some cleaning supplies. For the next thirty minutes, we dusted, vacuumed, scrubbed, and mopped, while softly chanting the words Mila had chosen:

> *"Bless this place*
> *Cleanse this space*
> *Death erase*
> *Let in grace."*

With the door open, it quickly cooled off in the back room, but the exertion of cleaning kept me warm. My suit had gotten dusty and my hair was falling out of its bun, but I was too focused on the task at hand to notice.

Toward the rear of the room were two inner doors side by side, one leading to a small bathroom and one to a broom closet. While Mila cleaned the bathroom, I decided to check the closet to see if it ought to be cleaned, too. When I pulled open the closet door, I heard a small ping, as if the bottom of the door had tossed a stone across the floor. I turned around to look for it and spotted something a few feet away. I picked it up and turned it over. It wasn't a stone. It appeared to be a fragment of bone.

Mila came out of the bathroom, wiping her brow. "I think that about does it. I'm going to close the back door now."

I nodded and continued to turn over the bone in my hand. It was brownish yellow and about one square inch. I figured it must have chipped off of a larger piece.

Mila shut the door and slid the deadbolt into place, then turned to me. "What do you have there?" she asked.

"I'm not sure," I said, handing her the fragment. "I found it on the floor."

She walked over to her computer desk, where she sat down and held the piece under a lamp.

"You don't sell animal parts, do you?" I asked. I knew some shamanic traditions used animal parts in their rituals, but I didn't recall ever seeing any in Mila's shop. I also remembered my research about the illegal ivory and rhino horn trades. Mila could find herself in a whole other kind of trouble if she were to sell any elixirs or powders made from the horn of an endangered rhino. I was relieved to see Mila shake her head.

"No. Sometimes I use found feathers or similar items left in nature, but I don't sell anything like that. I don't know where this thing came from."

"Hmm. I suppose someone may have tracked it in from the alley," I said. "Mind if I keep it?"

"Go right ahead," said Mila, handing me the piece. Then she allowed a small smile. "You know, I feel as if a weight has been lifted since we cleaned in here. Can you feel the difference?"

"I do," I agreed. "But, Mila, it still worries me that someone keeps finding a way to get in. You did change all the locks, right?"

She opened her mouth to respond when a thud at the back door caused us both to jump.

Chapter 15

Catrina stumbled in from the alley, her arms full of canvas bags containing an assortment of jars and bottles. She set the bags on the floor with a clatter and kicked the door shut behind her.

"That new lock is kind of sticky," she began. Then she spotted me, and her eyes flashed. "You! Why haven't you returned my calls? I've been trying to reach you all day!"

"I'm sorry, but—"

"A person was killed here!" she interrupted. "This shop could be ruined. You need to defend Mila. I think you should write an op-ed, and—"

"Catrina!" Mila said sharply. Catrina looked at her, startled. Frankly, I was startled, too. Mila straightened her spine and looked pointedly at Catrina.

"Keli is not my publicist," said Mila. "In fact, she's not even my lawyer. I don't need a lawyer. She's my friend, and she stopped by here to help me out as a friend. Now, I think you should apologize and stop bothering her with my problems. I can handle them myself."

For a moment, Catrina was speechless. She jutted out her chin and took a deep breath. "I'm sorry," she said to me. "This whole thing just has me so upset."

"I know," I said. "It's okay. Don't worry about it."

Mila patted Catrina's shoulder. "Thank you," she said.

I checked the clock on my cell phone. "Mila, I'm going to have to get back to the office soon. Should we do the ritual now?"

"Yes," said Mila, clapping her hands together. "Catrina can assist."

We gathered around the altar, where Mila cast a circle and invoked the God and Goddess. She picked up the bowl of salt and blessed it. Then she sprinkled some of the salt into the chalice of water. Lifting the chalice, she intoned an intention for the space-cleansing ceremony. "By the powers of earth and water, may all darkness, all negativity be banished from this space."

She poured some of the water into her cupped hand, then flung the droplets around the circle. Next, she raised the bronze bell and said, "By the power of this chime's vibrations, all toxic chi will flow away and be gone."

Mila and Catrina kicked off their shoes. Catrina gave me an arch look until I removed my boots as well. She then opened a cabinet and took out a wooden shaker. "Do you want a sound maker?" she asked. "Or do you just want to clap your hands?"

"Me? Oh, um, I'll just clap."

Catrina shrugged. She dipped her fingertips into

the chalice of salt water and sprinkled it on her shaker. Then she offered it up to Mila, who blessed it with the same words she had said over the bell.

"All right," said Mila. "Let's concentrate on this room. We'll begin in the corner where . . . where Mr. Morris left this plane. May his soul be at peace as he transitions to his next life."

I watched as Mila walked to the corner, raised her arm high, and flicked her wrist to sound the bell. Then she crouched low and rang it at the floor. Slowly and deliberately, she moved along the perimeter of the room ringing the bell in a sweeping motion, high and low.

Catrina followed with the shaker, mimicking Mila's motions. Up and down, up and down, around the room. Feeling slightly awkward, I trailed behind them, clapping my hands at the walls. I was so used to performing my rituals in private that it was hard not to feel self-conscious.

After a minute, Mila added her voice to the cacophony, chanting, "Om," over and over. Catrina joined in, compelling me to do likewise.

Once we had traced a complete circle around the room, Mila returned to the altar and closed her eyes. She moved her lips in a silent prayer to close the ritual. When she opened her eyes, she reached over and gave me a hug.

"Thank you so much for your help. It feels immensely better in here. Catrina and I will cleanse the front room now. I know you need to get back to work."

"Okay. I'll check in with you later." I put my

boots back on and grabbed my coat as I said my good-byes.

As I hurried down the sidewalk, I noted that clouds had rolled in, making it feel chilly and later than it was. Still, I took the time to make a quick stop at Callie's Health Food Store and Juice Bar to grab a container of premade lemony lentil salad and a green smoothie. I would eat at my desk to make up the hour or more I had spent at Mila's shop.

By the time I reached my office building, I was wishing I had opted for hot tea instead of a cold drink. I was still shivering as I fumbled to open my office door without dropping my lunch.

"Do you need a hand?" asked a deep voice behind me.

I turned to see Crenshaw standing in the hall with his arms folded across his chest.

"Sure," I said, handing him my smoothie.

I could tell he was about to comment on the color of my beverage when he looked at my face and raised his eyebrows.

"Have you just come from your second job at a coal mine?"

"Huh?"

"You have a smudge," he said, pointing at my cheek.

"Oh. Thanks." I opened my door, set my salad on my desk, and turned to take my smoothie from Crenshaw. He handed it to me, then lingered in my doorway.

"So," I said, changing the subject from my disheveled appearance, "I've been meaning to tell you, I enjoyed your performance the other night. The show was really entertaining. You made a very convincing butler."

Crenshaw gave me a half bow. "Thank you very much. I relish the opportunity to expand my range. And the Cadwelle Mansion provides a unique venue."

"Will there be other shows at the mansion?" I asked.

"*Murder at the Juice Joint* runs for twelve weeks," he said. "After that, we'll see. The venture can't be profitable, considering the actors' union rates, the four-course meal, and the limited seating. However, the Thomisons said they would like to host other shows."

"Well, I hope it all works out," I said politely.

"As a matter of fact," Crenshaw went on, "the Thomisons have been quite receptive to my recommendations for a future performance. You see, I have this idea for an adaptation of a Sherlock Holmes story. I would play Holmes, of course, and—"

My cell phone began to ring.

"Excuse me," I said to Crenshaw, taking out my phone. I recognized Wes's number and felt a flutter of joy. I couldn't keep the smile off my face as I answered the call.

"Hey, Wes," I said, as I backed into my office.

I was about to nod a silent farewell to Crenshaw when he pursed his lips and turned on his heels. I shook my head and closed the door.

The temperature continued to fall throughout the afternoon, so by evening I was beginning to think Tish might get her wish for a winter wonderland after all. Of course, the Groundhog Festival was still a few days off. Since this was Illinois, the weather was bound to change a few more times before then.

After work, I took a long warm shower and decided I'd have to bundle up for my date with Wes. He wanted to take me to a new vegan restaurant in the next town over. Looking in my closet, I selected a short heather-gray wool dress, sweater tights, and black boots. I was just adding the finishing touches to my makeup when the doorbell rang.

Here I thought I was eager for the date, I thought, glancing at the clock. He was a good fifteen minutes early.

I trotted downstairs to the living room, swung open the front door—and found myself face-to-face with a stranger.

"Oh!" I said, taken off guard.

The man on my doorstep was stocky, with a broad face and receding hairline. I took in his attire—a brown leather bomber jacket over a shirt and tie with tan pants—and his serious expression, and tried to place him.

"Keli Milanni?" he said.

"Yes?"

"I'm Detective Adrian Rhinehardt, Edindale P.D." He held up an ID case containing a badge and allowed me to read it. "May I come in for a minute?"

"Uh, sure." I gestured him inside.

We sat down in the living room, the detective taking the armchair adjacent to where I sat on the edge of the sofa. He pulled out a steno pad and ballpoint pen.

"I was wondering if you could tell me about your day last Sunday. Walk me through your activities that day and night, up to the moment when you called nine-one-one early Monday morning."

"Okay," I said. I took a deep, centering breath, determined to tell the truth as much as I possibly could. "That morning I got up around seven A.M. and did some yoga in the living room. Then I had breakfast, cleaned the kitchen, started some laundry—"

"You have laundry facilities here?" he asked.

"I have a washer and dryer upstairs," I answered, pointing toward the stairs.

He nodded and made a note.

"Let's see," I said. "I sent some e-mails and did some online shopping from about eleven to twelve-thirty or so. Then I ran out to the grocery store to stock up for the week."

"Which store?"

I told him, then continued to describe my bland day of cooking, cleaning, and chatting on the phone.

"And then," I finally said, "I got up early and dressed warmly. My friend Farrah came over around three A.M., and we drove downtown to go for a run."

He looked up at me. "Do you always go for a run at three in the morning?"

"No, not usually. Though, I've been known to run at almost any hour of the day or night," I said truthfully. "Lately work has been really busy, so I haven't been able to run as much as I'd like to. And, there's this 10K coming up on Saturday."

"Okay," he said, jotting down another note. "Then what?"

Beginning with the light I saw in Moonstone Treasures, I related the subsequent events pretty much as they happened. I was no longer afraid to admit that Mila was my friend. I told Detective Rhinehardt that I was worried about her, and that I called her right after I called 911.

When I finished speaking, the detective was silent, as if pondering everything I had said. I cleared my throat. "Um, I do have something else to share with you."

"Yes?" he said, regarding me with interest.

"Well, as I said, Mila is a friend of mine. She showed me the, uh, poison-pen letters she's been receiving. I understand you have them now?"

The detective nodded.

"Well, I think the harasser chose each quote purposefully, to foreshadow the next incident. The vandalism, the fire, the murder. It seems very intentional."

Detective Rhinehardt had a good poker face. I had no idea what he was thinking—or how he judged my credibility. He nodded, almost as if to himself.

"Is there anything else you can think of that might be relevant?" he asked.

I thought about Tish's disdain for Mila's business and Yvette's overall reticence. I wasn't sure how relevant these things really were. Before I could say anything, however, the doorbell rang.

"That's probably my date," I said.

The detective stood up and closed his notebook. "I'll let you go. If you think of anything else, please give me a call anytime." He handed me a business card, then headed to the front door.

I followed him and watched with some amusement as he opened the door to a startled Wes. The two men sized up one another. Rhinehardt nodded curtly and moved past Wes to descend the steps to the sidewalk.

Wes watched him go, before turning to me with a questioning look.

"Are those for me?" I asked, indicating the bouquet of wildflowers in his hand.

His face softened and he smiled, then leaned in to kiss my cheek. "Do you have a vase? I can arrange these for you."

"I do, yes. That would be great." We went inside to the kitchen and chatted lightly, while Wes trimmed the flowers and I filled a vase with water. It felt so natural to be with him. He was a welcome distraction from the week's troubling events—especially considering how fine he looked in his dark jeans. With his plaid scarf and the upturned collar on his peacoat, I thought he looked handsomely mod.

A short time later, we were in Wes's car driving through town toward River Road. It would have been the scenic route if it were daytime. Still, it was a quieter and less hurried way to travel. Along the way, I told Wes about Rhinehardt's questions.

"So," Wes said, "you just happened to be going for a jog downtown in the middle of the night."

"Well, yeah." I paused. *Am I really going to lie to Wes, too?* I seemed to be bending the truth a lot lately. I didn't want to deceive Wes, like I had everyone else.

"No," I said, making up my mind. "Actually, that's not quite right." I told Wes about Farrah's fixation on the burglaries and our stealth mission through the downtown alleyways.

"Good God, Keli," said Wes. "What if the burglars were armed?"

"We weren't going to confront them," I said defensively. "We were just going to spy on them."

He glanced over at me to see if I was serious. I met his eyes, and we both burst out laughing.

"You know, this isn't really funny," he said, still chuckling.

"Yeah," I said. Then I turned serious again. "But, Wes, how are the burglars getting in? And why did they kill Charlie?"

"You think the burglars killed Charlie?"

"Who else?" I said. "Granted, nothing has been stolen from Moonstone Treasures. Still, don't you think the break-ins at Moonstone have to be connected to the other burglaries?"

Wes was silent for a moment. I looked at his profile and saw that he was chewing on his lips.

"Charlie must have seen something," he said, almost as if to himself.

"I think you're right," I said.

Then I had a disturbing thought. What if Charlie had been walking at night, had seen a light or a door ajar, and had decided to check it out? What if he had done the exact same thing Farrah and I had done?

More to the point, what would have happened if *we* had gotten there before he did?

Chapter 16

Craneville was a small lake town about fifteen miles north of Edindale. It was known for its bustling main strip, which featured a variety of eateries including Layla's on the Raw, a new vegan bistro specializing in "high raw" cuisine. As it was a cold Tuesday night in February, the restaurant was pleasantly quiet. Only a few other diners occupied the cozy, candlelit space.

Wes and I sat knee to knee at a small round table near a window in the back. After placing our orders—a creamy cauliflower and arugula salad for me and veggie-stuffed collard wraps for Wes—we sipped warm tea and munched on an appetizer of hummus and crudités, while chatting companionably about food, work, and the weather.

Before long, however, our conversation returned to the demise of poor Charlie.

"Do you know if he had any family?" I asked.

Wes shook his head. "I got the impression he didn't. I haven't heard anything about funeral arrangements yet. I was thinking of stopping in at the place he lived, St. Xavier House, to see what I can find out. I'd like to pay my respects."

"Mind if I come along? I'd like to pay my respects, too. Especially since I . . . found him."

Wes reached over and squeezed my hand. "I'm sorry, Keli," he said. "That must have been traumatic for you."

"Yeah," I said. "But mostly it was sad."

Wes took a sip of tea. "Sheana thinks there's something weird going on with the psychic shop. She's been trying to get an interview with the owner, but the woman keeps brushing her off. Sheana thinks the owner is a witch who's into some kind of voodoo practice."

I put down the carrot stick I had been about to bite into and regarded Wes in the candlelight. *How much should I tell him?*

I cleared my throat. "I know Mila. She's a practicing Wiccan, but she's not into voodoo. Someone is harassing her. She's the victim here, not the perpetrator."

"Well, she and Charlie," Wes said.

"True." I gazed out the window, where a street lamp cast a circle of light on the empty sidewalk. A misty fog was rolling in from the lake.

"I'm going to miss Charlie's funny songs," Wes said wistfully. He chuckled softly. "The last time I saw him, he was reciting the words to 'Down in the Valley' in combination with that children's song 'Down Down Baby.'"

Our dinner arrived, and we ate in silence. My thoughts returned to Moonstone. Why *had* Charlie been killed? Was he just in the wrong place at the wrong time? Or was it premeditated, to fulfill the threat in the notes? If it was planned, would the killer kill again?

Wes cleared his throat, and nudged my foot under the table. "Hey. On a lighter note, want to help me pick my next tattoo?"

I raised my eyebrows. "You're getting another tattoo?" I knew he already had two—a tribal armband around his left bicep, and a dragon on his right shoulder.

"Yeah, on my back, as soon as it gets warmer. What do you think? Hamlet's hand with a skull? Da Vinci's *Vitruvian Man*? Or a geometric design?"

"Wow, I don't know. Those all sound kind of cool." I smiled. I could tell Wes was trying to cheer me up.

After dinner, we held hands on our walk back to the car. Cruising back down River Road toward Edindale, Wes offered his hand to me again, palm up, and I readily clasped it, feeling a grin tug at my lips in the dark car. Before long, I spotted a sign touting Briar Creek Cabins as a romantic weekend getaway. It may have been just a coincidence, but Wes gently pressed my hand as we passed the sign.

Hmm. An overnight camping trip would definitely up our relationship status.

I shook myself. Better not to let my imagination jump ahead like that.

"So, how did you learn about Layla's on the Raw?" I asked. "I can't get over how fresh and tasty that was."

"Sheana told me about it," he said. "She wrote an article on the restaurant when it first opened." Wes chuckled. "She wants to be a crime reporter, but there's not enough crime in Edindale to keep her busy. So, she has to write pieces for the 'Lifestyle' section, too."

"Ha. That makes sense," I said. But inside I wasn't really that amused. I was hung up on the fact that Wes had mentioned Sheana twice during our date.

I gave Wes a sidelong glance as I tried to come up with a way to ask him how much time he spent with the pretty, young reporter.

"Dang!" exclaimed Wes, slamming on the brakes. "Where the hell did he come from?"

I jerked my eyes forward to see a black car peeling out in front of us. Wes had pulled his hand from mine to grip the steering wheel, and he now accelerated as if to catch the car.

"What are you doing?"

"I just want to get a look at the license plate," he said. "Who pulls out like that right in front of another car? There's no one behind us. Why couldn't he wait?"

As Wes gained on the other vehicle, I held on to the edge of my seat. The dense woods on either side of the road flew by, the rolling landscape becoming a blur.

"Can you see the plate?" Wes asked as we gained on the black car.

I squinted through the windshield. "I think it's a California plate," I said. "6Y—"

The car in front of us sped up even more and rounded a curve, kicking up dust as its tires hugged the shoulder. Thankfully, Wes let up on the gas and fell back.

"Not worth it," Wes said. "What a jerk."

"Yeah," I agreed, with relief.

Wes glanced at me and smiled sheepishly. "Sorry if I scared you."

This time it was me who reached over and took *his* hand. "That car was acting weird. But it's not our job to chase it down."

For the next several minutes we listened to classic rock on the radio and chatted about music. Wes mentioned that a band he liked was going to be playing at the Loose Rock on Friday, and he asked if I'd like to go with him to see it. I readily accepted, ignoring the fact that I'd have to run a 10K the next morning.

When we reached Edindale, we came up to a stoplight behind a small black car. I glanced at the license plate and realized with a start that it was the same car that had cut us off on River Road. Wes saw it, too, and frowned.

"I guess he's not in a hurry anymore," he remarked.

When the light changed, we followed the car until it turned onto Archer Avenue. After a slight hesitation, Wes turned the same way. I didn't object. I was feeling increasingly curious about the car myself.

A mile and a half later, the black car switched on its turn signal. Wes slowed down, and we watched as the car drove into a long driveway leading up to a large Victorian mansion. And not just any Victorian mansion.

It was the Cadwelle Mansion Bed and Breakfast.

Wes shrugged and drove on. "Guess he was in a hurry to go to bed."

* * *

After checking in at the law firm Wednesday morning, I headed to the office of Edin Title Services for a real estate closing. I represented the buyers, a young couple who were purchasing their first home. Their nervous excitement was contagious, and I found myself grinning as they signed the final papers. At one point, I even caught myself imagining what it would be like if Wes and I were the ones buying a house together.

When the seller's agent handed over the house keys, my brain switched gears. I suddenly thought about all the burglaries around town and the fact that there was no evidence of a forced entry. Farrah had said something about a potential master lock picker . . . or someone with a master key. Someone like a real estate agent?

Of course, Mila had changed the locks on her store after the first incident of vandalism. Nevertheless, when I found Charlie's body, the back door was standing open. Maybe Mila or Catrina had forgotten to lock it. Or maybe the new lock didn't work properly—I remembered Catrina saying it was "sticky." Either way, if the door had been left open, then it wouldn't matter if the lock had been changed. The killer could still be someone who had somehow possessed a key to the original store locks.

That is, assuming the killer and the vandal were one and the same.

As I left the title company and walked to my car, I made up my mind to reach out to Yvette. I would make an appointment with her to talk about house hunting—and then see how much other information I could wheedle out of her.

Now, though, it was time to call Wes. We had agreed to meet up as soon as I was finished with the closing and then proceed together to St. Xavier House.

After making the call to Wes, I started my car and shifted into gear when my phone rang. With a sigh, I shifted back to PARK and pulled the phone out of my purse again. I saw it was Farrah and picked up.

"What's up, Kojak?" I said by way of greeting.

"Hiya, Tootsie Pop," she said. "You know me well. I've got an idea."

"Uh-oh. Why does that statement make me nervous?"

Farrah laughed. "Hear me out. You think the 'Mystic of Moonstone Treasures' is innocent, right? But there was a dead body found in her shop. And it was covered in some kind of herbal juju stuff."

"Yeah," I said uncertainly.

"The psychic lady has to be involved somehow," Farrah said. "So we have to talk to her, ideally at the scene of the crime. And I thought of the perfect way to do it—we'll make an appointment for her psychic services."

"You want to have a tarot reading?" I said, surprised.

"No, not tarot," she said. "In movies, the death card always comes up in tarot readings. I don't want to play around with anything that has a death card."

"Well, it's not meant to be taken literally," I said. "The death card can signal the ending of any number of things—the end of a phase, the end of a bad habit. It all depends on what question you asked before shuffling the tarot deck."

There was a pause on the other end of the line. "How do you know so much about tarot cards?" Farrah asked.

"Oh, well, you know . . . I dabbled in stuff like that when I was a teenager. My high school friends and I were all about the esoterica. Made us feel hip and important." This much was true enough, if not the whole story.

"Gotcha," she said. "Well, I still don't want to take any chances that a death card might pop up. I was thinking more along the lines of a palm reading."

"Okay. And how is this going to help again?"

"You'll sit next to me while I'm having my palm read. We'll look around, ask questions, get a read on the woman. You know. That sort of thing."

I shook my head, glad that Farrah couldn't see my expression. I knew there was absolutely no reason to investigate Mila, yet I couldn't think of a single excuse to get out of this.

"All right," I finally agreed. "I'll make the appointment for you."

Chapter 17

St. Xavier House was a cube-shaped brick apartment building on the same block as Our Lady of Mercy Catholic Church. A small rectory built from the same red brick sat between the apartment house and the tall, steepled church. Less than fifteen minutes after I left the title office after my real estate closing, I pulled up behind Wes's car on the street in front of the rectory and joined him on the sidewalk.

He gave me a brief smile and nodded toward the rectory. "Shall we start there?"

"Makes sense to me," I said.

We walked up the stone path, which was lined with neatly trimmed hedges, and rang the doorbell. A moment later, the door opened, revealing a clean-shaven man who appeared to be in his midthirties. Based on his black shirt and clerical collar, I gathered he was the priest.

"Hello," he said pleasantly, looking from Wes to me.

"Good morning, Pastor," Wes said, sticking out

his hand. "If you have a minute, we were hoping to talk to you about Charlie Morris."

"Certainly," he said. "Come on in."

We followed the priest to a tiny but warm and inviting parlor off the front hall and sat down on an old-fashioned, upholstered love seat. He took the adjacent wing chair and folded his hands in his lap.

"I'm Father Gabe," he said. "How can I help you?"

Wes and I introduced ourselves and explained how we were acquainted with Charlie.

"I have some photographs I took of him," Wes said. "If he had any family or friends who would like the photos, I'd be happy to share them."

"That's very kind of you," said Father Gabe. "I would love to see the photos. Charlie had one sister, who lives in a facility for Alzheimer patients. I don't know if she would recognize her brother, but I can arrange to have a picture sent to her."

"Did Charlie have Alzheimer's, too?" I asked. I didn't want to come out and say it, but what I really wanted to know was how sharp his mental faculties were.

"I don't know about that," said Father Gabe. "He had a number of health problems from years of drinking too much. And he had his eccentricities. But he got along okay, living by himself. Some ladies from the church would look in on him from time to time, but he was largely independent."

"How long did he live at St. Xavier House?" I asked.

"Oh, nearly three decades, I would say," answered Father Gabe. "He was a resident there long before I became the parish priest. I was told he had been laid off from his factory job and had no place to go. He also struggled with alcoholism, but he had a good heart. He was a gentle, Christian man."

Wes and I offered our condolences. The priest's mention of alcoholism reminded me of Reverend Natty's A.A. meetings. Was it possible Charlie had attended one? If Father Gabe had any knowledge about that, I doubted he would tell me. Those meetings were supposed to be confidential.

I tried to keep my tone casual. "I wonder if Charlie was familiar with the Church of the New Believers. I believe they have support programs for recovering alcoholics."

"Ah, yes," said Father Gabe. "Reverend Natty's church. I don't know if Charlie ever had any contact with the New Believers."

Something about the way the priest referred to Reverend Natty made me think Father Gabe didn't hold a very high opinion of his fellow pastor.

I cleared my throat. "I understand Reverend Natty has been outspoken about a number of things, including the psychic shop where Charlie's body was found. I recall reading something the reverend wrote about the shop owner being a witch."

Father Gabe pressed his palms together. "You're correct about Reverend Natty. He is well known for his outspokenness. While much of what he says is technically accurate, his methods are . . . not the most effective."

"Oh?" I said.

"Yes. You see, I don't think Reverend Natty realizes that most modern folks who call themselves 'witches' or 'Wiccans' are actually on a genuine spiritual quest. I prefer to take a more charitable approach and offer guidance and education, rather than make unkind accusations."

"Oh," I said. As sincere as the priest sounded, I couldn't help feeling a bit queasy at his words. Maybe it was time to change the subject.

Wes made a move to get up from the love seat, but I put my hand on his leg. "Father Gabe, I have another question about Charlie. Do you know if he had a habit of going out late at night? And, if so, where he would go?"

The priest looked thoughtful. "The police detective asked me the same thing. As I told him, Charlie preferred to be outdoors no matter the hour of the day or the season. To my knowledge, he generally spent most of his time in one of two places: a bench outside the courthouse and a bench in Fieldstone Park."

"Do you happen to know which park bench?" I asked, hoping he wasn't growing weary of my interrogation.

He nodded. "It was one of the benches along Clarke Street. Charlie liked to watch people go by as he fed the pigeons."

Just then the doorbell rang, and Father Gabe stood up. "Won't you excuse me for a moment?" he said.

As soon as the priest left the room, Wes turned to me and cocked his head. "Well, aren't you a regular Veronica Mars? Are you ready to go yet? Or do you have more questions?"

I smiled at him and rolled my eyes. "I guess I'm ready," I replied.

A minute later, Father Gabe returned carrying two large cardboard boxes. Wes jumped up to help him.

"Thanks," said Father Gabe, after Wes took the top box. "Let's just set these here by the wall. I can take them over to the church later."

"Are you sure?" asked Wes. "I'd be happy to carry them over for you."

"I'm sure," Father Gabe replied. "We don't need these until Saturday. These boxes contain the candles we'll use at our Candlemas service Saturday evening."

"Candlemas? Is that related to Christmas?" asked Wes.

"It is related," Father Gabe affirmed. "Candlemas is the Feast of the Presentation of the Lord. Forty days after Christ's birth, the Blessed Virgin Mary brought the infant Jesus to the temple for the first time. Therefore, as Jesus is the Light of the World, we bless all the year's candles on February second."

I listened to the priest without comment. Of course, Father Gabe didn't mention that Candlemas had been a Pagan festival of lights long before the Christians adapted it for their purposes.

"This is a celebratory holy day," Father Gabe added. "You are more than welcome to join us at the service."

Wes buttoned his coat and offered up a mildly apologetic grin. "I'm agnostic, Pastor. But thanks all the same."

"I won't hold that against you," Father Gabe said with a smile. "But I guess that rules out my original assumption when you two showed up at my door. Usually when a young couple comes knocking they want to talk about having a wedding."

Something flickered across Wes's face in reaction to the priest's words, but I didn't have time to analyze it. Father Gabe had turned toward me.

"Unless, of course, you have ties to the church?" he asked.

"I . . . I'm a . . . lapsed Catholic," I finally said, shifting my eyes to the floor.

"Well, like the prodigal son, you can always come home," the priest said, walking us to the door. "Our Lady of Mercy will always be here for you."

After work, I went straight home, changed into comfortable clothes, and slipped on my favorite pentagram necklace. I had taken to wearing the necklace more often lately. Feeling the silver pendant against my chest was comforting, like being wrapped in a well-worn security blanket. It also made me feel close to the Goddess—my Earth-Mother of a thousand names.

I flipped on the TV to catch a snippet of local news. It had been three days since I'd discovered Charlie's body, and the police were still being tight-lipped about their investigation. The only bit of news tonight was that the coroner had released his report, which confirmed that Charlie had been hit from behind. There was no question it was homicide.

I turned off the TV and went to the kitchen, where I filled my teakettle and placed it on the stove. Then I sat down in my breakfast nook and called Mila. In typical fashion, she expressed concern for me before I could even ask her how she was doing.

"Keli, I have this new herbal tea blend you have to try. It's a tisane made from chamomile, lemon balm, and valerian root. Wonderful for calming the nerves."

"That sounds nice," I said. "Have you been drinking it? You sound remarkably calm right now. I take it you haven't received any more threatening notes."

There was a silence on the other end of the line.

"Mila?"

"I haven't received any other notes," she said. "But I have received a couple of phone calls."

"What! When?"

"Two on Monday night. One on Tuesday night. None yet today—knock on wood."

"What did the caller say? And what did they sound like?"

Mila paused again. She clearly didn't want to talk about this.

"Well," she finally said, "they spoke in a whisper. I couldn't tell if it was a man or a woman. And they didn't stay on the line for more than a few seconds."

"What did they say, Mila?" I asked again.

I heard Mila sigh. "In the first call, they said I need to take down my sign at the shop and move out. Or else . . . someone else will die. In the next two calls, they said I have until Saturday, or else there will be more innocent blood on my hands."

"Jeez, Mila. Did you go to the police?"

"No. I can handle this. Besides, I'm not sure the police would believe me. It's not like I have any proof."

"Mila," I said firmly, "call Detective Rhinehardt. Please. He needs to know about this."

Another sigh.

"All right," she said. "I'll do it for you."

"Thank you. So you're not going to reopen the shop until this person is caught, are you? I walked by earlier today and saw that you were still closed."

"Actually, I plan to reopen on Imbolc," Mila said, using the Gaelic word for the February 2nd holiday. I understood her thinking. The early spring sabbat was auspicious for any new beginning. It also happened to fall on Saturday, the day of the killer's deadline. I had to hand it to Mila—she was not easily intimidated.

"Um," I began, "would you still be willing to give a private reading even though you're not open yet?"

"For you? Of course," she said.

"Actually, it's for my friend Farrah. She . . . has some issues with her love life." I cringed. Why was it I couldn't be honest with anyone anymore? *Ugh.*

After arranging to meet Mila at Moonstone the next day after work, I hung up and rested my face in my hands. *Three days.* That's when the killer would strike again if Mila didn't do as she was told. Why wasn't Mila more freaked out? She must believe the killer would be caught by Saturday. Maybe she planned to hex the person or something. Well, spells and rituals could be very effective for many purposes, but I wouldn't rely on energy work alone. Not in a matter of life or death.

I gazed around my kitchen. I didn't have much of an appetite, but I supposed I ought to scrounge up some dinner.

A bit later, I took my plate of improvised mashed

chickpeas with veggies and olives to the table and opened my laptop to check e-mail while I ate.

I saw I had a message from my mom. I stopped chewing and dropped my fork when I read the subject line: "About Your Aunt Josephine."

Holy cow.

My mom rarely talked about her older sister. From the little she did share over the years, I knew she was heartbroken when Josie left home. She was hurt that Josie hadn't confided in her—and she was angry about the turmoil Josie had caused for their parents. It was a painful topic.

I quickly read my mom's e-mail:

Hi Keli,

I've been doing genealogy research, and I found something in Grandma O's papers. It has to do with Aunt Josephine, and it's somewhat odd. I know you're busy, but you may want to follow up on this. I'll send it to you by registered mail as soon as I can get to the post office. Call me when you get it.

Talk to you soon.

Love,
Mom

I stared at the computer screen feeling utterly perplexed. I had always been curious about my aunt Josephine. I couldn't imagine what my mom could have found, or why she would send it to me.

As I finished my dinner, I let my mind wander down a rabbit hole of possibilities. I was about to draft a reply to my mom's e-mail when my phone rang. Seeing that it was Wes, I answered right away.

"Hi there," I said.

"How ya doin', Perry Mason?" he said by way of greeting.

I smiled. "Just dandy. What are you up to this evening?"

"I just got off work. And, unfortunately, I have to cancel our Friday date. A new assignment just came up."

"That's a bummer," I said. "I know how much you wanted to see that band."

"I'll catch 'em next time," he said. "Sheana is doing a feature on the new bed-and-breakfast, and a room just became available Friday night."

My heart dropped like an anchor as I realized what he was saying.

"You're going to spend the night there? With Sheana?"

"Yeah. Get the full effect. You know."

All I knew was that I had better have my palms read along with Farrah. Because I had no idea what my love line would show.

Chapter 18

I tossed and turned Wednesday night, troubled by dreams of whispering stalkers, grim exorcists, and my lost aunt Josephine, who had been wandering for years in a dark, tangled forest. Walking to work, I tried to shake off the residual unease. I needed to focus on the child custody negotiation I had scheduled to take place in the firm's conference room first thing that morning. I had no time for phantom mysteries.

Three hours later, I shook hands with my client and watched as she left the office suite with her ex-husband and his attorney. Their mood was positive and relieved—we had managed to iron out all remaining issues. Still, there was an undercurrent of sadness. In spite of an amicable divorce, it was always hard to break up a family with small children.

Well, at least I did my part in smoothing the process, I thought, as I put away the case file. Now if I could only work out my own issues.

After freshening my makeup and slipping on my coat, I told Julie I was leaving for a lunch meeting.

Then I headed to the Cozy Café, where I had arranged to meet with Yvette Prime. I found her sitting in a window booth, reading something on her smartphone. She shoved the phone in her purse when she saw me approaching the table.

"Good afternoon," she said, as I slipped into the seat across from her. "I'm glad you suggested we meet here. It's been a while since I've had one of their BLTs, and I remember it being very tasty. Love those home fries that come with it, too."

I smiled. "The food here is always really fresh. And the service is fast, which is another plus."

A waitress arrived to take our orders. I chose the same sandwich as Yvette, except I requested avocado slices in place of the bacon and Dijon mustard instead of mayonnaise.

"You got it," said the waitress, who was used to my substitution requests.

While we waited for our food, Yvette brought out a small stack of printouts showing various property listings.

"So, you said you're interested in moving from your town house into a single-family home with more yard space, right?"

"Yeah. At least I'd like to see what's available. I mean, I have a nice little backyard now, with a small garden. But it would be nice to have side yards as well."

Yvette nodded, and fingered through the stack of papers.

"I do get a lot of sunlight in my town house," I continued, "through the front and back windows and the skylights upstairs. Sunlight is important to me, as I have a lot of plants."

Yvette nodded again and handed me some listings. "Here are a few you should take a look at. They're really nice properties with an abundance of green space."

I glanced at the first one and saw that it was on the edge of town, not far from Mila's subdivision. "Oh, I should also mention that proximity to downtown is important, too. I like to walk to work as often as possible."

Yvette frowned and took back the papers she had given me. Our food arrived then, and we were quiet for a moment as we savored our first bites.

"So, how are your renovations coming along?" I asked, breaking the continued silence.

"Slowly but surely," she said. "I'm having my kitchen updated and the whole house painted. Luckily, the B&B is such a lovely place to stay. If only I could have Danielle cook for me all the time." She smiled pleasantly and took a bite of her sandwich.

"The B&B isn't too noisy?" I asked. "I heard the rooms are all booked up now."

"Weeknights have been quiet. It will probably be louder on Friday evening. There's another mystery dinner show, as well as a private party in the speakeasy."

"Oh?" I said, surprised. "I didn't think the speakeasy was quite finished yet."

"Finished enough, I guess. Tish rented the space for a small gathering she's hosting. She didn't want to wait."

So Tish is going back to the B&B. For some reason, I found this very interesting.

Yvette took a sip of her soda, then picked up the stack of listings again. "Did you say you wanted two bedrooms and one bathroom, or did you want something bigger?"

"Well, right now I have two bedrooms plus a den, which is about right for me. I have a full bathroom attached to my bedroom and a half bath downstairs. Since I live alone, this works pretty well."

"Okay," she said. "So we'll look for a small bungalow or cottage that's—"

"Of course," I cut in, "I won't always live alone. I imagine I'll get married and have kids someday."

Yvette looked at me with slightly raised eyebrows. How flaky must I sound to her? "I suppose," I went on, "that, when the time comes, that'll require a whole new search, right?"

I laughed self-consciously. I really needed to change the subject before Yvette could ask me any more questions about a house hunt I clearly wasn't really into.

"Oh, by the way!" I said, as if a thought had just popped into my head. "My friend Mila Douglas may be interested in selling her downtown store space. She owns Moonstone Treasures."

That got Yvette's attention. She sat up straighter and leaned forward. "Really?" she said.

I nodded, crossing my fingers under the table. "I told her she should give you a call, since you specialize in downtown real estate. Do you know anyone who might be interested?"

"Yes," she said, a little too eagerly. "Please give

Ms. Douglas my number." She pulled a business card from her purse and slid it across the table toward me.

I looked at the card and pressed my lips together. As much as I hated to, I was going to have to be blunt. I looked up at Yvette. "So, who do you know that might want to buy it?" I asked, putting on my most innocent face.

"I don't divulge information like that," Yvette said plainly. She dipped a fry in ketchup and popped it into her mouth.

"Oh. Well, I was just wondering what kind of business might move into the space. Another gift shop? Or a clothing store? Probably not a coffee shop, right?"

"Time will tell," Yvette said. The waitress came to clear our plates, and Yvette asked for the check. "Lunch is on me," she said.

I thanked her and took the stack of property listings. She asked me to call her if I wanted to go see any of them.

I think we both knew I wouldn't be calling anytime soon.

After work, I waited for Farrah in the downstairs lobby of my office building. She arrived on time and we walked over to Moonstone Treasures together.

"I'm kinda excited about this palm reading," she said. "This could be fun."

"I thought you were a skeptic," I said, giving Farrah

a sidelong glance. "Do you think you might actually learn something about yourself tonight?"

"Who knows?" said Farrah. "But let's not forget our real mission. We want to find out why that old man was killed . . . or sacrificed."

I winced. Earlier in the day, I had called Mila to remind her that Farrah didn't know I was Wiccan. She promised not to reveal my secret. I only hoped Farrah wouldn't do anything to offend Mila.

The door to Moonstone Treasures was unlocked, so we let ourselves in and looked around. Catrina was in the front of the store dusting off merchandise. She held a feather duster in one hand and a cloth rag in the other. Farrah regarded her with interest.

"Hi there," Farrah said brightly. "Your earlobe plugs are wild. How big are you going to let them stretch? Will they grow closed if you change your mind someday?"

Catrina narrowed her eyes and curled her lips as she sized up Farrah, who was still smiling innocently. With her golden-blond ponytail, blue eyeshadow, and snug-fitting skirt-suit, Farrah looked like a prototypical sorority sister. Pointedly ignoring Farrah's questions, Catrina turned her back and returned to her dusting.

Farrah turned to me with an amused expression, and I shrugged. Then Mila came out of the back room.

"Hello," she said, shaking Farrah's hand. "I'm Mila Douglas." She touched my arm and smiled. "Come on back."

Mila led us to the round cloth-covered table in

her divination parlor. The Japanese folding screens hid the area where we had found Charlie's body.

Next to the table was a painted bureau, decorated with an assortment of exotic statuettes and lit candles. The candles gave off a cozy glow and scented the air with jasmine and vanilla. In the center of the table was a brass desk lamp with an extendable arm. Mila sat down with her back to the bureau, and Farrah and I sat across from her. She turned to Farrah and spoke in a soothing and confident voice.

"Before we begin, I always like to set an intention for the reading and help my clients enter a relaxed, receptive state of mind. So, let's all take a deep breath."

Farrah grinned and winked at me. "Okay," she said.

"Now," Mila continued, "gently close your eyes and take another full, deep breath."

We did as she asked, and I noticed the room seemed quieter. I wondered if Catrina had left.

Mila spoke softly about what was going to happen, and she asked us each to call to mind an issue that felt central to our lives at the moment. I immediately thought of the witch-hating killer I was trying to track down.

But then I thought of Wes. By the end of our phone conversation the night before, I had figured out that he and Sheana would be staying in separate rooms at the B&B. Still, I wasn't particularly happy about it. I wondered if my palms would reveal anything about the future of our relationship.

As I continued to breathe quietly, I started to feel a peacefulness settle in. Then Farrah jumped in her seat, jarring the whole table. "Did everyone feel that?" she hissed.

I opened my eyes and looked at Farrah. She had a frightened expression in her eyes. "Feel what?" I asked.

"I felt something on my legs, like a cold breeze." She looked around the room as if expecting to see something.

Mila frowned slightly but remained serene. "Perhaps it was my cat, Drishti. I'm sorry she disturbed you."

Farrah shook her head. "No, it was more like a . . . breath of air. It felt ghost-like."

I snickered, trying to dispel Farrah's fear. "This isn't a séance, Farrah. You probably just felt a draft."

She dropped her shoulders and giggled nervously. "Right. Sorry. But a person did die here, after all."

I raised an eyebrow. Was this Farrah's way of getting Mila to talk about the murder? Somehow I didn't think so. Farrah's alarm had seemed genuine.

Mila folded her hands on the table in front of her. "Yes," she said, addressing Farrah. "But the room has been fully cleansed. I believe the gentleman's spirit has moved on. Are you sensing an ethereal presence?"

Farrah hesitated, then shook her head. "I guess not."

"Okay," said Mila. "Let's take one more deep breath. Now then, who wants to go first?"

I smiled. Without me saying anything, Mila had picked up on the fact that I would like my palms read, too. I nodded toward Farrah. "It was her idea. Let her go first."

Farrah held out her hands and Mila took them in each of hers. Running her thumbs over the grooves and curves, Mila studied Farrah's palms and fingers under the light.

"You're a passionate woman," Mila began. "Adventurous, outgoing, strong, and independent."

Farrah glanced at me and shrugged. "That's all true enough."

"While you're independent and self-sufficient, you have strong ties with your family and friends." Mila looked up for a moment. "Do you have a sister?"

"Uh-uh," said Farrah. "I'm an only child."

"Then perhaps it's another family member or a close friend." Mila looked back down at Farrah's hands. "I see a strong female bond."

I looked over at Farrah, and she looked at me. "Oh!" she said. "Duh. Keli's like a sister to me."

Mila nodded. "You're fiercely protective of your close friends. From the time you were a small child, you were always a leader among your peers."

Farrah fell silent as she listened to Mila continue to describe her. It was as if Mila had known Farrah her whole life. I smiled to myself as I observed Farrah become totally absorbed in the reading.

"Your marriage lines show that you've had several romantic relationships," Mila said.

"Marriage?" Farrah echoed.

"That's an old label for these lines," Mila explained, rubbing her thumb over the fine lines along the edge of Farrah's hand. "These generally represent your more serious romantic relationships."

Farrah leaned forward and tried to see the lines herself.

"One of these lines is more prominent than the others," Mila said. "It's a little fractured in places, but it's longer and deeper. The others are fading in importance. I see a lot of potential with this line." Mila met Farrah's eyes. "You'll be very happy with this one," she said.

"Jake," Farrah whispered.

Mila concluded Farrah's reading, and then turned to me with a questioning look.

I cleared my throat. "I wouldn't mind having a reading myself," I said.

"Go for it!" said Farrah. "I'd like to hear yours."

Mila took my hands into her cool, strong fingers and examined them as she had with Farrah's. I took a deep breath and waited to hear my fate.

"You're very intelligent, Keli," Mila said. "You're careful, cautious. You tend to weigh your options before making any decision. You also have a big heart. You're intuitive and emotional."

She nodded, as if my life line made perfect sense. "I see your Gemini personality. Your two sides, the serious and the playful. One of these sides has been neglected lately."

"Mm-hmm," said Farrah knowingly.

"I've been swamped at work," I murmured.

She moved her thumb to the space between my fingers. "As a child, you were surrounded by a close, loving family. Lots of siblings and cousins and friends. Close grandparents. You respected your parents, though you didn't always agree with them."

I found myself nodding. So far, Mila was spot on with everything she had said.

"You have a strong love interest," she continued. "New within the past year. There is a deep attraction, a real connection. We're talking soul mate serious here."

"Aww," said Farrah beside me. "Is Keli in love?"

Mila smiled softly but didn't look up from my hands. "I see a lot of energy around your feelings for this man. You're worried. You're feeling possessive and defensive. You want to remove the uncertainty. This comes from your practical nature. You want to define the relationship and make it clear that his heart belongs to you, and yours to him."

Hearing this truth made me nervous. My heart started beating faster.

"I also see that your heart line is conflicted," Mila said. "I see the stress you feel from the effort of hiding an important part of yourself."

I stiffened at Mila's words. She glanced up quickly and let go of my hands. An apologetic look crossed her face.

"All right then," she said. "I think our time is up. Do you have any questions?"

I shook my head. "No, I'm good. Thank you for the readings."

I stood up and grabbed my purse before Farrah could ask any questions. I was ready to leave.

Chapter 19

After leaving Moonstone, Farrah and I hopped on over to the Loose Rock, our favorite nightspot. Over bruschetta and beer, we discussed our palm readings.

"That was actually *very* cool," Farrah said. "Do you think the lines on our palms really revealed everything Mila told us? Or is she just extremely perceptive?"

"Probably a little bit of both," I said. "She interpreted the lines using her natural psychic abilities."

"Hmm." Farrah gazed out over the empty dance floor. "You know what? I think you were right about Mila. She didn't strike me as a murderer. In fact, she was quite lovely."

Inwardly, I thanked the Goddess and breathed a sigh of relief. "You see why I want to help her now? I don't know what's going on, but it looks like someone is trying to drive her out of business."

"Could be," Farrah said. "So when the dark threats and property damage didn't work, somebody decided to frame her for murder?"

I scrunched up my face. "I don't know. Maybe? But get this—yesterday Mila told me she's getting creepy phone calls now, too. The caller is saying someone else is going to die if she doesn't permanently close her shop by Saturday."

Farrah widened her eyes. "Are you kidding me? I just got massive goose bumps. That is so freaky. How was she so calm tonight?"

"I know. I think she's trusting in a higher power, or something." I tore my napkin into little pieces of confetti on the table. "I was really hoping to solve this thing, but time is running out."

Why is the deadline on Candlemas anyway? Does the killer know it's a Wiccan sabbat?

Farrah tapped her fingernails on the side of her beer bottle. "Time hasn't run out yet. Tell me—who are the suspects again?"

"Well, one of them could be Yvette's mystery client." I told Farrah about my lunch with the real estate agent. We agreed it seemed odd that she wouldn't reveal her client.

"After all," said Farrah, "if the person ends up buying the place, his or her identity will be a matter of public record. What's the point of keeping it a secret now?"

"I know, right?" I finished off a piece of bruschetta and wiped my fingers on what was left of my napkin. "You know, here's another thing I wonder. Who were the prior owners of Mila's shop? And who handled the sale? I'm still thinking about who else might have had a key."

"I can look that up," Farrah said. "I might have time tomorrow."

I was about to tell Farrah about Tish's apparent disdain for Mila when two guys approached our table. The taller one slid into the booth next to Farrah.

"I thought we might find you here," he said. He reached over and grabbed her glass of beer, tipped it toward me in a salute, and took a swig.

Farrah rolled her eyes. "Next round's on Jake," she said, brushing the floppy bangs off his forehead.

I scooted over to make room for the other guy, a burly young man with light brown hair, whom I recognized as Jake's friend, Dave. He was the police officer who had helped me out over the summer as a favor to Farrah.

"Catch any thieves lately?" he asked me with a grin.

"I'm working on it," I said, smiling back at him.

"Actually, don't." His grin fell away. "Unless you're thinking of joining the police force."

"Now there's an idea," Farrah joked. She signaled a waitress to bring two more beers, then turned to Dave. "So what's with all the crime in Edindale lately? Do y'all have any leads, or what?"

"You know I can't comment on pending investigations," Dave said. "However, I can tell you about my theory on crime."

"Here we go. . . . " Jake chuckled and took another drink from Farrah's beer bottle.

Dave folded his hands on the table and leaned forward. "It's almost always about greed," he said. "Any crime—you name it. The root is greed."

"Arson," said Farrah, giving Dave an arch look.

"Greed for power and notoriety," Dave said. "See,

greed is just a supremely selfish desire for something. It's usually money. Think of theft, embezzlement, fraud, et cetera. But it can also be greed for other things, like sex or power or control."

"What about murder?" I said. "The motive for murder can't always be greed."

"No, not always," said Dave. "It can be hatred or revenge, or some other warped emotion. But greed is right up there, like I said."

The waitress brought beers for everyone and a fresh plate of bruschetta. I wasn't sure if I agreed with Dave's theory, but it was interesting to consider. My thoughts drifted back to the anonymous notes Mila had been receiving.

"Hey," I said, "have any of you heard of the First Church of the New Believers?"

They all gave me blank looks.

"The pastor is this outspoken dude who calls himself 'Reverend Natty.'"

"Oh!" said Dave. "You mean Brother Nat?"

"Brother Nat?" I looked from Dave to Jake.

"Oh, yeah," said Jake, nodding. "I remember him. He used to stand on the quad at SCIU yelling through a bullhorn. He harassed students as they walked by, calling them sinners for drinking and fornicating."

"Nice," Farrah said sarcastically.

Jake laughed. "What a nutcase. That was a few years ago, though. Is he still doing that?"

"If he's the same guy I'm talking about, he has his own church now. And he's still against drinking, among other things."

"To Brother Nat," Dave said, lifting his beer.

"To Brother Nat," Jake echoed.

We clinked bottles, then moved on to other topics of conversation. Yet, in the back of my mind, I kept wondering about the person harassing Mila. What was that person's motivation?

When I came home from the Loose Rock, I should have been tired. It had been a long day, both at work and afterward. But my thoughts wouldn't slow down. I couldn't stop thinking about murderers and vandals and thieves. *Oh my.*

To relax my mind, body, and soul, I decided to do some yoga. I dragged my coffee table to the edge of the living room and rolled out my yoga mat in the center of the floor. I started with some standing poses, stretching my arms to the sky and breathing in rhythm with each move.

I wonder what Wes is doing right now?

Dave had insisted on giving me a ride home. He was a nice guy—he talked about his two little boys, a toddler and a baby, the whole way. There wasn't a hint of flirtation, which I appreciated. However, if anyone had observed me being dropped off by the nice-looking off-duty cop, they might assume I was coming home from a date. *If Wes saw, would he care?*

Sighing, I lowered myself to the floor for some easy forward folds. As I held each posture, my mind drifted back to the night Farrah and I found Charlie's body at Moonstone. I shuddered at the memory.

I sat up straight and crossed my legs for a seated spinal twist. Inhaling, I lengthened my back. Exhaling, I twisted gently to the right. After a few seconds, I switched sides and twisted to the left. As I looked over my left shoulder, my eyes fell upon the stack of books on the end table next to my sofa. On top of the stack was the booklet Farrah gave me the day before we conducted our late-night reconnaissance of downtown Edindale. I untwisted from the pose, shook out my legs, then crawled over to the end table to retrieve the book.

I read the title: *Twentieth Century Edindale: A Pictorial History.* I had been so preoccupied during the week, I hadn't had a chance to look at the booklet. Now, I leaned against the sofa and flipped through the pages.

It was a neat little compilation. I especially liked the oldest photos showing the early town citizens in their charming hats, often standing outside next to horses and buggies or Model Ts. Some of the most striking photos showed the working-class folks: a group of somber coal miners after a hard day's work, a class of barefoot children next to their one-room schoolhouse.

Most of the pictures featured the town's businesses. There was the first general store, the old movie theater, and a few long-gone manufacturing companies. On a couple of pages, Farrah had inserted sticky notes. Next to the picture of a 1920s cigar shop, the note attached said, "now Handbags and More." And next to a photo of a former tavern, the note said, "now Gigi's Bar and Grill."

As fascinating as the book was, I yawned and rubbed my eyes. *I should be able to sleep now.* I thumbed through the remaining pages to see if there were any more sticky notes. There weren't, but something else jumped out at me. It was the word *commune*.

I flipped back to the section covering the 1960s to the 1970s and searched for the word again. When I found it, my heart skipped a beat. In the midst of photographs showing soda fountains and discos, wide lapels and bell-bottoms, there was a snapshot at the entrance of a farm. According to the hand-drawn sign, it was the "Happy Hills Homestead." The caption stated it was an experimental commune on the edge of Shawnee National Forest. Three smiling young people stood in front of the sign, next to a brightly painted boulder. Two women and a man, each with long hair and ruddy cheeks.

Based on photos I had seen in my mother's old scrapbooks, I would have bet my bottom dollar one of the women was Josie O'Malley—aka Aunt Josephine.

Now I was more curious than ever about what my mom had discovered relating to Aunt Josephine. I couldn't wait to receive the package she had sent— and to send her a copy of this photo.

On the downside, I was also wide awake again.

Chapter 20

As I cut through Fieldstone Park on my walk to work Friday morning, I remembered what Father Gabe had said about Charlie people watching from a bench somewhere in the park. On a whim, I changed course and made my way over to Clarke Street on the north side of the park.

Green painted benches appeared every few yards along the broad sidewalk. *Which one did Charlie favor?* My question was immediately answered when I observed a flock of pigeons congregating around one bench more than the others. I walked over to the bench and sat down.

"Sorry, guys," I said to the birds. "I've got nothin' for you."

And your bread-crumb supplier won't be coming back, I thought sadly.

I gazed around, taking in the Charlie's-eye view. The morning air felt cool on my face, but the bright sun made me wish I had brought sunglasses. Traffic was moderate on Clarke Street. A school bus passed by, as well as a few cars carrying commuters

to work. Pedestrians were sparse on the sidewalk
in front of me. I saw only one jogger and one dog
walker in the five minutes I spent sitting on Charlie's
bench.

*Why did he have to die? Did he see something he
shouldn't have? Or was he just a convenient scapegoat?*

For the next few minutes, I sat on the bench
wondering about Charlie's whereabouts the previous Sunday night. Before long, I was reminded of
the extra-large green juice I downed for breakfast
and recalled seeing a small sign pointing to the
public restrooms. *Might as well take advantage of the
facilities before heading on to work.* I knew the city park
amenities were usually well maintained.

With a backward glance at the pigeons, I left
Charlie's bench and followed a concrete path to a
pavilion featuring picnic tables, a park directory,
and a ramp leading to an underground shelter. At
the bottom of the ramp were the public restrooms,
as well as a door labeled PARK OFFICE. To the left was
a pedway leading to an underground parking
garage for city maintenance equipment.

When I came out of the restroom, I paused outside the door to the park office. The glass window
was dark. It occurred to me that Charlie had probably frequented the facilities here, considering how
much time he used to spend outside.

I took a few tentative steps down the pedway as
an idea began to take shape in my mind. Along the
concrete wall were several metal grates approximately
three feet high by four feet long, fastened by old,
rusty screws. Except for one grate, which was held
in place with four shiny, silver screws. Frowning, I

peered through the slats, but it was too dark to see anything.

A noise behind me caused me to jerk my head around. A young man in torn jeans and a ragged sweatshirt appeared at the bottom of the ramp and went into the men's room. I took that as my cue to get going.

Once back up in the sunlight, I walked downtown as rapidly as I could. Along the way, I pulled out my phone and called Farrah.

"What's the story, morning glory?" she said upon answering.

"Hey, can you stop by my office today by any chance?"

"I can be there in half an hour. Does that work?"

"Yeah, that would be perfect. Oh, and bring your iPad. I want to take a look at that map you made, the one that points out all the burglary locations."

When Farrah arrived at my office, we had to talk quickly before my 10:00 client meeting. I ushered her inside and closed the door. She pulled out a sheet of paper from her purse and set it on my desk.

"I printed out the map," she said, taking the seat across from me. "Should we tack it to your corkboard and mark it up with colorful pushpins?"

"Like in the movies?" I grinned. "That won't be necessary. However, I do want to draw on it."

I took a pencil from my desk drawer and drew a faint line connecting all the businesses that had been robbed. Then I continued the line to Moonstone

Treasures. Finally, I made an *X* on Fieldstone Park and another on the street between the courthouse and the county jail.

Farrah watched me mark up the map, then looked at me with raised eyebrows. "What are you thinking, captain?"

"I'm thinking maybe the burglar is breaking in from the inside."

"An inside job like the police indicated?"

"No. More like an underground job." I pointed at the map with my pencil. "See how there's a relatively straight line connecting all the businesses? What if there's a tunnel under there? Just like the tunnel here—from the jail to the courthouse—and here, in the pedway to the park's underground garage."

"Ooh!" Farrah's eyes gleamed. "Ingenious! So we're looking for a mole person."

She scratched the back of her head. "Wait. Wouldn't all these businesses know if there was a tunnel into their buildings?"

"Not necessarily," I said. "Not if the tunnel is secret. These are all old buildings. I imagine the tunnel, if there is one, would predate all of the current occupants."

I studied the map again. "Any guess why someone would create a secret tunnel?"

"Underground railroad?" Farrah said.

I took the pencil and drew another *X* on the map, this time on the edge of the paper, about two miles from the downtown business district. I wrote

"Cadwelle Mansion" next to the *X*. "How about for smuggling bootlegged liquor?"

Farrah's eyes grew wide. "Of course! The original owner of the B&B was a bootlegger!"

My desk phone buzzed. The caller ID display told me it was Julie. "My client is probably here," I said. "What's your afternoon like?"

"I'm giving a guest lecture on legal research techniques at the law school," Farrah said. "But I'll be there less than two hours. Why?"

"Think you could do some research of your own? Like maybe check city and county records to see what the government knows about what lies beneath Edindale?"

"You bet."

"I'd also like to know what year the tunnel to the courthouse was constructed," I added.

"You got it, Daphne," she said, folding the map and re-placing it in her purse. "If my knowledge of history is correct, that tunnel was probably dug in the early part of the twentieth century."

"You're the best, Velma," I said, as I opened my office door.

"So, shall we meet up at the Loose during happy hour and compare notes?" Farrah asked.

"Sure thing. Unless . . ."

"Unless what?"

"Unless I can get Wes to let me stay with him at the B&B tonight. I really want to get a closer look at that speakeasy."

"Ooh. An overnighter at a B&B. How very 'coupley' of you. Maybe the psychic was right."

"Maybe." I didn't know whether to frown or grin at the idea.

Guess I'll wait and see how Wes reacts.

"You want to join me on my assignment?"

I had called Wes right after my last client meeting of the day. It wasn't easy to concentrate on work with the dark deadline looming. Now I sat at my desk gazing out the window at the street below. Although the late afternoon sun cast long shadows, I was heartened to note that the daylight hours were noticeably longer. Tomorrow I would have to find time to officially welcome the return of the light in my own private Candlemas celebration.

"I need a cover," I said to Wes. "An excuse to snoop around the B&B. I figured no one would think it odd if you brought your girlfriend along for the evening."

There. I said it.

I held my breath as I waited for Wes to respond.

If he hesitated, it was only for a second. "True. I'd love to have you come along. But I still don't understand why you want to snoop around."

Yes! I twirled in my chair. Then I filled Wes in about my tunnel theory.

"I think Charlie found the tunnel, Wes. Remember you said his last song was 'Down in the Valley' mixed up with 'Down Down Baby'? He could have gone *down* the ramp to the Fieldstone Park restrooms and then heard something that prompted him to crawl through a grate, leading him further down into a tunnel. He probably even did it more than once."

And then he was caught. I swallowed as I recalled the appearance of Charlie's body when Farrah and I found it. The back of his suit and head were black, as if he had been dragged through dirt.

I shuddered involuntarily. *Who could have been so heartless?*

"You could be right," Wes said. "Don't you want to go to the police with this information?"

"This is all conjecture right now. Still, I'll stop by and see Detective Rhinehardt on Monday morning. In the meantime, I can't help but wonder if there's an entrance to a tunnel from the Cadwelle Mansion speakeasy."

I had already called Mila to see if she could meet me at her shop so we could scan the walls there for a hidden opening. Unfortunately, she was on her way out the door when I called. Her husband had insisted on taking her for an overnight getaway to help her forget her worries, at least for a little while. Under the circumstances, that sounded like an excellent idea to me, for Mila's sake. While it made me nervous to think the killer might be using a tunnel to enter the shop, my search of Moonstone would have to wait.

"I'll help you," Wes said. "If I can do anything to help track down Charlie's killer, I'm in."

"Thanks, Wes. That would be great."

"There's just one problem."

"What's that?"

"It's my assignment," he said, with a teasing note in his voice. "I'm afraid sharing a room with you will be too distracting. How am I going to keep my mind on my job?"

I felt a rising blush heat my face as I smiled into the phone. "I guess you'll just have to figure out a way."

Chapter 21

The minute I arrived home after work, I dashed around like a madwoman. I showered, fretted over what to pack in my small overnight bag, and tried on four different outfits before settling on a simple black jersey dress. I couldn't believe I was really doing this. Though, whether my nervous excitement was more about spending the night with Wes in a romantic B&B or surreptitiously searching the mansion, I wasn't quite sure.

"I wish you could come with me," I said to Farrah when I called her after I finished getting ready.

"Yeah, right," she said. "You've got lover boy to play Ned to your Nancy. You don't need me."

I laughed as I peered out the front window to watch for Wes's car.

"I do wish I could be there to help you snoop, though," Farrah said. "I found out the tunnel to the county jail was built in 1920, a year after Prohibition began. If somebody wanted to 'smuggle them some moonshine,' having a tunnel already started would have been mighty convenient."

"I take it official records didn't show an underground passageway beyond the courthouse and the park."

"No. Not that I could find. I'll make some phone calls on Monday to try to 'dig up' some more info. I still need to research the title chains for those downtown businesses, too."

I saw Wes pull up, so I told Farrah good-bye. I stepped outside into the chilly evening air and locked the door behind me.

On the way to the B&B, Wes told me he and Sheana would be receiving a private tour of the mansion and then attending the mystery dinner. "Mrs. Thomison told me that you're more than welcome to join us for the tour, and stay the night and have breakfast in the morning, but that the mystery dinner is sold out. She said she would make you a plate of food to eat in our room. I hope that's okay."

"Yeah, of course," I said. "That's fine. I've already seen the show." I wasn't too concerned about Wes feeling like he was on a date with Sheana. I knew he'd be on his feet taking pictures during most of the performance.

After I got a look at Sheana in the mansion's parlor, however, I wondered if I should be worried after all. With her peekaboo hairstyle and low-cut, form-fitting ruby gown, she looked like she could be one of the evening's performers. Wes, wearing jeans and a button-down shirt, raised his eyebrows when he spotted her. "Did I miss the memo? No one told me this was a black-tie affair."

Sheana laughed and hung her head. "I thought it was going to be an audience participation kind of thing. I figured everyone would be in costume. Marco just set me straight."

I glanced over at Marco, standing by the fireplace and holding a tumbler of bourbon on the rocks. His cheeks were rosy and his eyes sparkled with glee. He looked like he was trying to hold back his laughter. "You look fine to me, honey," he said.

Wes furrowed his brow as he held back a smile, too. "You look like a 1940s film star. Isn't this play set in the 1920s?"

Sheana turned red, so I elbowed Wes. "Don't be mean," I said. "There's no shame in being over-dressed. So what if you've got the nicest outfit in the room? It's far worse to be underdressed."

"Sorry," said Wes, looking duly humbled. He took his camera out of its case and fiddled with the lens.

Sheana gave me a grateful look and introduced herself. "Wes has told me so much about you."

He has? For some reason this surprised me.

"If we have time later, I'd love to ask you some questions about last Sunday night. I know finding that body must have been upsetting. I'm working on a follow-up story focusing on the psychic shop. I'd love to have a firsthand account of what you saw."

She pulled a tape recorder out of her sequined clutch as if she were ready to start recording my comments that instant.

"We'll see," I said noncommittally.

A man dressed as a bellhop entered the room to gather our bags and take them upstairs. I didn't recognize him from last week's tour. I wondered if he was a new actor or if he was an actual servant. I glanced over at Marco, who wasn't paying any attention to the bellhop. Instead, he was refilling his drink.

"Ready for the tour, folks?" Marco asked. "Danielle is overseeing things in the kitchen, but she may join us in a bit."

Marco began his spiel about the history of the mansion and pointed out various antiques he had acquired. Sheana held her recorder up and asked questions while we walked through the downstairs rooms. Wes trailed behind us, snapping pictures along the way.

When we entered the library, Yvette was reading in an easy chair. She jumped at the sound of Marco's voice and dropped her book. I was nearest to her so I leaned over to retrieve it, but she snatched it up first. She tucked the book beside her in the crevice of the chair before I could see the title.

"Where did you get all the books?" Sheana asked Marco. She pointed to a wall of floor-to-ceiling shelves filled with an assortment of titles.

"We purchased some from secondhand stores, but many were donated. Like these here," he said, kicking a cardboard box on the floor. "I'm not sure what to do with these."

"Are those Bibles?" I asked, glancing down at the blue paperbacks in the open box.

"Yeah." Marco snorted. "The good Reverend Natty brought them by the other day."

"You mean Reverend Nutty," said Danielle, entering the room in a rush. She wrinkled her forehead and bit her lip. "That man gives me the willies. I came downstairs yesterday morning and found him wandering around the house. He scared me half to death."

"You don't lock the doors?" I asked.

"Overnight we do. But in the daytime, guests are always coming and going." Danielle turned to Marco and frowned. "We may have to do something about that."

Marco took a sip of his drink and tugged playfully on the frilly apron Danielle wore over a burgundy silk dress. "Don't let the reverend get to you, dear. I'm sure he's harmless."

Danielle looked down at her apron and winced. She untied it, slipped it off, and folded it over her arm. "The dinner guests will be arriving soon. So, if you'll all excuse me . . . " She hurried out of the room.

"All right," said Marco. "Let's continue the tour upstairs. I'll show you the two rooms you all will be staying in. The other bedrooms are occupied."

"What about the speakeasy?" I asked. "I bet Sheana and Wes would like to see it."

"That'll have to wait until tomorrow morning," he said. "We have a private party down there tonight."

"Oh, that's right." I glanced at Yvette, who hadn't moved from her seat. "I heard Tish booked the space."

"Yep," said Marco, heading for the door. "She's trying to impress some muckety-muck investors and convince them to come to Edindale." Marco winked at me. "See how the Cadwelle Mansion is benefiting the town already?"

Sheana, Wes, and I followed Marco out of the library and toward the grand staircase in the front hall. Marco and Sheana were already on their way up the steps when the door to the dining room opened and Crenshaw emerged. He stopped short when he saw me and straightened the vest on his butler costume.

"Why, Mademoiselle Milanni! You decided to see my performance a second time? I'm flattered."

I couldn't tell if he was joking or not. Wes looked curiously from Crenshaw to me.

"Hello, Crenshaw," I said. "That's actually not why I'm here. I'm just . . . having a tour with Wes here."

Crenshaw narrowed his eyes almost imperceptibly as he stared at Wes. In turn, Wes raised his eyebrows.

Ugh. I resisted the urge to roll my eyes.

"Wes, this is my coworker, Crenshaw Davenport. Crenshaw, this is Wes Callahan."

I sensed Wes tense up beside me, so I quickly added, "My boyfriend."

Crenshaw abruptly stuck out his hand, and Wes clasped it. It might have been my imagination, but they each appeared to be putting quite a bit of muscle into the handshake.

"Wes!" called Sheana from upstairs. "Come up

here and see this furniture! We need pictures of this."

"Excuse us," I said to Crenshaw, while Wes gave him a curt nod. We proceeded up to the second floor, where we found Marco standing in the hallway reading something on his cell phone. Sheana was perched on a windowsill, scribbling in her notebook.

Marco looked up. "As I was telling Miss Sheana, we have four guest rooms on this floor. These two here are for you all." He indicated the nearest two rooms, one on each side of the hallway, their doors ajar. "The third floor is where Danielle and I stay, so we ask folks not to wander up there. We have one more nice guest room in the carriage house next door by the vineyard. It's occupied, too, but Danielle can show you pictures."

I peeked into the bedroom called the "Sunflower Room," which was decorated in an abundance of yellow and white. There was a suitcase sitting on top of a cedar chest, so I figured Sheana must have claimed this room. I turned to the other room. According to a sign on the door, this was the "Rose Petal Room."

Although I had seen the rooms during last week's tour, I was struck anew by all the romantic elements. From the whitewashed stone fireplace and rose trellis wallpaper to the heavily pillowed four-poster bed draped with a red and white quilt, and the crystal vase of pink rosebuds, the room could have been called the honeymoon suite.

I looked around as Wes took pictures and Marco described the antique furniture. After a few minutes,

Wes asked Marco how soon the show would be starting.

Marco glanced at his phone. "We'll start serving cocktails right about now. Show starts in twenty."

Sheana stood up. "I'm going to go down and interview the guests. I want to find out where they're from and make sure some of them will stick around afterward to give me a quote."

"I'll be down in a few," Wes told her.

Marco led Sheana down the back staircase. Wes joined me in the bedroom and pulled the door shut behind him.

"I'm sorry you can't come to the dinner," he said, setting his camera on the bureau. "I feel bad about that."

"Don't," I said. "That's not why I'm here, remember?"

Wes drew near me, the corner of his mouth twitching. "I know," he said, reaching for my hands. "You're here to play detective."

My heartbeat quickened at his touch. "That's right," I said. I looked into his eyes and recalled what Mila had said during my palm reading. *Was I here to stake my territory as well?*

Wes leaned in and lightly kissed my lips. Impulsively, I pulled my fingers from his and encircled his shoulders. At the same time, we deepened the kiss, and I felt Wes's hands move up my back. I had a fleeting thought that maybe he would skip the dinner.

He pulled back and gently touched the side of my face. "What did I tell you? Here you are distracting me from my job."

I smiled and lifted one shoulder. He kissed me once again, then stroked my hair and played with the necklace at the back of my neck. He playfully pulled the necklace chain outside the collar of my dress.

It was my pentagram. I wore the necklace to work and forgot to remove it in my rush to get ready for the evening.

"What's this?" Wes touched the pendant. "A good luck charm?"

"You could say that," I said, taking a step back. I turned around, afraid he would see the apprehension I suddenly felt.

"I've seen that symbol," Wes said. "What does it mean?"

Without answering, I walked over to the window and looked outside.

"Keli?" Wes came up behind me and put a hand on my arm.

I'm not going to lie. This is who I am.

I swallowed. "It means a lot of things. The five lines represent the five ancient elements: earth, air, fire, water, and spirit. The circle around the star represents infinity. Together, the continuous line symbolizes life, spirituality, and protection."

I turned around to gauge Wes's reaction. He seemed slightly puzzled, but interested. "Isn't this symbol used in New Age religions?" His eyes moved from the pentagram to meet my gaze. "Does it represent *your* religion?"

Slowly, I nodded. Then I set my jaw.

"Yes. It does. I'm . . . a Wiccan. I keep this part of

my life private, because it's a misunderstood religion. But this is the spiritual path I follow."

Now that I had begun, I felt the need to explain. "I try to live my life in tune with the natural rhythms of the earth," I continued. "I believe the divine is within us and all around us, and it manifests in nature—in the trees, the wind, the plants and animals." I took a step back. "But I guess you wouldn't know anything about that, would you?"

Moving around Wes, I walked over and sat on the edge of the bed. I trembled slightly and needed to feel grounded to the earth.

This is so not what I planned for this evening.

Wes came over and sat down next to me. "Why didn't you tell me before? What do you mean I 'wouldn't know anything about that'?"

I looked up. "You're agnostic, right? A cynic? A doubter?"

Wes scoffed. "So? Just because I question things doesn't mean I can't be sympathetic. It doesn't mean I'm gonna dismiss people who do believe."

"But how can you not believe in anything?" I said, my voice rising. "How can you look around at the amazing, exquisite planet that supports all life and still doubt the existence of God? I just don't understand that. It seems closed-minded."

He frowned. "Look," he said, "maybe there is a God. I'm not saying there's not. I just don't happen to believe we can know for sure. There's no proof."

I started to argue but caught myself. What was I doing? How could I judge him? I knew my path wasn't for everyone. I looked down at my hands, before looking up to search his face.

"So . . . you don't mind that I'm Wiccan? You don't think I'm weird?"

"No, I don't think you're weird." He gave me a reassuring smile. "This doesn't change how I feel about you. I love that you're unique. I love that you're true to yourself and that you've shared this part of yourself with me."

Feeling a rush of relief, I let out my breath. I also felt a surge of affection for Wes and wanted to wrap myself in his arms. Then his cell phone buzzed.

He pulled out his phone and opened the text. "It's Sheana. The show's about to start." I nodded and sighed.

"We'll talk more when I get back," he said, standing up and grabbing his camera. "I can't wait to hear all about your religion."

After Wes left, I wandered around the cozy "Rose Petal Room" in something of a daze. I hadn't intended to reveal my secret tonight. I was so accustomed to holding fast to the truth that I was left feeling a little unmoored for having let it go.

Yet I trusted Wes. I had almost opened up to him back when we first started dating last summer. I was sure he would keep my secret. *Wouldn't he?*

I halted in front of the mirror above the bureau and looked at my reflection. "Stop dwelling," I commanded.

I lifted the pentagram and dropped it back inside my dress. Then I left the room and quietly descended the back staircase. It was time for some snooping.

At the bottom of the stairs, I turned toward the

kitchen and opened the door a crack. A woman I took to be the caterer was assembling trays of food with the assistance of two uniformed waiters. A heavenly aroma of sautéed onions, garlic, and herbs met my nostrils, causing my mouth to water.

Guess Danielle forgot about making me a plate.

I remembered seeing a fruit bowl in the parlor, so I headed there next. Entering the room, I flicked on the light switch and looked around. Everything was neat and tidy, except Marco had left the liquor cabinet open. For a second, I considered making myself a drink, but then I thought better of it. I needed to keep my wits about me.

I settled for a banana from the fruit bowl and polished it off as I sauntered through the parlor and over to the library. Yvette was gone.

What had she been reading?

Strolling past the bookshelves, I perused some of the titles and tried to determine whether any books might have been moved recently. It was impossible to tell.

When I turned around to take one last sweeping glance around the room, my eyes fell upon a stack of brochures on the coffee table. I didn't recall seeing them before. I picked one up and read the cover: *Live Your Life According to the Bible. A Publication of the First Church of the New Believers.*

Goose bumps rose on my arms. I looked around the quiet room once again. Were these brochures here all along? I wished I knew for sure. I didn't like to think Reverend Natty might be lurking somewhere in the shadows.

I re-placed the brochure and left the library,

heading next to the entry hall. I walked over to the front door and peered out the window. The pathway was lit up, but the yard and street beyond were dark.

Lively sound effects from the adjacent dining room prompted me to move on. I made my way back to the rear of the house. Near the kitchen, I paused at the door to the basement. It was closed, but I heard muffled chatter below. Then Tish's blaring voice cut through. I craned to make out what she was saying when the basement door flew open. I jumped back and found myself face-to-face with the tourism director herself.

Tish swayed unsteadily as she squinted at me. "Oh, the lawyer. Have you seen Marco? He needs to get his cute butt down here and tell these prospects all about the winery. I told them it will open in the spring—which I have no idea if that's true or not—so Marco needs to come back me up." She ended her rambling sentence on a hiccup.

"I haven't seen him," I said.

"I have to go to the little girls' room," she said, pushing past me.

Yikes. I raised my eyebrows as I watched Tish stumble down the hall.

Did she say "cute butt"?

Chapter 22

It was after 10:00 P.M. when Wes finally came back. I was lying on the bed, scrolling through Facebook on my phone, when he tapped on the door.

"Are you decent?" he called, opening the door a crack.

"That depends on what you think of my yoga pants and hoodie," I said, sitting up. Then I spotted the covered plate in his hand. "Ooh! What did you bring?"

"I asked the caterer for a salad and some roasted vegetables. Danielle seemed frazzled, so I decided to take matters into my own hands."

"You're so sweet," I said, taking the plate. He pulled a napkin-wrapped fork from his pocket and handed it to me.

While I dug into the food, Wes stood in the middle of the room with his hands in his pockets. "It sure is flowery in here, isn't it?"

"It is a bit rosy," I agreed. "Don't you like it?"

"I like the view from here," Wes said, looking at me. He smiled and waggled his eyebrows.

I laughed and said, "Has everyone left or gone to bed yet?"

"The dinner guests and actors are gone, and Sheana called it a night. Some cleaning people were just finishing up in the dining room when I left. I don't know what happened to Marco and Danielle. They probably went to bed."

I was about to ask about Tish's party when a car door slammed shut. Wes walked over to the window and looked down at the parking lot below.

"Check it out," he said.

"What?"

"I recognize this car."

I joined Wes at the window and saw immediately what he meant. "It's the car that cut you off on River Road the other night. Can you see the California plates?"

"It's dark down there, but I think so." A back porch light cast a dim glow that just reached the rear of the car.

"Who is that?" I peered out the window and saw a man open the trunk of the car. Wind whipped the edges of his long coat and flapped his blue scarf. His bald head was bare. *He must be cold.* We watched as he lifted a crate from the trunk and carried it to the back door of the mansion.

"I'm not sure," Wes said. "He could be the guest staying in the carriage house. Danielle mentioned he's a single guy who didn't want to go to the show tonight."

A few minutes later, the bald man returned to his car and drove around the side of the mansion. We couldn't see the carriage house from our window, so we didn't know if that was where he headed.

"Well, what do you think?" said Wes. "Do you want to investigate the speakeasy now?"

I checked my phone. "Let's wait until after midnight, or later, just to be sure everyone is asleep."

"Okay." He kicked off his shoes, walked over to sit on the bed, and leaned back on the pillows. "So, tell me about Wicca. How did you get started?"

I took a deep breath. I crawled onto the foot of the bed and sat cross-legged facing Wes.

"I was a young teenager," I began. "My Goth friends liked to play around with 'magick.' We learned about tarot cards and runes, made up spells. It was harmless fun."

"Goth?" Wes grinned. "Did you do the whole black hair, black eyeliner, emo thing? I'd love to see pictures."

"Nah. Well, maybe. For, like, half a second." I smiled. "I was attracted more to the nature-worship aspect. I read some books and became fascinated. The religion spoke to me. It made so much sense."

Wes looked thoughtful. "So when you said you know the owner of Moonstone Treasures, I guess you meant you know her pretty well."

"Yeah. I've been to her shop many times. In fact, I'm trying to help figure out who's been harassing her." I told Wes about all the break-ins and threatening notes.

"Are you saying someone murdered Charlie to drive Mila out of business?"

"It looks that way. I mean, I still think Charlie was in the wrong place at the wrong time. But the notes threatened death. And now the calls are threatening further bloodshed if Mila doesn't permanently close her business. By tomorrow."

"Whoa! That's crazy."

"You're telling me."

We speculated about the crimes for a while, then segued into a discussion of religion, philosophy, and pop culture. I was surprised when I checked the time and saw it was half past twelve.

"Ready to do this?" I said, jumping up from the bed.

"I'm right behind you," he said, running a hand through his unruly hair.

Wearing only socks on our feet, we slipped out of the Rose Petal Room and tiptoed down the hall. A loud snore from the third floor made me stop short. Suppressing a giggle, I rolled my eyes at Wes and led the way down the back stairs.

When we made it to the first floor, I told Wes I wanted to check the front door before heading to the basement. He nodded and said he'd take a peek in the other downstairs rooms.

Without making a sound, I snuck to the front door and tried the knob. It was unlocked.

Darn. Had Danielle and Marco forgotten to lock up? It bothered me to leave the door unsecured, so I turned the latch. *Hopefully, I'm not locking anyone out.*

I met up with Wes near the dining room, and we proceeded down the small hallway toward the basement door. He opened the door, felt for a light switch, and started down the steep stairway. I pulled the door shut behind us. As we descended the steps and entered the speakeasy, the pungent odor of hard liquor accosted us.

"Whoa," I said. "I guess the cleaning crew didn't make it down here."

The single overhead light was enclosed in a vintage leaded-glass fixture. It was a classy look, but it didn't give off much illumination. Wes turned on a floor lamp and then walked over to the old-fashioned bar. "Watch your step," he said. "There's broken glass on the floor."

Treading carefully, I scanned the room. Since the last time I was here, a green velvet sofa and another cocktail table had been added to the sparse furnishings.

"I can't believe I didn't bring a flashlight," I said. "What kind of detective am I?"

"Well, don't go lighting any candles," Wes said. "There's alcohol spilled everywhere."

I joined Wes and hopped up on a stool. He slid behind the bar and looked around. Seeing him there, in the bartender's spot, reminded me of our first date over the summer. I smiled at the memory.

He examined the labels on some of the bottles behind the bar. "I wonder how much the Thomisons charged Tish for the open bar. They have some expensive stuff here."

"Hey," I said. "Maybe that's what the bald guy was delivering—bottles of liquor."

"Maybe," said Wes. "I don't see a crate back here, but it could be upstairs someplace."

Looking around at the stone walls, I tried to imagine how there could be a secret exit down here. The walls appeared to be solid. Maybe there was a trapdoor?

Swiveling on the stool, I looked at the floor. It was covered in wall-to-wall carpet. I sighed.

I was beginning to think my notion about a secret tunnel was nothing more than a flight of fancy. Then my eyes fell upon the wood-paneled wall on the side of the staircase. Usually one would expect to find a storage closet under the stairs, but I didn't see a door.

Leaving the stool, I walked over to the staircase and inspected the wall. Wes saw me tapping on the wall and came over beside me.

"Is it hollow?" he asked.

"Yeah, but that's not a surprise. I don't know why anyone would completely seal this off, though."

I ran my fingers along the edges of the paneling, hoping something would catch. Wes studied the edge of the wall. "You know, this very well could slide open. We just have to find the trigger."

For the next several minutes, we pushed, pulled, pressed, and tapped on everything on and around the staircase. All to no avail.

Feeling frustrated, I flopped into a club chair. "I don't know why I thought this would be easy," I said. "Old man Cadwelle wouldn't have wanted anyone accidentally opening the panel. I guess you have to know the secret."

Wes looked at me. "You could be onto something there. There was usually a secret password to get into speakeasies. Maybe we have to enter a code someplace."

I swept the room with my eyes until my gaze settled on the antique telephone at the end of the bar. Wes had the same thought. He was near the phone, so he picked up the receiver.

"Any dial tone?" I asked.

"No. It's not connected."

"Is it plugged into the wall?" I stood up and joined Wes by the bar.

He looked closely at all sides of the phone and then tried to lift it off the bar. It didn't budge.

"It seems to be bolted to the wood."

"Seriously?" I perked up. For the first time since we started our search, I actually felt like we might be getting close. "Try dialing some numbers."

Wes tried each number, from zero to nine. With each turn of the dial, we watched for the wall panel to move. It didn't.

I sat down and propped my elbows on the bar. "Of course, it would have to be a sequence of numbers, right?" I said. "Probably not a long sequence, though. The door would have to be able to be opened in a hurry."

Wes randomly dialed numbers while I scratched my head and tried to divine a code Orion Cadwelle might have used. "Hmm. When did Marco say Cadwelle built the mansion? 1901? Try that."

Wes tried, but it didn't work. "I wonder when he married his wife," Wes said. "I'll start with 1900 and work my way back through the 1800s."

With every failed attempt, I felt my frustration rise. None of the dates caused a secret door to open.

"Okay," I said, trying to stay positive. "His wife's name was Violet. Can you spell that on the phone?"

"It's kind of long, but I'll give it a try." When that didn't work, Wes tried spelling "Orion." Nothing.

Staring at the numbers and letters on the phone,

I had another thought. "Why not just try spelling 'open,'" I said. "Six, seven, three, six."

I stifled a yawn as I watched Wes turn the numbers. When he dialed the fourth number and we heard a metallic click beneath the stairs, I almost didn't realize what was happening.

The wooden panel slid open, just as we had imagined, revealing a dark passageway within. A rush of cool, dank air blew into the room. I was too astonished to move.

"We did it!" I exclaimed.

"You're a genius," Wes said, grabbing me by the shoulders. "This is amazing! Man, I wish I had brought my camera down here."

I stood up from the stool and moved cautiously toward the opening under the stairs. At that moment, I had two questions in my mind: Where could I find a flashlight? And would the same code work to close the door?

I needn't have wondered about closing the door. It must have been designed to stay open for only a few seconds and then close automatically. Before I reached the threshold, it started sliding closed.

"What do you—" Wes started to speak as he moved toward the center of the speakeasy but then froze.

"What's the matter?" I asked.

He put his fingers to his lips and shook his head. I turned to see what had alarmed him. A pale arm stuck out from behind the velvet sofa.

A woman was sprawled on the floor between the wall and the couch.

Chapter 23

I ran over to the still body on the floor. It was Tish. Her dress was rumpled and her shoes were missing. Her smeared makeup looked garish on her pallid face. Fearing the worst, I leaned down and touched my fingertips to her wrist. She groaned. Startled, I jumped back and bumped into Wes, who was hovering right behind me.

"Is she okay?" he asked.

"She's alive, at least." I turned back to Tish and scanned her body for any visible signs of injury. My first thought was that she had been attacked. For a fleeting moment, I had even wondered if the killer had struck again. After all, it was officially Saturday now. However, it soon became apparent that Tish's troubles were self-inflicted. She reeked of alcohol.

Supporting her back, I helped her sit up. "Tish, can you hear me? Are you okay? Does anything hurt?"

She groaned again and lifted her hand to her head. "My pound . . . my head pounding. An' my mouf . . . firsty."

I glanced up at Wes, and he dropped his shoulders in relief. He had dealt with plenty of drunk bar patrons. "Tish, let's get you off the floor," he said. "Keli, could you get her a drink of water?"

I hurried over to the sink behind the bar and filled a glass with water, while Wes lifted Tish and carried her to the sofa. I sat next to her and held the glass to her lips. She took one sip, then leaned her head back and closed her eyes.

"Tish?"

"Huh?"

"How did you end up on the floor? Why are you still here?"

She groaned again, then opened one eye. "Marco. It's all his fault."

Wes and I exchanged a look. "What about Marco?" I asked.

She sighed, shut her eye, and mumbled her response. "He . . . he said he'd come back here after all the guests left. My party ended. Everybody left in taxicabs. Marco and I had it all planned out. Our little . . . *rendezvous.*" She whispered the last word as a small smile flickered across her lips.

Wes whistled softly under his breath, and I shook my head. I had heard enough. I wasn't entirely sure if Tish had passed out before the alleged tryst could take place or afterward, but at least I knew she hadn't been assaulted.

Surely Marco didn't know she was still on the floor of the basement when he went to bed.

After a quick huddle, Wes and I decided it would be best for Tish to spend the remainder of the night right where she was on the sofa. I ran up to the main floor to snatch an afghan from the library, and then we tucked her in as best as we could. We turned off all the lights except for one lamp, so she wouldn't be left in complete darkness. Finally, we snuck back up to our room.

I'd had more than enough surprises for one night.

I sprinted down Main Street, separating myself from the other runners. They were an enthusiastic crowd of colorfully dressed women, men, and children, unfazed by the gray sky and clammy air. As a light drizzle began to pelt cold droplets on my face, I ran even faster—not only to warm up, but also to wake up and get the race over with. This was Candlemas. D-day according to Mila's harasser. I was a little on edge.

"Hey, speedy!" Farrah caught up with me and matched my stride. "Did you forget about a little thing called 'pacing'?"

"Sorry." I slowed down slightly. "I have to take advantage of my early momentum. Otherwise, I'm afraid I won't be able to finish."

"Just stick with me," she said. "I'll see that you make it to the end."

She slowed her pace to a more moderate speed and kept talking, so I had no choice but to fall into step. Following the signs for the "Groundhog Shuffle," we entered Fieldstone Park for our first loop. After a jaunt through the park, we would make our way downtown, around Courthouse Square, and then back to the park. At that point, runners who had signed up for the 5K would cross the finish line. The rest of us would branch off and do the whole course all over again.

It was going to be a long morning.

At least I was beginning to warm up. As for waking up, I probably should have been used to operating on less than a full night's sleep by now. When Farrah had picked me up at the B&B at the crack of dawn to get us to the 8:00 A.M. race in plenty of time, Wes was still snoozing under the covers. I would have given anything to be able to sleep in with him.

Then again, I was more than happy to miss the community breakfast with Danielle, Marco, and the other guests. I could only imagine how awkward it would be when Tish came stumbling up the stairs from the basement.

When Wes and I had finally made it back up to our room, we had laughed at the absurdity of finding Tish on the floor—and bemoaned the fact that we didn't get to explore the hidden exit we had found in the speakeasy. We went round and round over what to do about that. Wes thought we should go straight to the police, but I told him the police couldn't just knock on the door of the mansion and ask to search the passageway. They would need probable cause to obtain a warrant. I thought we should focus instead on finding an entrance in one of the downtown businesses. I told Farrah as much when I filled her in this morning, and she agreed.

"Did you hear a word I just said?" asked Farrah.

"What?"

"That's what I thought. You're still thinking about the secret passageway, aren't you?"

"Among other things," I said. "I'm eager to start searching for other tunnels."

"Me too," said Farrah. "As soon as we're done with this thing, I'm going to call Ted. He should be able to get us into Gigi's."

"That would be great." I wasn't sure what time Mila would get back from her weekend getaway, but I planned to try reaching her as well.

We exited the park and followed the route I took to work every morning. A roadside marker told us we had passed mile number two. While my body continued on autopilot, my mind raced ahead.

Who knew about the secret exit from the speakeasy? Danielle and Marco had lived in the mansion for only a few months, so it was conceivable they might not know. Although they could have stumbled upon it, or read about it someplace.

As the Thomisons' real estate agent, Yvette would have seen the property records. Plus, she was spending a lot of time at the mansion. Tish had spent time there, too, especially in the speakeasy. And Tish was a city official, so she would have had ready access to information about the town's history, as well as any maps of the town's underground infrastructure.

On the other hand, whoever was using the tunnels could have found an access point from somewhere other than the mansion. That person could have emerged in the speakeasy and then gone out through the front door of the mansion—leaving it unlocked behind him or her.

As my feet pounded the pavement, I continued to mull over the possibilities. When Farrah and I crossed the alley that ran behind Moonstone Treasures, I automatically looked to the right. I caught a glimpse of a pale girl wearing an army jacket and combat boots.

"What's Catrina doing back there?" I said.

Making a split-second decision, I veered into the alley and jogged to the back door of the shop.

"Keli!" called Farrah, chasing after me. "What are you doing?"

When I reached the back door, Catrina was gone. The knob didn't turn when I tried it, so I knocked. No answer.

I turned to Farrah, jogging in place next to me. "I saw Catrina, the clerk who works here. I thought maybe she could let us in to search for a tunnel."

Farrah looked over her shoulder. "I hope this little detour doesn't disqualify us."

"You know, this isn't going to be our best time anyway," I pointed out.

"Right," said Farrah. "I'll check the front." She darted around the corner. I pounded on the door again, waited a few seconds, then ran around to the front of the building to join Farrah.

"There's no one in there," she said. "Can we go back to the race now?"

"Yeah." I nodded, and we sprinted back to the racecourse, falling in with a group of runners we had passed several minutes ago. Farrah continued at a brisk clip, as if to recapture the lost minutes. I managed to keep up, though I wasn't quite sure how. It must have been the adrenaline.

When we rounded the courthouse, we came upon a row of antique cars, decorated trucks, and vibrant floats, lining up in preparation for the parade. I spotted Pammy and Crenshaw standing next to the law firm's float and waved.

"Go, Keli!" Pammy yelled, clapping. "Woo-hoo!"

Crenshaw folded his arms and raised one eyebrow as he watched me run by.

"He *so* wants you," Farrah said.

I was trying to think of a suitable retort when something caught my attention up ahead. A large banner fastened to a flatbed truck bore the words "First Church of the New Believers." As we drew near, I heard raised voices. On the sidewalk behind the truck was the most unlikely pair I could imagine: Reverend Natty and Catrina. They appeared to be arguing.

"How did she get here so fast?" asked Farrah. "Are you sure it was her you saw in the alley?"

"Positive. Maybe she biked over or drove. Or maybe she took a shortcut."

"Like through a tunnel?" Farrah asked.

I dropped to a slow trot in hopes of catching a snippet of their conversation. All I heard was Catrina say, "You wanna bet!"

After we passed them, I looked back over my shoulder. That's when I saw the sign on the back of the truck: REPENT! THE END IS NEAR!

Oh boy.

Farrah saw it, too. "Seriously?" she said, as we

turned the corner and headed back to Fieldstone Park. "People still say that?"

"Apparently so," I said. "Even fanatics are free to say whatever they want."

As long as they don't harm anyone.

We fell silent as we jogged into the park and began the second half of the race. The rain had let up and the sun peeked through the clouds. I was reminded that this was supposed to be a festive day. Imbolc—Candlemas—was meant to celebrate the waning winter. I didn't exactly feel spring in the crisp wind, but I did feel that change was in the air. Something was definitely brewing.

Twenty minutes later we were back for our second pass along the parade lineup. Pammy and Crenshaw were gone. I imagined they had probably joined the throngs heading to the park to see "Eddie," the Edindale groundhog. However, Reverend Natty was still next to the church truck. Now he was speaking to a young police officer.

"Hey, that's Dave!" said Farrah.

I squinted. Sure enough, the officer nodding and listening attentively to Reverend Natty was our friend Dave. I saw him look to where the reverend was pointing, at the tires of the truck. They were all flat.

"Ooh," said Farrah. "Do you think that Catrina chick is responsible for that?"

"If she is, then she's even more of a radical than I thought."

"I'll call Dave later and find out what he can tell me."

We continued trudging down the street, pushing through our last half mile. I didn't know about

Farrah, but my lungs burned and my legs had turned to spaghetti. It was sheer willpower that kept me going.

When we rounded a curve in the park and the large FINISH sign appeared in our line of sight, Farrah turned to me.

"Thelma and Louise?" Farrah offered her hand, so we could cross the finish line at the same time.

"No way," I huffed. "You go."

"Okay," she said. "If you insist."

She burst forward like a powerful spring, cruising through the finish line in a blur. I, on the other hand, stumbled over the line several seconds behind her. Someone handed me a cup of water, which I splashed on my face. Then I walked in circles, holding my arms above my head, until Farrah found me and pulled me to a nearby picnic table.

"You did it, girlfriend! I knew you could!"

"Ugh," I replied, unable to form any actual words.

Farrah laughed. Her face was flushed and her T-shirt was damp, but she looked remarkably perky. "What can I get you?" she asked. "Water? Fruit? A towel?"

I shook my head and stretched my legs. Now I knew what would happen when I failed to train properly. I was going to feel this for a while.

A voice over a loudspeaker announced that Eddie would be coming out of his burrow soon.

"Do you want to see the shadow ceremony, or whatever it is?" Farrah asked.

"I'm spent," I said. "You can go if you want."

"No. I'll take you home," Farrah said. We removed the numbers pinned to our shirts and walked toward the parking lot. "Can you believe how much trouble the town's going to over a silly groundhog superstition? They're going to kick off the parade next. Then, there's a luncheon at the courthouse and a street fair, and tonight there's a concert at the university featuring some famous country music band."

"It does seem like a lot for one day," I agreed.

"Not that I mind any excuse for a good party," Farrah added.

We walked past a side street where a marching band was rehearsing and stamping their feet to keep warm. A gust of wind ruffled the plumes on their hats and blew dried leaves and litter in a small swirl on the sidewalk. Looking down, I saw a long-stemmed white rose among the debris.

"I could use this," I murmured, picking up the flower.

If Farrah heard me, she didn't say anything. She was distracted by the shiny black car that zipped into the parking lot in front of us and pulled haphazardly in front of a handicapped parking sign. The door swung open and out stepped Tish Holiday wearing a long leopard-print coat and dark sunglasses. She slammed her car door shut and hurtled toward Fieldstone's gazebo.

"I guess she recovered," said Farrah.

"Guess so," I said, noting Tish's bright red lipstick and pop star hair.

I couldn't help wondering how close she had become with Marco. Or how much she knew about the speakeasy. I was just glad she was still in one piece.

Chapter 24

I slipped into the hot, silky bathwater and sighed. With a deep inhale, I breathed in the soothing aroma of sweetgrass and lavender, as the oiled water washed over my aching body. White candles and gentle guitar music completed the stage for my ritual purification bath—which today did double duty as a postworkout recovery soak.

When Farrah dropped me off at my town house after the 10K, we agreed that we would check in with each other later. She planned to make some phone calls and arrange for us to snoop around in Gigi's Bar and Grill tomorrow morning before the restaurant opened. She also said she would stop off at the library and see what she could learn about Orion Cadwelle—especially his bootlegging days.

I had some phone calls to make, too. First, I went to the kitchen and blended up a smoothie with coconut water, cucumbers, orange slices, and chia seeds. As I sipped my drink, I dialed Mila's number. There was no answer, so I tried Max next.

"Max Eisenberry," she answered, in her professorial voice.

"Hi, Max. It's Keli."

"Oh, hello, Keli. How's it going?"

"Good," I said. "Do you know when Mila is due back?"

Max hesitated. "Um . . . she'll be back this afternoon. I'll be seeing her later. Do you have a message you'd like me to relay?"

"You can ask her to call me," I said. "Say, Max, how well do you know Catrina?"

"Fairly well, though it's been less than a year since we first met. I do know Mila trusts her."

"Hmm. Catrina used to date a girl named Andi. Do you know if they're still together?"

"They're not. Andi used to be in Circle, but she stopped coming when they broke up. It's too bad. She was a sweet girl."

"Yeah. Do you happen to have Andi's number?"

Max found the phone number for me. As soon as I hung up, I tried reaching Andi but there was no answer. I left her a message, then kept my phone within arm's reach as I soaked in the tub.

I leaned my head back on a folded terry cloth towel and closed my eyes. As the fragrant water cleansed my body, I visualized the release of all of my anxiety, stress, and confusion. All negativity would be washed down the drain.

After a few minutes, I realized I should get out of the tub before the water became too cool. I pulled the plug, stood up, and toweled off. I was in the midst of applying a thick herbal body cream when the phone rang. I wiped off my hands and grabbed the phone.

"Hey there, supergirl. How was the race?" Wes said.

I smiled at the sound of his voice. "It was long, but I finished it. How was your morning?"

"Interesting. Danielle canceled our photo shoot in the speakeasy. She said the place was a wreck after the private party, making her rethink the whole idea. Marco was nowhere to be seen. I never saw Tish come up either."

I told Wes about seeing Tish downtown. "Maybe Marco was cleaning up the speakeasy."

"I don't know. There was a weird vibe during breakfast. Sheana kept trying to ask Danielle about her recipes, but Danielle was distracted. All the guests seemed uncomfortable. Yvette left abruptly without saying a word to anyone."

"That's odd," I said.

"Yeah." He paused. "So, do you want to get together later? Maybe have some dinner?"

"I'd like that," I said. "Before I do anything, though, I need a nap. How about if I call you later?"

"Sounds good."

After saying good-bye to Wes, I went to my bedroom and drew the curtains against the late morning sun. I put on my pentagram necklace and donned my white hooded robe. Then I cleared off my altar, moved it to the center of the room, and draped it with a white cloth. Using an assortment of white and green candles, I decorated the table. In the center, I placed a bud vase containing the white rose the wind had delivered to me. Finally, I cleared a workspace, on which I placed a ceramic pot, a container of soil, a bottle of melted snow, and an amaryllis bulb.

In my usual fashion, I cast a circle around the altar. Then I lit the candles while chanting a spell I had composed on a previous Candlemas:

> *"One flame to purify*
> *One to transform,*
> *One flame to beautify*
> *One to keep warm.*
>
> *One flame for innocence*
> *One for desire,*
> *One flame for benevolence*
> *One to inspire."*

Finally, I lit the two largest candles, saying:

> *"A flame for the god, born anew*
> *A flame for Brigid, goddess true."*

By the light of the candles, I proceeded to plant the flower bulb. As I did so, I contemplated the significance of Candlemas, a cross-quarter sabbat marking the midway point between the winter solstice and the spring equinox. At this point on the wheel of the year, the mythical god, who was reborn at Yuletide, was now beginning to mature as the sun grew stronger in the sky. At the same time, the mother goddess had recovered from birthing the god and could now return to her maiden form. Thus, the earth could begin a new cycle of growth and fertility.

When the bulb was securely ensconced in the pot, surrounded by soil, and watered with the melted snow, I whispered my wish for the amaryllis and for myself: "That you may bloom to your full potential, bring joy to all who see you, and fulfill your true purpose in this life. Blessed be."

I closed the circle, then allowed the candles to burn out while I sat on my bed writing in an indigo cloth-bound journal. I didn't always take the time to document my spells and rituals in a "Book of Shadows," but sometimes I felt called to do so. As I jotted down notes about my observance of Candlemas, I started to feel sleepy. With a big yawn, I set down my book and closed my eyes.

The sound of my phone woke me up. I didn't know how long I had slept, but the light outside was much dimmer. I grabbed my phone from the bedside table and was surprised to see it was Max calling.

"Hi, Max. What's up?"

"Keli, you're not going to believe this."

"What is it?"

"Mila has been arrested."

With all the street closures for the Groundhog Festival, I had to park on a side street three blocks from the police station. Wearing the same running shoes from the 10K earlier today, I jogged up to the front door of the small brick building and went inside. I informed the officer at the front desk I was an attorney there to see Mila Douglas and showed her my identification. She wrote down my information in a log book and said it would be a few minutes.

"Is Detective Rhinehardt here?" I asked.

"No. He left a while ago. Would you like to leave a message?"

"No, that's okay. I'll catch him later."

I turned around and headed to the waiting area in the lobby. It was empty except for Max. She stood up when she saw me.

"Thanks for coming," she said. "I'm sure this isn't how you planned to spend your Saturday evening."

"It's no problem," I said, putting a hand on Max's arm. "How are you doing? Have you heard anything about what's going on with Mila?"

"I'm fine. Poor Mila is still in processing, or so I'm told. They seem to be taking their time about it."

"Tell me exactly what happened," I said, taking the seat next to Max. She sat back down and sighed.

"We were performing a binding ritual on the sidewalk in front of Moonstone. There were nine of us, all members of Magic Circle. Mila had created a poppet to represent her harasser, and—"

"A poppet?" I interrupted.

"Yes. A dummy, made from a large rag doll. She put a piece of duct tape over its mouth."

I tried not to cringe. "Oh. That sounds really creepy."

"Well, taken out of context, I suppose it does. Anyway, we gathered in a circle, each of us holding one end of a black cord. Mila pinned the other ends to the doll, which she propped on an old wooden chair from her shop. Then we danced around the poppet, winding the cords around it like a maypole."

"To magically bind the perpetrator?" I said.

"That's right. We chanted a binding spell as we went."

I took a deep breath. "Why did you do this outside? Couldn't the ritual have been done inside the shop? Or at someone's home?"

"Well, Mila wanted to psychically seal all the openings to the shop. Our plan was to start with the front door and window, since that's where the violations started. We were going to do the back door next."

"I imagine you attracted a lot of attention."

Max grimaced. "I wanted to wait until after dark and perform the ritual by the light of the waning moon. But Mila was anxious. She had received another threatening phone call, so she didn't want to wait."

I shook my head. *Was stress or fear clouding Mila's judgment?*

"So," I said, "someone called the police?"

"Not just anyone," said Max. "That tourism director, Tish Holiday. You should have seen her." Max chuckled. "I know it's too soon to laugh about this, but she looked like a crazy woman. She came running up, yelling and waving her arms, carrying on about voodoo dolls and bad publicity. Apparently, that big shot country singer Rhett Shelby and his entourage saw us from their limo and said something to the mayor."

"Yikes."

"Yeah. The police officer told us to disperse, but Mila didn't hear him."

I frowned. "What do you mean?"

"Mila had entered a trancelike state to channel

the Goddess Hecate," Max explained. "She had closed her eyes to shut out all distractions. She wouldn't have heard anything until the ritual was complete."

"What about the rest of the group?" I asked.

"It was a little chaotic, I must admit. I touched Mila's hand to bring her gently out of the trance. Only she thought I was signaling her for the final step in the ritual—the burning of the poppet."

"Uh-oh."

"Yeah." Max rubbed her temples. "Mila took her candle and lit the doll on fire. I managed to put the fire out quickly by stepping on it, but the damage was done. Tish insisted that Mila be arrested for disorderly conduct. She claimed Mila was a trouble-maker who was disturbing the peace. Tish said she was pressing charges."

"Poor Mila."

"Actually, Mila seemed unfazed by the whole thing. When she realized what was happening, she told me not to worry. She said she had had a vision of her spending a night behind bars, so she wasn't even surprised. She was more concerned about the rest of us."

"So only Mila was arrested?"

Max nodded.

I glanced around the empty police station. "Where's Catrina? I would have expected her to jump at the chance to be locked up for civil disobedience."

"I don't know where Catrina is," said Max, frowning. "She took off the second she saw the police officer approaching."

Max checked her watch. "I need to get going. I'm already late picking up Janie from the babysitter."

I nodded, regarding her curiously. "How do you do it, Max? How do you manage to be a public Wiccan? Aren't you worried about your job?"

Max looked surprised. "Oh, everyone in the English department knows about my religion. Most students find out eventually, so I get questions sometimes. Occasionally, someone tries to convert me. I don't pay them much attention." Max laughed. "It's a free country, remember?"

The steel door next to the front desk opened and a police officer stepped out, looking our way. "Attorney Milanni?"

Max left, and I approached the officer. She searched my purse and patted me down. Then she led me through the steel door and down a hallway to a small conference room with a metal table and two chairs. Mila was sitting in one of the chairs. She was wearing an orange jumpsuit.

"Mila!" I exclaimed the moment I caught sight of her. "You shouldn't have to stay here overnight! You should be able to post bond and go home."

Mila gave me a resigned smile. "Apparently, the judge left already. The next bond hearing won't be until tomorrow morning."

I opened my mouth to protest. Surely I could make a couple of calls and find somebody to handle this tonight. Mila held up her hand.

"It's okay. I already discussed it with my husband. He's reaching out to a bail agent now. This is how it's supposed to be. I had a vision. This is the consequence of my binding spell, but it's worth it. It had to be done."

I studied Mila for a moment and saw there was no use arguing with her. "Would you like me to attend the hearing with you in the morning?"

"That's not necessary," she said. "I know this isn't your area of law. Besides, my husband said he would find a defense attorney."

I couldn't help feeling Mila was declining my assistance in order to protect my privacy. I felt bad about that. As if reading my mind, Mila reached over and squeezed my hand. "There is one thing you can do for me," she said.

"What is it?"

"Ask the police officer for the ring of keys in my personal effects—I'll tell her it's okay. Then go by Moonstone and check on Drishti."

"Drishti is in the shop?"

"Yes. She's fine staying there, but I didn't have a chance to refill her food and water bowls. You can find them in the back room. The cat food is in the bottom drawer of my desk. I would be so grateful if you would do this for me."

"Of course," I said.

Mila smiled, while I marveled at her serenity. "It's just one night," she said. "I'll be fine."

Suddenly, Mila's smile faded and a look of worry crossed her eyes. "Be careful, Keli. The shop is enchanted with the most powerful protection charms I know. And the police should be watching it, too—I told them about the caller's deadline. But this person is not predictable. First, it was notes and graffiti. Then a fire, phone calls . . . murder. There's no telling what the killer will do next."

Mila's words made me shiver. I knew she was right.

"Watch your back," she continued. "I'm afraid this person is getting desperate. And desperation spells danger."

Chapter 25

I decided to leave my car where it was and walk the short distance to Moonstone Treasures. A few holdovers from the street festival loitered in Courthouse Square, but most partiers had relocated to the concert hall at the university. I thought I could hear the strains of Rhett Shelby's country band echoing through the night air.

Using the key the police officer retrieved from Mila's purse, I let myself in through the front door of the shop. With Mila's cautionary words still ringing in my mind, I locked the door behind me. I turned on a light and moved through the front half of the shop.

"Drishti!" I called. "Here, kitty-kitty. Where are you, Drishti?"

After a quick check in the clothing section upstairs and the book section downstairs, I went through the curtain to the back room and turned on a lamp in Mila's divination parlor. There was still no sign of the cat, but I found her food dish and water bowl.

I filled them with dry pellets and fresh water. Then I stood in the center of the room and gazed around.

If I were a hidden tunnel, where would I be?

Underground, obviously.

I looked down at the wood plank floor. In the divination area, it was covered with an Oriental rug. On the storage side, the floor was mostly bare except for a carpet runner in front of the back door.

Slowly, I walked around the room, bouncing my feet as I went. The floor felt pretty solid to me.

When I reached the round table where Mila had read our palms, I recalled Farrah's jumpiness. For a minute there, she looked like she really had seen a ghost. I wasn't sure what I believed when it came to ghosts. Was it possible Charlie's spirit could still be lingering on the earthly plane? Thinking about it now—and being alone in this place—made the back of my neck prickle.

I dropped into a chair at the table and peered into the shadowy corners of the room. This was a century-old building, I reminded myself. Was it so far-fetched to imagine it contained residual energy from long-ago occupants?

Yet, when Farrah had felt the breeze on her ankles, neither Mila nor I had felt any ghostly presence—and we were both intuitive Wiccans. I bent over to look under the table.

I had been sitting closest to the curtain that evening, and I didn't feel anything. The air must have come from the back of the room.

I stood up and considered the gap between the two Japanese screens. As I walked around to the other side of the screens, my eyes fell upon the closet next to the bathroom. I opened the closet door, pulled the cord for the overhead lightbulb, and looked inside. Along the right wall were a vacuum cleaner, a couple of brooms, and a mop in a plastic bucket. On the left was a set of wooden shelves holding folded tablecloths and other linens. In the back, across the width of the closet, was a steel rod on which hung a few cloaks and dresses.

I turned around. If the door had been open that night, a current of air coming from the closet could have touched Farrah's ankles. Of course, that meant there would have had to have been a source of air in there.

My heart beat faster as I searched the closet. Pushing aside the hanging clothes, I studied the wall and floor. *Is there an opening in here?* The floor seemed solid, but the walls were made from knotty pine. I pressed the knots in the wood and felt along the edges of the wall.

Remembering the old phone in the speakeasy, I searched for something that could hide a trigger mechanism. Nothing in the closet was bolted down except for the coat hooks behind the mop and brooms. For good measure, I tried twisting each hook—with the final twist, a part of the back wall clicked open.

Holy Goddess!

I rushed forward to examine the opening. It was only about three feet high, but I could see stone steps leading into the blackness below. I was tempted to climb down the steps and have a look, but I didn't want to be foolhardy. I backed out of the closet, found my purse where I had left it on Mila's desk, and pulled out my phone.

I had to call Farrah. Never mind if she thought it was strange that Mila had given me the keys to her shop. I would worry about that later.

I was about to press CALL when my phone buzzed in my hand, nearly causing me to drop it. I glanced at the display and saw a number I had seen many times before—Catrina's. She probably wanted to tell me about Mila's arrest.

"Hello," I said, hoping to end the call in a hurry.

"Keli, are you doing anything right now?" Catrina asked. "Can you meet me at Moonstone?"

"Why?"

"There's something I want to show you."

I frowned. "Actually, I'm at the shop now. I saw Mila at the police station and she gave me her keys."

"I'll be right there." Catrina hung up, leaving me to stare at my phone.

Now what?

Before I could decide what to do, my phone buzzed again. This time it was an unknown caller.

"Hello?"

"Hello, Keli? This is Andi Roark. You called me earlier."

"Oh! Right. Hi, Andi. I'm not sure if you remember me. We met at Mila's shop last summer."

"I remember," said Andi. "Your message said you wanted to talk about Trina?"

Briefly, I told her about seeing Catrina argue with Reverend Natty—and then seeing the tires slashed on his truck. "Do you think Catrina would do something like that?"

"She would totally do something like that," Andi said without hesitation. "She's gone off the deep end."

Whoa. I didn't expect that. "What do you mean?"

"I mean she's certifiable. She's nuts. She used to be okay, or so I thought. Then she got it into her head that everyone's against her. Everything's a conspiracy. She lost touch with reality."

I paced the room, suddenly worried about Catrina showing up any minute now. "Andi, forgive me, but that sounds really harsh. When did things change?"

Andi sighed. "It started when she was fired from her job as a teacher's aide. She loved that job, but she was let go. She claimed it was discrimination, because someone found out she was a witch. To add insult to injury, she started to get hate mail, and someone even egged her car."

So Catrina was being targeted just like Mila. That explained a few things.

"Then what?"

"Then we left the Chicago suburbs and moved to Edindale. Catrina had filed a grievance with the school district, which she continued to pursue even after we came here. A few months ago, she learned she lost her case. I think that started the downward spiral."

"Hmm. It kind of sounds like she had a legitimate reason to be upset."

"Well, maybe at first. But she wouldn't let it go. She got so negative. I mean, she could put on a normal face for the public—that's how she got the job at Moonstone. Behind closed doors, it was another story. She'd troll on the Internet, anonymously picking fights with people. She lost her sense of empathy, only seeing the bad side of people. She became unbearable."

"Wow. I'm sorry to hear that, Andi. That's really sad."

As I spoke with Andi, I wandered into the front part of the store and turned out the lights. Standing at the front window, I looked out onto the empty street. There was no sign of any police officers watching the shop.

"Yeah," said Andi. "It *is* too bad. I couldn't handle it anymore. Trina became too scary for me."

I was beginning to think Catrina was too scary for me, too. After thanking Andi for being so open, I hung up and bit my lip.

Could Catrina be the person behind all the anonymous notes and calls to Mila? Could she have vandalized the shop and burned the books just to draw attention to the discrimination that some Wiccans suffer—and that she experienced when she lost her previous job?

Was she crazy enough to burn the hand that fed her?

Gazing out the window, I looked at the dark courthouse across the street and the empty bench where Charlie used to sit. I couldn't believe Catrina would have killed Charlie . . . at least, not on purpose. Maybe she was in the midst of causing more destruction at the shop when he came along, and she . . . what? Hit him over the head with a candlestick?

The sight of headlights on the other side of the square drew my attention. A car was coming this way. As it grew closer, I was pretty sure I recognized Catrina's lopsided hairdo behind the wheel.

Crap.

My first instinct was to hide. Moving quickly, I returned to the back room and rummaged in Mila's bureau for a pillar candle and a book of matches. Then I grabbed my purse, cut the lights, and closed myself in the closet. After only a slight hesitation, I gingerly ducked into the dark stairwell and pulled the secret panel shut behind me. I heard the jingle of the front door right before the panel clicked into place.

Holding my breath, I held on to the cool, stone wall as I descended the rough steps. Being careful not to misstep in the darkness, I proceeded with caution, counting as I went. Eleven steps in all.

I stood still at the bottom of the stairs listening intently for any hint of sound. It was completely silent. The soft ground beneath my feet felt like bare earth. The air was dank and musty, making me wish I had a scarf to wrap around my mouth and nose. I pulled my coat closed and waited.

After a few seconds, I struck a match and lit the candle. As I suspected, the steps had led to a narrow, cave-like tunnel. By the light of the flickering flame, I could see only a few feet in front of me, but I imagined the tunnel was long and winding. I shivered.

Well, I wasn't going to explore it now. I would wait a few minutes for Catrina to leave, and then I'd go back up into the shop and call Detective Rhinehardt. As much as I wanted to investigate it myself, I knew the tunnel might not be safe.

I strained to make out any sounds in the shop above me, but I couldn't hear a thing. I was counting on my belief that Catrina didn't know about the tunnel. If she was harassing Mila for her own twisted purposes, then it was unlikely she was also the one committing the burglaries. The crimes must be unrelated after all.

Right?

A twinge of doubt tugged at my mind, but a small pile of debris on the ground by my feet distracted me. I lowered the candle and squinted. *Are those bones?*

Reaching down, I picked up a dusty piece and turned it over in my hand. It was definitely part of a bone. I remembered the fragment I found on the floor when I helped Mila clean the storeroom. The bones on the ground were the same color and texture.

I frowned. Was Catrina playing around with sorcery? Were these bones used as part of some black magic ritual? Or could there be another Pagan who didn't like Mila? I would have to ask Mila or Max about the other members of their coven.

Puzzling over the possibilities, I glanced up at the door to the shop. If Catrina knew about the tunnel, surely she would have entered it by now. It was probably safe to go up.

With the candle in one hand, I used my other hand to hold on to the uneven wall as I carefully climbed back up the steps. Shining the light on the backside of the panel, I looked for a doorknob or handle. There was none.

Uh-oh.

There had to be a way to open the closet from this side. I held the candle close to the door and examined the wood, inch by inch, using the fingers of my right hand to feel for a latch. Finally, I found something. A keyhole.

You've got to be kidding me. My heart thudded in my chest. I couldn't get out of here without a key?

Alarm coursed through me, as the truth sank in.

I was trapped.

Chapter 26

Without a second thought, I pounded on the locked door. "Catrina!" I yelled as loudly as I could. "Catrina! Are you in there?"

I paused and listened. It was as quiet as a tomb.

What have I done?

Trying not to panic, I pulled my phone from my purse. As I feared, there was no signal. Not a single bar.

The clock on my phone told me it was after 7:00 P.M. I groaned. I was supposed to have called Wes about having dinner this evening. Would he think I was still sleeping? Or worse, that I was standing him up?

Gathering my nerve, I climbed back down the stone steps and into the dingy cellar. I would have to find another exit. Holding the candle out in front of me, I took a few tentative steps forward.

The silence was unsettling. Not to mention the impenetrable darkness in the tunnel ahead. The crumbling walls and dirt floor seemed ancient, like something in a medieval dungeon. The sound of my own breath called to mind a found-footage horror movie—with me as the star victim.

Get a grip, Milanni!

After only a few yards I came upon a metal ladder. I looked up and saw the bottom side of a trapdoor. With my long coat on, the purse on my shoulder, and candle in hand, it would be a tricky climb, but I didn't hesitate. I scrambled up the ladder and pushed on the hatch with my free hand while bracing my legs for balance. The door didn't budge.

"Come on!"

I held the candle above my head to see the trapdoor better. That's when I saw the keyhole. My heart sank and I climbed back down the ladder.

Continuing down the tunnel, I thought about the map Farrah had printed. The trapdoor probably led to the handbag store next to Moonstone Treasures. If I was remembering the map correctly, I should come upon Elena's Boutique next. Would it be locked, too?

As I trod along, I noticed the dirt floor seemed to be exceptionally black, and I wondered if the trapdoors could have been coal chutes years ago. Maybe the tunnel was used to transport coal. Then I remembered the back of Charlie's suit when we found his body, and the black dirt in his hair, and it suddenly hit me. He had been dragged through this tunnel. The murderer had definitely been here.

Icy fingers of fear crawled up the back of my neck. I swallowed hard as I inched my way forward. By the light of the candle, I examined the walls as I went. They were also made of dirt, reinforced with concrete cinder blocks. No wonder it was so dusty in here. I felt a tickle in my nose and sneezed. The loudness of it startled me, as it echoed through the tunnel.

After sneezing three times in quick succession, I stood in the silence and rubbed my nose. *What was that?* I froze. I could have sworn I heard something in the tunnel ahead.

For a second, indecision paralyzed me. Should I blow out the candle? Run the other way? What should I say if I encountered someone down here?

Something moved in front of me, and I let out a yelp. Then I saw the candlelight reflected in jewel-like eyes.

"Drishti!" I said, relief flooding through me. "What are you doing in here?"

The gray cat sauntered over and rubbed her face against the side of my leg. I reached down to pet her.

"You little sneak," I said softly. "You scared me half to death." I realized she must have slipped into the closet and through the secret door while I was talking on the phone in the shop.

With Drishti for company, I continued down the tunnel. It might have been a false sense of security, but I felt immeasurably better when the cat decided to stay with me.

After a while, I checked my phone. I had been in the tunnel for more than thirty minutes. *Maybe I should start walking faster.* No sooner had I picked up the pace than I came upon a fork in the passageway.

The new tunnel was smaller than the main one.

I would have to keep my head down to avoid scraping it along the dirt ceiling. Still, I was hopeful this branch would lead to a way out. I was rewarded a few minutes later when I came upon a wooden door.

"Check it out, Drishti! I wonder if we're under the courthouse or the jailhouse now?" At this point, with all the twists and turns, I had lost track of where I was in relation to the town above.

I grabbed the doorknob and tried to turn it. It was locked. I looked around for something I could use to force the door open, but the tunnel was empty. Disappointed, I made my way back to the main passageway and kept going. Drishti stayed close to my ankles, sometimes padding ahead and then circling back.

For the next half hour or so, we scuttled down the dark tunnel, following every fork—and then backtracking when it took us to a dead end or locked door. At first I spoke softly to Drishti as a way to comfort both of us. Then my mouth became dry, and I decided I had better conserve my energy. I was also hungry and weary, not to mention exceptionally sore from the race.

At some point, I gave up on the tunnel offshoots and resigned myself to the fact that I was going to have to see the main path to the end. I was pretty sure I knew what that end would be—I only hoped I would find it soon. My candle was now a stub of wax.

Gradually, I noticed the tunnel floor and walls had become smoother. Instead of bare earth, the floor seemed to be made from poured cement. It was still very dirty, but it felt harder under my feet. The walls appeared to be made from concrete as well.

Finally, I came to another fork, but this time the main path reverted to dirt, while the fork continued in concrete. I took the concrete path and soon found myself in a room that looked like a wine cellar. One wall was made from a familiar-looking wood panel.

I had made it to the Cadwelle Mansion.

"Thank Goddess!" I murmured.

Putting my ear to the panel, I listened for signs of life in the speakeasy. All was quiet. By this time, I was so desperate I would have pounded on the door regardless of who was on the other side. As it happened, I didn't have to. I saw a latch, lifted it, and slid the panel open.

The speakeasy was nearly as dark as the tunnel. I felt Drishti streak by me into the room. She was as grateful as I was to be out of the passageway. Stepping into the basement, I blew out what was left of my candle.

Using my cell phone for illumination, I hurried across the room and up the stairs. Slowly, I opened the door a crack. The hallway was empty, but I heard voices in the kitchen. After placing the candle stub in my pocket, I slipped into the hall and listened by the kitchen door. It sounded like Danielle was arguing with Yvette.

"I thought you were my friend!" said Danielle. "Was that all a ruse, to give you an excuse to search the mansion?"

"Danielle, listen to me," said Yvette. "Do you know—"

"I bet you're not even having your condo renovated," Danielle said. "I can't trust a word that comes out of your mouth."

I heard the front door open and my heart skipped a beat. Pivoting on my feet, I dashed into the powder room and locked the door. In the relative safety of the small room, I breathed a little easier. If anyone heard me in here, they would probably assume I was one of the guests—that is, if there were any other guests.

I turned the light on and looked at myself in the mirror. *What a mess.* I almost laughed at the sight of my tangled hair and dirt-streaked face. Instead, I used the sink to wash my hands and face. I let the water flow into my cupped hands and drank from the tap until my thirst was quenched.

Running my fingers through my hair, I tried to decide what to do. I was so fatigued, I couldn't think straight. *I should text Farrah*, I decided. *Ask her to pick me up here.*

I fumbled in my purse for my phone when a knock on the door made me jump. *Maybe if I ignore them, they'll go away*, I thought hopefully.

The person knocked again.

"Danielle? Are you in there?" It was Marco.

I plastered a smile on my face and opened the door.

"Hello," I said.

"Oh!" he said, appearing startled. "Sorry."

"No worries," I said. "I was just freshening up."

Danielle rounded the corner from the foyer and started down the hall. She was wearing a fur-trimmed stocking cap and a bright purple ski jacket. She stopped short when she saw us.

"There you are," said Marco. "I was hoping you hadn't left yet. You forgot . . . your list." He held up a folded piece of paper and handed it to Danielle.

"Thanks," she said, eyeing me. "That's what I came back for."

I batted my eyes and continued to smile. I knew I should make up a story, but my mind was blank. Luckily, Marco and Danielle both seemed too distracted to ask me what I was doing in their home. Maybe I could just excuse myself and walk out the front door.

Danielle slipped the folded paper into her white leather purse and turned to go.

"I'll walk out with you," I said quickly.

"Oh, don't go yet," said Marco. "I'm going to have a nightcap with Yvette. Won't you join us?"

"Well . . . " I trailed off. I supposed it would be better to wait for Farrah inside than start walking outside in the cold, dark night.

Wait. I hadn't even called Farrah yet. I needed to pull myself together.

"I'll see you later," said Danielle, turning on her heels. As I watched her walk away, I felt a slight queasiness come over me. It was probably because I hadn't eaten in more than ten hours. Alcohol was probably not the best idea for me right now.

"Come on into the parlor," Marco said, leading the way.

I looked around as I followed him. The B&B was quiet, and when we entered the parlor it was empty. Marco headed straight for the liquor cabinet.

"Where's Yvette?" I asked.

Marco gave me an expressionless look and then laughed. "Oh, right. She's probably in the library. I'll go see."

I trailed him to the library, but it was dark. Marco shrugged.

"Maybe she went downstairs to the speakeasy," he said. "She likes it down there."

We walked down the hall toward the basement. The door was still open a crack, just as I had left it, and the lights were off.

"You know what," said Marco, opening the door wider and flipping on the light switch, "we should have our drinks in the speakeasy anyway. You go on down and decide what you'd like. I'll go upstairs and knock on Yvette's door and let her know where we are."

I nodded and headed down the steps. This would give me a chance to look for Drishti. The poor thing was probably hiding somewhere. I had no idea how I was going to sneak her out.

When I reached the bottom of the stairs, I walked over to the bar and slipped behind the counter. I crouched down and peered in the corners.

"Drishti?" I called. "Where ya hiding, kitty?"

There was a cardboard box of spirits on the floor in front of some shelves. I imagined the dark shelves would make a perfect hiding place for a skittish cat, so I dragged the box away from the corner to have a look. As I did so, I noticed the shipping label on the box. It was addressed to "Gigi's Bar and Grill."

I stood up and felt the room spin. It could have been hunger and fatigue causing my light-headedness— or it could have been my sudden realization. I now knew for sure who was using the tunnels.

Either Marco or Danielle, or both of them, was the burglar.

Which meant one of them was most likely the killer, too.

The creak of a floorboard upstairs spurred me to action. With a trembling finger, I dialed the OPEN code into the antique telephone, causing the secret panel to open. I scanned the room, but there was no sign of Drishti. *She's a good hider. She'll be fine until I come back with help.*

I dashed inside the hidden room and watched as the door automatically slid closed.

I didn't have a plan. All I knew was that I had to get the hell out of there.

Chapter 27

It was a nightmare come true. I was fleeing a bad guy, stumbling in the dark, lost in an underground labyrinth. My only thought was escape. After darting through the speakeasy exit, I tore blindly down the tunnel, my arms outstretched in front of me.

I didn't get far. In the pitch blackness, I failed to see the curve of the tunnel wall. I bumped into it at full speed and bounced back, landing on my rear end.

Stunned, I sat on the cold ground and rubbed my knuckles where they had scraped the wall. Other than a few scratches and a stubbed toe, I seemed to be okay. I closed my eyes and inhaled slowly and deeply. *Goddess, help me.*

Reaching into my purse, I found my cell phone, then pulled it out and turned it on. Of course, there was still no signal to the outside world. My battery power was now at 20%. Holding the phone up, I used its dim light to try to get my bearings.

The ground was soft dirt. That meant I had already passed the last fork I had encountered, right before I found the speakeasy in my earlier trek through the tunnels. *Well*, I thought, *that fork didn't seem very promising anyway*. It headed farther away from downtown. I wanted to head back toward civilization.

I stood up and began walking. There had to be another way out. I would use my phone sparingly, I decided, turning it on long enough so that at least I wouldn't bump into any more walls.

No sooner had I resolved to stay calm than a sound behind me caused my heart to jump to my throat. Straining in the darkness, I heard it again, a scuffling noise, like someone moving around. It was coming from the direction of the speakeasy.

Before I could react, I heard another noise, this time the jingle of keys. Worse, it was coming from the tunnel ahead of me.

I inched forward with my hand on the wall, hoping desperately that I would come upon an opening, a crevice, anywhere to hide. The bright beam of a flashlight played across the ground in front of me.

There was nothing I could do but wait for the person to find me. For a fleeting moment, I dared to hope it could be a friend. A rescuer. But I knew that wasn't likely. Farrah and Wes had no idea I had even gone to Moonstone, let alone entered the tunnels. Mila was in jail. Catrina was clueless, and possibly unstable.

With a mental plea to Morpheus, I prayed for invisibility as I flattened myself against the wall. The beam from the flashlight brightened, and soon a person's brown boots came into view. It was a man. A bald man.

As soon as I recognized the stranger who had been driving the car with the California plates, I knew he was no friend. He must be working with Marco. Frantically, I thought about the contents of my purse, trying to determine whether I had anything I could use to defend myself. Wallet, makeup, tissues—nothing useful. *Why didn't I carry pepper spray?*

I reached into my coat pockets. My fingers closed over something with sharp edges. It was the broken clock face I had found outside Moonstone Treasures after it was first vandalized. I had forgotten to return it to Mila.

Still grasping the clock face, I pulled my hand from my pocket and kept my eyes glued to the figure approaching me. When he was a few feet away, he halted. He had spotted me. In the next moment, he raised to his toes as if he was about to lunge. I was two seconds ahead of him. With all my might, I hurled the clock face at the man's head. It struck him in the forehead, causing him to drop the flashlight as he grabbed his face in pain. I brushed past him and grabbed the flashlight, leaving him in darkness as I bolted.

With the light to guide me, I flew down the passageway as fast as my feet would carry me. As I ran, absurd thoughts swirled in my head. I longed for sleep. I wished I could just go to bed and wake up to do the whole day over again differently, like Bill Murray in the movie *Groundhog Day*.

I just clocked a guy with a clock, I thought madly.

Fighting hysteria, I sprinted as if my life depended on it. In fact, I realized, it probably did. Danielle or Marco, or their bald cohort, must have killed Charlie because Charlie had found the tunnels. Charlie had probably interrupted a burglary in progress. From what I had heard at the B&B, Yvette must have found the tunnels, too—and now Yvette seemed to be missing.

Now that I knew their secret, there was no way they would let me out alive.

When I came to a split in the tunnel, I skidded to a stop. It was a fork in the path I hadn't tried before. It could very well lead to a dead end, but if I kept going the way I had come, I knew I would wind up at a locked door. Without sparing another second to think about it, I turned off the main passageway.

By this time, I couldn't run anymore. I was out of breath and plagued by a side cramp I couldn't ignore. With labored breathing, I limped along, shakily shining the flashlight ahead of me.

After a few minutes, the roof of the tunnel sloped downward, and the winding tunnel became less like a human-made passage and more like a warren burrowed by a small mammal. *Like Eddie the groundhog.* I stifled a giggle and wondered if I was becoming delirious.

I continued to follow the path, stooping in places to avoid hitting my head. As I advanced, I noticed a small opening in the side of the tunnel wall. And then another. I couldn't tell if these were smaller tunnels that led anywhere, or just the abandoned start of new passageways.

After passing three such openings, I paused. I had detected a change in the air. It smelled different. I closed my eyes and tried to place the faint odor. It was like old fuel or motor oil—like the smell of a garage.

As I tried to make sense of this information, I noticed a shadow on the wall. *What in the world?* I tilted my head, trying to figure out what it was. At the last second, I knew.

I swirled around in time to see Marco raise a thick board. I screamed and ducked. Without a word, he raised the board again as I backed away.

"Please!" I begged. "Don't do this!"

Apparently, he wasn't in the mood for conversation. With a headlamp strapped tightly around his stocking cap, his face appeared pinched and distorted. His eyes had a murderous gleam.

Thinking fast, I pointed the flashlight into his face, hoping to blind him. It only made him angrier. He swung the board low, nicking my hip. I screamed again, as much from horror as from pain.

Scrambling backward, I came upon another gap in the wall. This time I darted inside. Marco followed.

"Marco, please," I repeated. "Can't we talk about this? Maybe I can help you."

There was no reasoning with him. He lifted the board again, and I covered my head, preparing to be hit.

But when I heard the thud of the board making

contact, I didn't feel a thing. I opened my eyes.
Marco had hit the ceiling instead. I watched as he
swung the board like a bat, striking upward at the
top of the tunnel before him. Dirt sprinkled down.

In a last-ditch effort to escape, I lunged at Marco's
legs and grabbed on. He elbowed me in the back
and kicked me off. I twisted away, landed hard on
my left wrist. As I curled on the ground, wincing in
pain, he kicked me again, his boot landing on my
lower back. He continued to strike at the ceiling
while he backed out of the crevice. Again and again
he broke into the crude structure until it began to
crumble.

Feeling clods of dirt and stone hit my head and
body, I rolled deeper into the gap, away from Marco.
My last thought, as I surrendered to the inevitable,
was that I had entered the belly of the earth. The
womb of the Mother Goddess.

The tickle in my throat was unbearable. Coughing and gagging, I tried to sit up. I needed to get
out of bed and go to the bathroom for a drink of
water. Then my hand clutched dirt instead of bed-
sheets, and I remembered.

Oh, no.

Lying in the coal-black earth and covered in dirt,
I tried to take stock. It was so dark I wasn't sure if
my eyes were opened or closed. My body hurt from
head to toe. With a dim recollection of all I had
been through, I halfheartedly wondered if any of

my muscle aches were due to the 10K I ran with Farrah so many hours ago. So many *lifetimes* ago.

At least I was alive. I was breathing. Somehow, someway, there was oxygen in here.

Carefully I touched the ground around me and felt clumps of dirt and rock. My purse was no longer on my shoulder. Searching my pockets, I found the remnants of the candle I took from Moonstone—and the book of matches.

I lit a match and looked around. By the light of the flame, I could see a huge pile of debris blocking the way to the main passage. Marco had succeeded in causing a cave-in. I wouldn't be getting out that way. Looking up, I wondered about the stability of the ceiling above me.

The match burned out, so I lit another one and pushed myself to my knees. Pain shot through my left wrist. Refusing to give up, I began crawling deeper into the tunnel. Every few seconds, I lit another match so I could see where I was going.

After a few minutes, I thought my eyes must be playing tricks on me. The light from the match showed that the texture of the dirt wall had changed. It was smooth and gray. I touched it, knocked on it. It was metal.

The match started to burn my fingers, so I dropped it and prepared to light another—only to discover I was out of matches. Crawling blindly now, I used my hands to feel my way along the metal wall, turning a corner. My fingers snagged on a sharp edge.

Ouch!

I pulled my fingers back, then realized I had

been crawling with my eyes closed. I opened them and noticed a variation in the darkness. It wasn't quite as inky as before. I reached my hands up to the wall again and felt slats.

Slats. Like in a vent or a grate.

I was behind the wall in the underground shelter at Fieldstone Park.

With a surge of hope, I put my face to the vent and called out. Or I tried to call out. My throat was so dry I couldn't make a sound. I licked my cracked lips and tried again.

"Help!"

It came out as a whisper.

Using the last ounce of energy I could muster, I banged on the metal grate with the palms of my hands. The muted noise was answered by silence. There was no one out there to hear me.

Based on the level of darkness on the other side of the slats, I guessed it must still be Saturday night. When would someone come along? More importantly, how much longer could I hold on?

My head started to swim, and I realized I was in bad shape.

Closing my eyes, I tried to visualize a divine white light. I mentally summoned the Triple Goddess— Maiden, Mother, and Crone—and begged for help. Like a flash, I saw an image of a glowing silver pentagram behind my eyes.

Understanding, I fumbled with my necklace and managed to unclasp it. I slipped it through the slats, allowing it to drape over the edge of the metal rather than fall through.

Maybe Wes will see it. I had told him about the grates by the Fieldstone restroom. I had told him my theory that Charlie may have entered the tunnels here.

Wes knows this is my necklace.

With a vision of Wes lifting me up in his arms, I finally lost consciousness.

Chapter 28

"Keli? Can you hear me? Wake up, buttercup. Time to rise and shine."

I opened my eyes and squinted into a haze of yellow light and confusion. My body felt like a lead weight, and there seemed to be a wire attached to the back of my hand. *Where am I?*

Someone squeezed my other hand, and then Farrah's face came into view. She looked tired and pale, her hair pulled back in a messy ponytail, but she smiled. "You all right there, sistah? Speak to me, hon."

"Hey," I said, my voice cracking. "What's going on?"

"What's going on is that you scared the living daylights out of me," said Farrah. "First you go MIA, so I'm frantically looking for you all over town. Then you go and get yourself trapped in an air duct.

"You're okay now. Have a sip of this," she said, holding a glass and bringing the straw to my mouth. "It's juice."

I tasted the juice and made a face. "Sour."

"Want water instead? The IV is supposed to keep you hydrated. If you can drink on your own, they'll probably remove it."

I shook my head. "Give me the juice again," I said. "It's better than the nasty taste in my mouth."

Farrah laughed and gave me the drink. I took a sip and gazed around the hospital room. Slowly the fog began to lift from my brain.

"What day is it?" I finally asked.

"Sunday, February third." She glanced at the wall clock. "Eight-twenty in the morning."

Closing my eyes, I leaned back on the pillow and breathed slowly. Yesterday had been the longest day of my life. Yet, something told me it wasn't quite over. I reopened my eyes and turned to Farrah. She had a worried expression, which she dropped when she saw me looking at her.

"How did you find me?" I asked.

She sat up in her chair. "I followed a hunch. At around eight o'clock last night, I tried calling to check in with you, like we agreed. When you didn't answer, I didn't think anything of it at first. I tried again twenty minutes later, and then every few minutes for an hour. I drove over to your house and saw that your car was gone. I assumed you were with Rock Star, but it bugged me that you didn't answer your phone, or at least send me a text."

"Did you call Wes?"

"I would have, but I didn't have his number. I decided to go to the Loose to track him down and ask about you. No luck there. Then I looked for your car at your office building and the municipal parking lot. Of course, with the festival and the concert, it wasn't easy to get around. I enlisted Jake to help, and made him call Dave to get the police looking for you, too."

I shook my head in wonder. All that time I was wandering around underground, there were all these people looking for me aboveground.

"I even drove by the Cadwelle bed-and-breakfast," Farrah continued. "But the house was dark, and your car wasn't there. Same for Moonstone Treasures and the places that had been burglarized."

Farrah stood up and looked out the window. She squeezed her fingers as she recounted her ordeal. "I thought about the old man who had been murdered, and I was afraid something had happened to you, too. Then I remembered what you said about a possible tunnel entrance in the park. So I went there. And that's when I found your necklace."

She turned around and pulled my necklace from the pocket of her hoodie. "Here it is, by the way," she said, smiling.

"You're an angel," I said, shaking my head. "An angel with mad detecting skills."

"Ha! I guess so. Now, are you ready to tell me *how* in the heckfire you ended up behind that grate?"

"Sure," I said. "But first, I want to know one more thing. How did you know that was my necklace?"

Farrah folded her arms and tilted her head at me. "Remember those 'mad detecting skills' you just mentioned? Well, girlfriend, I can put two and two together. I saw how friendly you were with Mila, the Wiccan psychic. She even said you were hiding something during your palm reading. And you told me about how you were into learning about the metaphysical when you were younger."

I raised my eyebrows.

"Besides," Farrah added, "I've known you for a while now. You're always doing weird little things—like collecting that white rose off the ground after the race yesterday."

Farrah came over and kissed the top of my head. "Don't worry, lady. I always knew you were a hippie-chick. I still love you."

Between nurse examinations to check my vitals, an interview with Detective Rhinehardt, and a visit from Wes, I finally managed to tell Farrah the whole story of my terrifying night in the tunnels. She bit her nails, cursed, and hopped out of her seat several times before my tale was complete.

"Jesus Christ, Keli! If you were a cat, I'd say you used up at least seven of your nine lives last night."

At the word *cat*, I slapped my forehead. "Drishti! I left Mila's cat at the B&B. I forgot to tell Detective Rhinehardt to look for her."

"Give him a call," said Farrah. "He's probably arrested Marco by now. This gives you a good excuse to find out what happened."

An orderly entered the room, pushing a food cart, so I had to eat lunch before calling the detective. Farrah had made sure the hospital was aware of my dietary restrictions, so my meal consisted of a passably decent salad and apple slices with peanut butter. Farrah drank coffee while I ate.

By this time, the nurse had removed my IV and told me that I would probably be discharged later that afternoon. I was eager to talk to Detective Rhinehardt again. I still had so many unanswered questions.

As it happened, I had to leave a message for the detective. Since my cell phone was still buried in the collapsed tunnel, I asked him to call me at the hospital. He still hadn't called by 3:00, when Mila stopped by.

She knocked on the door and peeked in. "Are you awake?"

"Hey!" I said when I saw her. "You're out of jail!" I sat up in the hospital bed and beckoned her in.

"Yes. They dropped the charges." Mila waved her hand dismissively and entered the room. She was carrying a large bouquet of red, yellow, and white daisies and a basket of assorted teas including jasmine and hibiscus. I knew she had carefully chosen these particular gifts to speed my healing process.

Farrah stood up, allowing Mila to sit in the chair next to my bed. "What lovely flowers," she said. She took the gifts from Mila and found a place for them on a table.

"Thanks," Mila said to Farrah. She sat down and took my hand. "Keli, I am so—"

"Mila," I interrupted, "I have to tell you something. It's about Drishti."

Mila smiled. "Drishti is fine. A police officer brought her home an hour ago. I hadn't been to the shop yet, so I didn't even know she was missing. The officer also told me what happened to you." Mila's eyes darkened.

I put my hand to my chest and sighed. "I'm so relieved Drishti is okay. But how did the officer know she was your cat?"

"Her collar says 'Moonstone Treasures,'" Mila explained. "Plus, the collar is enchanted. I cast a little spell to ensure Drishti always finds her way home."

"Cool," said Farrah. She perched on the edge of a chair in the corner and listened to Mila with interest.

"And she was okay?" I asked.

Mila nodded. "Perfectly okay. But how are you? Are you in pain?"

"I'm much better now. And it could have been worse."

"Well, I can't tell you how glad I am to see you in one piece. I was horrified when I found out what you went through." She reached over and placed her hand on my shoulder, sending me positive vibes. "Catrina sends her best wishes as well. She also wanted me to give you this." Mila reached into her purse and handed me a brochure.

It was yet another publication by the First Church of the New Believers. I read the title out loud: "Turn Away from Satan: What the Bible Says about Fortune-telling, Sorcery, and Witchcraft."

Farrah stood up. "Get out! What does it say?" She walked up to my bed and read over my shoulder.

I opened the brochure to find a smattering of

biblical quotations—including all the passages that were referenced in the threatening notes.

Mila pursed her lips. "Catrina did a little snooping of her own and found this at Reverend Natty's church. She thought she had found proof that he was the culprit."

So this is what she wanted to show me last night. I couldn't blame Catrina for thinking this implicated Reverend Natty. I might have thought the same thing. Of course, anyone could have seen a copy of this brochure. It was probably what gave Marco and Danielle the idea for the notes in the first place. What I still didn't know was *why* they wanted to scare Mila away. I voiced my thoughts aloud.

"Do you have any idea why the Thomisons wanted you to close your shop?" I asked.

Mila looked surprised. "I assumed it was their fear of alternative religions. There are certainly plenty of misguided people out there." She twisted the silver rings on her fingers. "I'm glad this is over, but I still feel awful that your life was endangered because of me."

"Oh, no." I shook my head. "It wasn't because of you. It was my decision to enter the tunnels. Twice." I grimaced. Then I squeezed Mila's hand. "You've taken enough blame for the actions of others. Now that we know who was behind it all, justice will be served. You can reopen your shop and reclaim your life."

Mila's eyes brightened and she lifted her chin. "That's music to my ears, Keli. I will never forget how you helped me."

I shrugged. "That's what friends are for."

* * *

Farrah brought me home from the hospital, after making me promise to call her the minute I heard anything from Detective Rhinehardt. She would have stayed the night in my guest room if not for the fact that Wes was coming over. He had insisted on making dinner for me.

At half past five, Wes showed up at my door with a bag of groceries and a bottle of wine. I kissed his cheek and showed him to the kitchen. I perched on a stool and watched with admiration and gratitude as he set about making pasta and a homemade marinara sauce. Other than a sprained wrist, a bruised hip, and a sore back, I was starting to feel almost normal again.

"I still can't believe what you went through last night," he said as he sautéed garlic and herbs. "I feel so terrible I wasn't out there searching for you with Farrah. I was holed up in my apartment watching bad television and thinking you didn't want to go out with me."

Not again, I thought with a frown.

I set down my wineglass and folded my arms. "After Friday night at the B&B? You really doubted I would want to go out with you again?"

He glanced up at me and hedged. "Well, I mean, I knew you were really tired after the run, so I figured you decided to stay in."

"That's not what you said." I wasn't going to let him off the hook that easily. This relationship was too important to me.

Wes shrugged. "Okay. Part of me thought you might have changed your mind about dating me." He stirred in the tomato sauce and avoided my eyes.

"I don't understand," I said. "Have I done something to make you think that?"

He shook his head but didn't say anything. I watched as he filled a pot with water, placed it on the stovetop, and turned on the burner. Then he turned the sauce down to simmer and walked around to join me at the counter.

"I'm sorry," he said. "I guess I have an insecurity thing going on again, just like a few months ago. I mean, hanging out and dating casually is one thing. I didn't really question that. But I was finding it hard to believe you'd want to get serious with me."

"Why, Wes?" I could tell this was difficult for him, but I needed him to articulate his feelings.

He looked away, but then finally met my eyes. "Because you're this successful attorney, surrounded by other successful professionals every day. Making good money, doing important things. And I'm . . . not on that level. Hell, until a couple months ago, I was living in my parents' house."

"You had extenuating circumstances," I said. "I knew that. Anyway, what do you mean 'not on that level'? You're a talented, professional photographer. I thought so even before you got the job with the newspaper. I've never thought I was somehow better than you. I hope I never made you feel that way."

"No. You never did." He smiled sheepishly. "This is my hang-up. It's stupid, I know."

He stood up and went back to the stove, where he added spaghetti to the boiling water and stirred the sauce again. I got up and followed him. When he put the lid back on the saucepan, I took his hand.

"Wes, let's be open with each other, okay? Completely open."

He lifted his eyebrows. "Okay," he said.

I took a breath and allowed my words to tumble forth. "I completely respect you and enjoy hanging out with you, and . . . I don't want to see anyone else. I want to see you exclusively."

His face broke into a wide grin. "Same here." He leaned down and softly kissed my lips. My heart soared.

All through dinner, we talked eagerly, like old friends sharing confidences. I admitted I had been slightly jealous of Sheana, and Wes admitted he was wary of Crenshaw—which made me choke on my wine from laughing. I even told Wes about the love spell I had cast before we met and how terrified I was that he might feel manipulated. To my relief, it didn't bother him at all. In fact, he found it intriguing.

I began clearing the dinner plates when the doorbell rang. Wes walked to the door with me and looked through the peephole.

"It's the detective," he said, opening the door. Detective Rhinehardt stood at my doorstep with a solemn expression.

"Hello, Detective," I said. "Please come in. Can I get you something to drink?" I was anxious to hear all about Marco's arrest and any confession he may have made.

The detective shook his head. "I can't stay. I just wanted to warn you to be careful. The suspects are at large."

I wasn't sure if I had heard him correctly. "I'm sorry. What did you say?"

"They've disappeared. All of them. The Thomisons. Their guests. Everyone. The Cadwelle Mansion is empty."

Chapter 29

I finally did it. After six years of perfect attendance at Olsen, Sykes, and Rafferty, I finally called in sick on Monday morning. Of course, I had a legitimate excuse. Being hospitalized—nearly killed, actually—after being trapped in an underground cave-in totally warranted a day off.

As sore as I was, though, my aches and pains were not the real reason I wanted to take a sick day. The real reason was that I couldn't stop thinking about Marco and Danielle. And their possible whereabouts.

How far could they have gotten? Would they really abandon their home and all their possessions? All those valuable antiques?

I guess that's what it means to be a fugitive.

The police had scoured the tunnels and were watching the mansion 24/7. Detective Rhinehardt assured me they had issued an APB for the Thomisons' arrest. Law enforcement officials in all the surrounding counties would be on the lookout. Naturally, they would also be watching for any charges on the Thomisons' credit cards.

After a careful shower, I pulled on a fluffy robe and hobbled to the kitchen to make breakfast, a hearty bowl of oatmeal with pecans and thawed blueberries from the freezer. While the oatmeal was cooking, I gazed out the glass sliding door onto my deck and the backyard below, my mind spinning.

Detective Rhinehardt told me most of the guests had checked out of the B&B earlier in the day yesterday. The only ones who appeared to have left suddenly were Yvette Prime and the guy who was staying in the carriage house. *He must have been the bald guy I clocked in the tunnels.* I shuddered to think of him on the loose.

Thankfully, the police found Yvette, safe and sound, at a friend's house.

I'll have to give her a call later, I decided. *Surely she'll have some interesting things to share.*

By Tuesday, I was tired of sitting around at home. It was time to get back to the real world. I had cases waiting and people to see.

Of course, I was the center of attention at the office again—much to my discomfort. Luckily, the fawning over me was tempered by all the gossip and speculation about the Thomisons. Most people assumed the couple had used the tunnels only to rob all the connecting businesses. I felt there must be more to it than that, but I didn't know what. And Yvette wasn't returning my calls.

At a quarter til noon, I hung up my phone after a conference call and stared at the purple amethyst on my desk. I couldn't shake my feeling of unrest. I felt like I had spent a month working on a complex jigsaw puzzle only to discover the last piece was missing.

"Ahem."

I looked up and saw Crenshaw hovering at my doorway.

"May I enter?"

I resisted the urge to roll my eyes at his formality. "Sure. Come on in." I gestured toward the chair facing my desk. He came in but remained standing.

"I, ah, was planning to venture outside for a bite of lunch. Given your recent . . . travails, I thought you might like me to bring something back for you. Perhaps a green . . . beverage?"

Will wonders never cease?

My lips twitched as I tried not to smile too broadly. "That would be great, Crenshaw. Thank you."

I grabbed a sticky note and wrote down my order for a pineapple, banana, and kale smoothie from Callie's Health Food Store and Juice Bar. My only regret was that I wouldn't be there to see him order it.

I handed him the square of paper. "Hey, I'm sorry your gig at the B&B has been cut short. That's a bummer."

Crenshaw opened his palms. "Oh, well. It's not

the worst that could have happened." He glanced down at his shoes, then back up at me. "I'm just glad you were not more seriously harmed. I—I'll be back with your drink." He turned on his heels and left.

I sighed. I was glad, too.

By the end of the week, there was still no trace of Marco, Danielle, or their mysterious guest from California. On my way home from work Friday evening, I resolved to call Detective Rhinehardt and press him for information. If that didn't work, I just might have to call Dave and try to coax him into sharing something about what the police knew. Any clue, any lead, anything at all.

When I arrived at my town house, I unlocked the front door and grabbed the mail from my mail-box. Once inside, I kicked off my shoes and dropped my purse on the couch. Then I headed to the kitchen, flipping through the mail as I walked. I stopped short when I saw a bulky envelope from my mom.

Finally.

Apparently one of my neighbors had signed for the registered delivery and stuck the package in my mailbox. Sitting at the kitchen counter, I opened the envelope and pulled out its contents: several sheets of printer paper folded around a white sta-tionery envelope. On the top sheet of paper, my mom had written a brief note.

Here's the letter I found at Grandma O's house. It provides the first inkling I've seen as to why your Aunt Josephine never came home all those years ago. It sounds a little oddball, but my big sister was always a free spirit, following the beat of her own drummer. Anyway, check out the return address. At least now we know where Josie lived when she was in Edindale in 1971.

For some reason, my fingers trembled a little as I carefully extracted Josie's letter and read the girlish handwriting.

Dear Mom and Dad,

First off, I am doing well, so you can stop worrying about me. I hope you're all doing well, too. I miss you, but I have to live my own life.

Secondly, I won't be writing again for a while. We've been forced off our land, so I'll be hitting the road soon. I can't tell you exactly where I'm going, because I've been entrusted with a secret undertaking. But once my mission is complete, and once it seems safe again, I'll be returning to Edindale. This is where my heart belongs.

I'll keep in touch as I can.

Love,
Josie

P.S. Roger moved to Canada to avoid the draft. You may have been right about him after all.

When I finished reading the letter, I had to read it again. *"Secret undertaking"? What is that all about?*

I turned over the envelope. On the upper left-hand corner, in the same handwriting as in the letter, it said, "Happy Hills Homestead, RR. 3, Edindale, IL." *I knew it.*

I hopped up to find the booklet Farrah had lent me and opened it to the page showing a trio of hippies at the Happy Hills farm. So, this *was* Aunt Josephine.

My mom hadn't directly asked me to find the commune, but she didn't have to. I knew she was hoping I would do it anyway.

I looked at the address again. *Hmm. Rural Route 3.* I recalled that Wes's grandfather used to have a farm out that way. Wes and I even picnicked in the area last summer. I grabbed my phone and sent him a quick text, asking if his family knew about a commune near his grandfather's farm. A short while later, my phone rang.

"Hey," said Wes. "Are you on to another mystery already?"

I smiled. "Maybe. But this one is personal."

"Ha. Sounds like a movie I'd like to see." Wes paused, and I heard the sound of shuffling papers. "Here it is. I called my mom and she knew exactly where there was a commune in the late 1960s and early 1970s. The entrance was near a roadside farm stand."

Wes gave me the directions, which I jotted down. I thanked him and asked if he had plans the next day.

"I've got to be at the Harrison Hotel all morning and most of the afternoon, taking pictures at a job fair. Can you wait til Sunday?"

"Yeah, sure. Or . . . maybe I'll see if Farrah can go with me." The truth was, I could hardly wait one night, let alone two. I was eager to trace down any clues to my mysterious aunt.

Wes chuckled. "Okay. I understand. You and Farrah go on and have fun. You two make a good team." Then his voice turned serious. "Promise me you'll be careful, though. You're still recovering from your ordeal. And there's still a killer out there somewhere."

"I promise."

Chapter 30

Saturday morning, right after breakfast, I downed a couple ibuprofens and dressed in long johns, jeans, and a sweatshirt. I was just packing up a backpack when Farrah arrived. I had explained to her about the letter my mom had sent, and she was totally on board for the adventure.

Half an hour later, we were cruising down Rural Route 3, up and down the rolling hills, past fallow fields and dormant vineyards. Eventually, we pulled into a small parking lot next to a shuttered farm stand, closed for the season. Farrah parked next to a picnic table, and we piled out to explore the area. There were barren fields all around with a cluster of barns and sheds in the distance. Nearby, behind a rail fence, a small flock of sheep munched at a haystack.

I wandered over to the fence and watched the sheep for a few minutes. The wooly creatures, symbolic of springtime and Candlemas, made me smile. As I gazed around, something caught my eye in a grove of trees at the bottom of a forested hillside.

It appeared to be a boulder. *Wasn't there a big rock like that in the picture of the Happy Hills Homestead?*

I called to Farrah, who was making her way toward the barns—trespassing on private property, no doubt. I waved her over, and we tramped through muddy brown grass to the woodsy glen.

Sure enough, the boulder was the one from the photograph in Farrah's booklet. I could tell by the flecks of red, yellow, and green paint that still clung to the surface of the rock.

We looked around. "Well, the sign is long gone, but this is definitely the right spot. See the overgrown lane?" I pointed to the ground near the boulder.

"How about a photo?" Farrah asked. I posed in the same place Josie had stood more than forty years earlier, and Farrah snapped my picture with her phone.

For the next ten or fifteen minutes, we wandered deeper into the woods until the trail disappeared. Farrah grabbed a stick to beat back the brambles, looking for any further evidence of the old lane. I sat on a tree stump to rest and look around. There was a lot to admire in the trees, hills, and cloud-streaked sky.

After a minute, I stood up and picked through the brush again. Meandering among the oaks and hickories, I recalled the last time I was able to get outside for an early morning nature ritual. It seemed like ages ago. I almost laughed out loud when I remembered how I had hidden from a purple-clad hiker.

Hang on.

An image flashed in my mind. It was Danielle in her ski jacket, the night I became trapped in the tunnels. Her jacket was the exact shade of purple as the one worn by the mysterious hiker. The hiker who had vanished into thin air in the forest behind Briar Creek Cabins.

Could that be where Danielle and Marco are hiding?

I called Farrah over and told her about the January morning I had had my close encounter with the purple-clad hiker. She laughed at my idea of communing with nature and asked if she should start calling me "Morgan le Fay."

It was so good not to keep secrets from her anymore.

"Let me get this straight," said Farrah. "You once saw Danielle wearing a purple jacket, so you think she was the person you saw skulking among the trees?"

"I do," I said. "I think something is going on out there. That bald goon with the California plates was coming from those woods when he pulled in front of Wes and me on River Road."

"Huh. River Road isn't far from here, is it?"

"No, it isn't. Let's go." I was already hurrying back toward the parking lot. I could delve into Aunt Josephine's past later. This suddenly seemed more important.

Farrah jogged to catch up with me. "Are you sure you're up for this?" she asked.

"I feel fabulous," I said, ignoring the aches that were slowly seeping back into my muscles.

A few minutes later, we drove to Briar Creek Cabins and left Farrah's car once again. This time, we followed the path the purple-clad hiker had taken. Patches of snow and dried leaves crunched underfoot as we inspected the landscape around us.

"There's something else I was thinking about," I said. "I never made it to the end of the tunnel that night. It kept going past the mansion—who knows how far? Maybe it came out this way."

"That would be a really long tunnel," Farrah pointed out.

"True. Maybe that's not very likely. The tunnel probably ended at the river behind the mansion. Still, I have a feeling about this. . . ." I trailed off as we reached the spot where I had seen the hiker drop out of sight. "Let's leave the trail here."

We crisscrossed the vicinity, following swales and breaks between trees, and muddying up our boots in the process. At one point, we came upon a bubbling creek blocking our way. Farrah held out her hand to help me across since I still wasn't quite at my full capacity.

After another twenty minutes of hiking, Farrah stopped and stretched her legs on a fallen log. "Should we come back later with more people? We could call Jake and Wes. Then we could split up and search in teams of two."

"Maybe," I said reluctantly. With Wes being on assignment, I knew it would be after dark by the time he was available.

"Or I could climb a tree," Farrah suggested. She stood up and eyed the nearest low-hanging branches.

"No, don't do that," I said. "I have another thought. The tunnels were originally created for bootlegging liquor, right?"

"Right," said Farrah. "That reminds me, after all the drama Saturday night I forgot to tell you what I discovered in my research that afternoon. It turns out Mr. Cadwelle's apothecary was in the shop your friend Mila now owns."

"That makes sense," I said, nodding. "He would have used the tunnel to get back and forth between the speakeasy and his place of business. What I'm thinking of now, though, is how he got the booze in or out of town. What if he used the river?"

"Like a rumrunner? I didn't think we had those in this part of the country."

"Why not?" I said. "The Muddy Rock River runs right behind the Cadwelle Mansion."

"True. It also runs through the forest somewhere around here, doesn't it?"

"Let's go back to that creek we crossed and follow it for a while," I said.

We found the creek and hiked in silence along its bank. To our right, a towering bluff stretched into the blue sky above. The terrain quickly became rugged, so we paused to rest and drink from our water bottles. I took the opportunity to pop another painkiller, while Farrah grabbed a stick and tried to scrape some of the mud off her boots.

I removed my hat and raised my face to the sun. "It's so beautiful out here."

"Yeah," she agreed. "It reminds me of Garden of the Gods, with all these rock formations. I'm kind of surprised we haven't run into anyone."

I shrugged. "I don't know. It's a cold day in February. We're off the official trail. Plus, you have to come from the Briar Creek Cabins to find the trailhead."

"I feel like such a scout," said Farrah. She took out her phone to snap a selfie of the two of us. Then we continued picking our way through the brush along the edge of the creek, carefully maneuvering all the twists and turns. Before long, the waterway broadened into a deep stream, wide enough to accommodate a canoe. We moved slowly to make sure we watched each footstep while also keeping a lookout for anything unusual. The sudden flutter of a bird's wings attracted our attention.

Farrah laughed. "What's got his panties in a bunch?"

We watched as a black-capped chickadee flapped its wings vigorously near the stream and then flew away.

I smiled. "The water must be too cold."

As I gazed in the direction from where the bird had flown, something else caught my eye. There was a piece of black thread caught on a bare twig. Balancing carefully on some flat stones in the creek, I made my way over to check it out.

"What is it?" asked Farrah.

I picked up the thread with my thumb and forefinger. "Somebody must have snagged a shirt or something."

"Way to go, eagle eye," said Farrah. "I can't believe—"

I gasped, cutting her off. "Look at that!" I pointed to the craggy rock face behind the bush. Hidden by a moss-covered overhang near the ground was an opening, just large enough for a person to enter. It had been camouflaged by the surrounding terrain, nearly hidden from view save from where I was standing—thanks to the little bird and the telltale thread.

Farrah walked over and bent down to peer into the hole. Then she dropped to her knees and crawled inside.

"Farrah!"

She backed out of the opening. "It's a cave all right," she said.

"Let's call Detective Rhinehardt." I reached into my backpack for my new cell phone. There was no signal. "Ugh. Why are my phones so useless lately?"

"Oh, yeah. Service is always spotty out here." Farrah rummaged in her pack and pulled out a flashlight. "I wonder how far this goes," she said, shining her light into the crevice.

I rubbed my face. *Now what?* When I removed my hands from my eyes, I saw Farrah disappearing into the hole again.

"What are you doing!" I called after her.

"Just taking a peek." She inched forward on the ground.

My heart thudded as I followed. I was loathe to enter any more dark tunnels, especially so soon after my nightmarish ordeal. But I was curious, too.

A couple of feet into the crevice, the cave opened up. I glommed onto Farrah and looked around in fascination as she directed the flashlight on the damp walls and ceiling surrounding us. I was about to say we should turn back when she clicked off the flashlight, leaving us in darkness.

"Why did you do that?" I hissed.

"Because I wanted to see if there was another light source," said Farrah. "And there is. Look."

Sure enough, a crack of daylight penetrated the gloom in a high corner of the cave. We gravitated to the light, climbed up onto a rocky platform, and squeezed through the opening. We found ourselves standing on a ledge overlooking a small cove.

"What do you know?" I murmured, squinting in the sunlight.

"Now we know where the river is." Farrah pointed to a ribbon of brown water beyond the cove. A thick stand of trees surrounded the area, shielding it from any boaters that might travel down the river.

In fact, the trees were so dense we didn't notice the approach of a speedboat until we heard the buzz of the motor directly below us.

We looked at one another, then silently ducked at the same time. From behind the cover of a smooth boulder, we watched as the boat drew up to the shoreline. The tinted windshield hid the driver from view.

We were so intent on watching the boat we both flinched at the sound of movement near the base of the cliff wall. At the same time, voices drifted up from the rocks below. Suddenly, two figures materialized from the underbrush, each person carrying a wooden crate.

Danielle and Marco.

We watched, enthralled, as they shuffled toward

the boat and set the crates on the ground. With wrinkled clothing and messy hair, they appeared far from the posh couple they once were. Shielding their eyes from the sun, they waited for the pilot to emerge from the cabin of the boat.

Finally, the hatch opened. Out climbed a figure—a striking, female figure—covered head to toe in a black wet suit. Oversized sunglasses obscured her face.

Farrah snickered under her breath. "Are we in a movie, or what?" she whispered. I shushed her and strained to hear what Marco was saying to the woman in the wet suit.

Moving quickly, the woman tossed Marco a rope. He tied it to a nearby tree, then scrambled into the boat. Standing on the deck, they spoke in undertones, their heads close together. On the rocky bank, Danielle stood by with her hands on her hips. That was when I realized who the woman must be. When she removed her sunglasses, I saw that I was right.

Tish.

"What is *she* doing here?" Farrah hissed.

I shook my head, keeping my eyes on the scene below. Marco leaned over to unfasten something from the floor of the deck. Tish scooted out of the way as he lifted a small kayak and heaved it over the side of the motorboat. Then he helped her step into the kayak and handed her a paddle. With a breezy wave to Danielle, Tish plunged the paddle into the water and maneuvered the kayak out of the cove. In a matter of seconds, she was on the river and out of sight.

Marco beckoned to Danielle. "Bring me a crate."

She obeyed. While Marco stashed the crate into the cabin of the boat, she grabbed the other one. He took it from her, placed it in the cabin, then clambered out of the boat. He headed back toward the rocky cliff, but Danielle lingered behind.

"Why can't we just go now?" Danielle whined.

"I told you," Marco said. "We have to wait until after dark."

"Do we have to wait in there? I'm sick of that place. It's so dirty."

"Now, pet, you know it's safer if we stay out of sight. It won't be much longer now."

Danielle glanced at the boat, then back at Marco. "Are you sure Tish knows where to leave us a car?"

Marco put his hands on Danielle's shoulders and steered her toward the cliff wall. "Yes, yes. It's all arranged. We won't be on the boat for long. Don't worry. You'll be on a beach sipping margaritas before . . ."

We missed hearing the rest of his sentence, as they vanished into an unseen opening in the rock face.

There must be another hidden cave.

Farrah and I looked at one another. The astonishment I felt was mirrored in her eyes. Without a word, we tiptoed back to the gap we had exited and scrambled back inside the cavern. Crouching on the dark ledge, we spoke in whispers.

"I can't believe we actually found them!" Farrah said.

"We have to alert the police," I said. "God, I wish we had a working cell phone."

"I know. By the time we find our way back to the car and get to someplace with a signal, it will probably be after sunset. They'll be gone."

"It shouldn't be too difficult for the police to find them on the river, even in the dark," I reasoned. "Except . . . it sounds like they won't be on the river for very long. And we don't know where they're going to dock."

"Yeah," said Farrah. "Apparently Tish is going to provide them with a getaway car. Why would she do that?"

I shrugged. "For love or money, I guess. My bet is on money."

"Well, what can we do?" Farrah flicked on her flashlight and shined it down onto the floor of the cave. "We can't very well stop them on our own. I mean, I could probably take Danielle, but not both of them. We're unarmed, and you're practically an invalid."

"Hey, I'm doing all right," I protested, even as a twinge of pain shot through my hip. I winced, then sighed. "I want to take another peek at that boat."

I climbed back up through the crack in the wall and peered over the precipice. The boat was a snazzy little cabin cruiser, white with a black stripe along the side. Two motors were attached to the rear of the vessel.

As I stared at the boat, a strong wind whipped my

hair into my face. Blinking, I watched the boat bob
in the water. It seemed to tug at the black rope se-
curing it to a tree trunk on the shore. *A black rope.*
Like the rope in the binding ritual Max had told
me about—the one meant to stop Mila's harasser.

I looked back at the boat, and then at the surrounding foliage, as an idea began to take shape.
Marco and Danielle had to be stopped.

Farrah crawled out of the cave to see what was
taking me so long. I whispered to her what I had
in mind and she agreed.

Leaving our backpacks in the cave, we moved like
cats along the ledge until we found a path down to
the cove. Keeping our eyes and ears peeled, we slunk
behind the trees until we were adjacent to the boat.
Now for the risky part.

Farrah played lookout, while I worked on the
rope. Struggling with the knot stressed my sprained
wrist, but I didn't let that slow me down. When the
rope was free, I tossed it into the boat. Farrah and
I gave the craft a shove, using all the strength we
could muster. It didn't move very far, but at least
it was unmoored now. The water lapped at its
hull, giving me hope that this plan would work.
Eventually, the boat should float away from the
shore and be caught up in the river's current. If
the Thomisons waited until dark to emerge from
their hiding place, they would find their means of
escape was gone.

I only hoped this would buy us enough time to
reach the police and show them the way back to the
hidden cove. With no time to lose, Farrah scurried

back the way we had come. I followed close at her heels.

As I climbed up the craggy bluff, I spared a backward glance at the concealed cave and narrowed my eyes. Under my breath, I muttered the words to an improvised curse:

"By your deeds, you are bound,
By my power, stay underground,
Til darkness falls, you shall not flee.
As I will, so mote it be!"

The wind blew my hair into my eyes again. I scrambled up the bluff, hand over hand, trying to catch up with Farrah. Suddenly, a sharp pain shot through my injured wrist. I lost my grip. In the same moment, my foot missed its toehold.

I plunged to the ground.

Chapter 31

I lay on the ground, stunned. As soon as I caught my breath, I turned my head to see if anyone had come out of the hidden cave. Luckily no one was there. I closed my eyes, trying to figure out which part of me hurt the worst.

"Keli! Oh my God! Are you okay?" Farrah knelt at my side.

"Yeah. I think so." I tried to sit up. Farrah put her hand on my back to help support me. Once I made it to a sitting position, I rubbed my head. "I can't believe I did that."

"You scared the shit out of me." Farrah bit her lip and cast a worried glance at the cliff face Marco and Danielle had entered.

"You and me both." I reached out my hand to Farrah, and she pulled me to my feet. The instant my right foot touched the ground, I collapsed into a heap again.

"What is it?" Farrah cried, trying to catch me.

I winced. "My ankle. It's either sprained or broken. I can't put any pressure on it."

"Oh, no. Are you sure?" Farrah helped me remove my hiking boot and gently moved my ankle to test it. I flinched and jerked away. "Oh, God," Farrah groaned.

"There's no way I can climb. You're going to have to go on without me."

Farrah widened her eyes. "There is *no way* I'm leaving you out here!"

I took a deep breath. Clutching Farrah's arm, I tried to stand again. This time, I held my right foot up while balancing on my left foot. I broke a sweat from the exertion.

"We have to hide." I looked around, then tilted my head toward a fallen tree in the thicket near the water. "There."

Leaning heavily on Farrah, I hopped on one foot as we scuffled forward. She carried my right boot. By the time we made it to the downed tree, I was out of breath. I dropped to the ground and groaned.

Farrah crouched next to me. "We should wrap your ankle." In a flash, she removed her sweatshirt and T-shirt, then put her sweatshirt back on. She folded the T-shirt into a long strip and wrapped it snuggly around my ankle. I gritted my teeth.

"I'll go get our backpacks," she said. "Then you can at least have a drink of water."

"You have to go for help, Farrah. Now. You have to get the police out here before the Thomisons come out and escape on foot."

"I'm worried about leaving you alone."

Forcing a smile, I showed her my pentagram necklace. "I'm not alone. I'm protected by the Goddess. Remember?"

"Fine. But I'm going to get your backpack first. You have some painkillers in there, right?"

"Yeah." *And I sure need them.*

In a matter of minutes, Farrah retrieved my backpack and came back to make sure I was safely hidden. She promised to come back as fast as humanly possible. I hunkered down and prepared to wait.

Over the next hour or so, I watched Marco's boat slowly drift away from the shore. Helped along by the stiff breeze, eventually it was out in the middle of the river. It was satisfying to see my plan work.

Except being stuck behind a log wasn't part of the plan.

The temperature plummeted as the sun sank behind the cliff. Before long, the cove was enveloped in darkness. I shivered.

Surely Farrah has contacted the police by now.

My legs had fallen asleep yet again, so I shook them out. There were only so many positions I could maintain and stay out of sight. I was in the process of drawing my knees to my chest when the sound of voices reached my ears. I froze.

With whisper-soft movements, I peeked over the trunk, through its dark branches. Marco and Danielle came out of the cave, each carrying crates again. They walked all the way to the water's edge before they noticed the cruiser was gone.

"Where's the boat?" Danielle asked as she looked around.

Marco let out a string of profanity so loud Danielle cringed and backed away. He dropped his crate and ran around the edge of the cove. "Get the flashlight! Help me look!"

Danielle set her crate on the ground and reached into her shoulder bag for a flashlight.

"Hurry up!" Marco barked.

She stumbled through the underbrush and handed him the light. He shined the beam onto the dark river.

"How did this happen?" Danielle wrung her hands. "I thought you said the knot was tight."

"Shut up! It was tight." Marco directed the light downstream. "There it is!"

He jumped into the water. Danielle screamed, "Marco! Don't leave me! You know I can't swim!"

Marco waded back to the shore. "Dammit. It's ice cold. I'll freeze before I ever reach the boat."

"Call Tish. Tell her to pick us up here."

Marco wiped his hand over his face. "She'll have to get hold of another boat. Jesus, there's at least two million dollars in cargo on that boat."

"Can't we just—"

"I said shut up! I'm trying to think." Marco stomped on a sapling, cracking it in two. Danielle whimpered.

Marco pointed the flashlight down the river again. "We have to keep the boat in sight. God, it's moving fast. You go put the other crates back in the cave, then catch up to me." He heaved a sigh. "I'll call Tish."

Danielle hurried back to the cave, while Marco tramped off in the other direction. I held my breath when he passed my hiding place. Luckily, he was so focused on the river he didn't even look my way. When Danielle ran back, her only concern was finding Marco. She didn't notice me either.

I waited until the sounds of their arguing and rustling had died away. Then I let out my breath. *Thank Goddess.* I unfolded my legs and pushed myself to my knees. Still moving quietly, I unscrewed the cap from my stainless steel bottle and finished off the last of my water.

Now that my adrenaline had subsided, I could feel how cold the air had become. My teeth chattered. I glanced toward the hidden cave. *Could I make it?*

During the time I crouched in the woods with nothing to do, I had noticed a broken tree branch nearby. It appeared thick and sturdy—a perfect walking stick. I grabbed it now and pulled off the protruding twigs. With all my weight on my good ankle, I pushed myself to a standing position.

Once I was sure of my steadiness, I took a tentative hop forward. Then another. I allowed the toes of my right foot to help with my balance. Thanks to the compression from Farrah's T-shirt and the ibuprofen, the pain was bearable. After each step, I paused to listen for any sign of Marco or Danielle. The only sound was that of water lapping against the rocky shore. I kept going.

When I reached the rock face, I stood squinting in the darkness for several seconds. By the light of the moon, I studied the rough, layered texture of the cliff and the fallen boulders jumbled haphazardly at its base. Inching forward, I finally spotted a narrow, triangular hole. I squeezed inside.

In the shelter of the cave, I paused and pushed my

hair out of my face. Leaning on the wall for support, I rubbed my hands together. It was warmer in here, out of the wind.

Without a flashlight, phone, or candle, I planned to remain by the entrance. But as I stared into the blackness of the cave, I detected a faint light. I followed it.

Shuffling forward, I rounded a corner and saw the source of the light. It was a battery-powered camping lantern, sitting on a table. Apparently, Marco and Danielle had forgotten to turn it off. I walked over to the table and picked up the lantern. I held it up to get a better look at the cavernous room.

What is all this? Against the wall next to the table was a pile of blankets and empty food containers. The better part of the room was filled with large barrels and rusty equipment of some sort. As I looked around, I realized what it was—an old distillery.

Of course. This must be where Orion Cadwelle made his illegal liquor.

And now it was being used to hide another kind of contraband. But what?

I scanned the room until my eyes fell on the crates Danielle had brought back inside. They were nailed shut. Hobbling around the antique distillery, I looked for a crowbar or other tool I could use to pry open the crates. My efforts were rewarded when I came upon a pile of abandoned woodworking tools on top of an overturned cask. I selected a hammer-shaped ax-like tool with a flat edge. Using it as a lever, I pried off the lid of the crate.

I gasped. In spite of the plastic wrapping, the contents were unmistakable.

Rhino horns.

The crate was packed full of rhino horns. From my research for Beverly, I knew a single horn could fetch upward of $300,000 on the international black market. Marco was probably right that two crates contained two million dollars' worth. With the two on the boat, plus these two, the Thomisons were sitting on four million dollars.

I was debating whether to open the second crate when I thought I heard a noise from the cave entrance. *Farrah must be back with the police.* I picked up the lantern with one hand and my walking stick with the other. I almost called out when something gave me pause. The hair on the back of my neck prickled.

To be on the safe side, I switched off the lantern and backed into the shadows. I waited and watched until I saw the faint glow of a lighter. Then I recognized the person holding the lighter. Danielle.

She mumbled under her breath as she entered the room. As she came closer, I made out some of her words.

"Damn him anyway. Making me come back alone. He thinks *I'm* holding *him* back?" She stopped when she reached the table and held up the lighter with a shaky hand. "Where's the lantern?"

I made a split-second decision. Taking a deep breath, I leaned my walking stick against the wall and stepped forward.

"Freeze!"

Danielle screamed and dropped her lighter.

I grabbed the woodworking tool and held it out in front of me. Then I flicked on the lantern and quickly set it on the floor. I shifted to the side, ensuring that I would remain hidden in the shadows.

"Put your hands in the air! I have a gun!"

Danielle complied. "Don't shoot!"

"Back up," I commanded. "Sit on the ground. And keep your hands up!"

She lowered herself to the ground and scooted backward. I could see her squinting in the darkness. "Keli? What are you doing here?"

"I'll be asking the questions." I tried to convey an authority I didn't really feel. My only hope was to fool Danielle. "I—I'm really an undercover agent. You've been caught, Danielle. You had better cooperate now, if you know what's good for you."

If you know what's good for you? I wasn't used to playing the role of a tough cop. I was afraid I sounded silly. But Danielle appeared none the wiser. She cowered in the corner, shivering.

"Fine," she said. "Whatever you say. This was all Marco's idea anyway."

I nodded curtly. "That's what I thought. How did he get mixed up in rhino horn smuggling?"

Danielle barely hesitated before blurting out an answer. "It started with antiques made of ivory. Marco was a middleman. Then he found out how valuable those nasty horns are. Crazy, if you ask me."

I had to agree with her there. "Go on."

"His buyer told him about this network that needed a Midwest dealer. The horns were brought in from Africa, one by one, hidden in people's luggage or something. They needed somebody to pick them up and consolidate them. Then a courier would take them from here and transport them to San Francisco, where Marco's boss lives. That's where the sale would happen. Most of the horns were then shipped to China or Vietnam."

"So Marco became the Midwest link. Where exactly did he get the horns?"

Danielle bit her lip, then shrugged. "There's this huge monthly flea market up north. People come from Chicago and other places. Marco would go up there with his van to 'hunt for antiques,' but he was really there for a pickup."

"At the first of the month?" I remembered Farrah's observation about the timing of the burglaries every month. Marco probably needed goods he could convert into cash to pay for the exchange.

"That's right," said Danielle. "He brought the packages back to the mansion to store there until a courier came to get them. Sometimes I didn't even know who the couriers were. They usually looked like regular B&B guests."

"Sounds like a risky business, Danielle."

"I know!" Danielle scoffed. "That's why we needed the store downtown. Marco was going to open an antiques shop. The horns would be concealed in antiques delivered to and from the shop. The tunnels provided a perfect hiding place."

"You knew about the tunnels before you even came here, didn't you?"

Danielle nodded. "I found them when I was a little girl. My grandfather's candy shop used to be a pharmacy run by Cadwelle, the bootlegger."

"Why did you think you could force Mila out of business?"

"We needed that shop! We knew we could outbid any other potential buyers, if only the owner would give it up. Marco was under pressure from his boss, who was afraid there were too many people hanging around the B&B. I figured it couldn't be too difficult to scare off someone who calls herself a 'witch.' There were these botanicas in California just like that shop. All the people there were so superstitious."

"So you left the notes? And vandalized the shop? And killed Charlie?" I felt my face get hot as I thought about everything this foolish couple had done. All because of greed—true to Dave's theory.

"I didn't kill anyone!" Danielle protested. "And Marco didn't mean to. He told me it was an accident. He . . . he just decided to make the most of a bad situation. He thought we could frame the psychic. Or at least scare her even more."

I didn't believe it was an accident, not for one minute. I doubted Danielle believed it either.

"Men," she grumbled. "See what happens when you let them call the shots? They mess everything up. He couldn't even coordinate a simple getaway. We had to hide out like animals in this stupid cave until Tish finally showed up with a boat. Then, when it's finally time to leave, what happens? The boat floats away."

I didn't say anything. My ankle had begun to throb, and I was feeling light-headed. I wasn't sure how much longer I could balance on one foot.

Danielle shifted on the floor. "Why don't you come out of the shadows? Why haven't you hand-cuffed me?"

Uh-oh. With Danielle becoming suspicious, it looked like I was about to lose the upper hand. I tried to think of a plausible explanation when the beam from a spotlight shone into the cave. *Please don't let it be Marco.*

"Keli?" It was Farrah. I breathed a sigh of relief and threw down the tool I had been gripping all that time.

"In here!"

I grabbed the lantern and limped out of the corner.

"Hey!" said Danielle. "You're not really an agent, are you?"

Farrah rushed in, with Detective Rhinehardt close behind. "I told you to let me go first," he growled. He stopped short when he saw Danielle, who was pushing herself to her feet.

"Hold it right there," he said.

She sniffed. "If you take me someplace warm and dry, I'll tell you where to find Marco and Tish."

The detective handcuffed Danielle and informed her of her rights. Farrah helped me outside to a waiting police boat.

"I do believe you're rescuing me again," I said.

"Girlfriend, if anyone is the hero here, it's you."

I shrugged. "I think we're both pretty awesome."

Chapter 32

The group assembled around the green bench in Fieldstone Park on Thursday evening was larger than I expected. Father Gabe was there with a handful of his parishioners. So were Pammy and a couple other lawyers, as well as some maintenance workers from the park. I stood between Wes and Mila as we listened to Mayor Helen Trumley say a few words about Charlie Morris and how much he would be missed.

"With his cheerful disposition and ready smile, Charlie touched us all," she concluded. "And so, we dedicate this park bench to his memory. May it remind us of his friendliness and inspire us to be friendly to others. Through a smile, a pleasant word, or a small act of kindness, we can lift one another's spirits, as Charlie lifted ours."

"Hear, hear," said Wes, clapping his hands.

We all applauded, then mingled for a few moments and shook hands with the mayor. I had approached her at her office in city hall earlier in the week to ask about dedicating Charlie's park bench. She readily agreed. In fact, she had just read about me in the newspaper, so she was more than happy to oblige.

The day before, news had broken of the arrests of Marco, Danielle, and Tish. Marco and Tish had been found on the river, trying to fit the two of themselves into a one-person kayak. They were not hard to catch.

Details about the smuggling ring continued to trickle out. So far, Marco refused to say a word, but Danielle kept talking. Thanks to her, the U.S. Fish and Wildlife Service could now trace other traffickers through the Midwest flea market and Marco's San Francisco contacts. Much to my relief, they had also captured the bald courier on his way back to California.

"I'm so glad you stopped by," Mayor Trumley had said, walking around her desk to shake my hand. "I want to personally thank you for your role in uncovering the wildlife smuggling operation happening right here, in our very own town. And also for exposing Tish Holiday. Between you and me, I was about ready to fire her anyway. She never seemed to understand the concept of staying within budget."

Now, as the sun began to fade in the sky above, the mayor thanked me again and left the park. Everyone else dispersed except for Wes, Mila, and me. We gathered at the bench to take one last look at the personalized brass plaque.

Wes put his arm around my shoulder and kissed my cheek. "Thank you again for making this happen."

"My colleagues were happy to contribute." I chuckled. "I think I could ask them for just about anything these days."

"That's not surprising," Mila said. "You have good karma." She reached into her cloth satchel and pulled out a plastic bag full of bread crumbs. She opened it, and we each reached in to grab a handful. As we sprinkled bread crumbs around the bench, and pigeons joined us to accept the offering, Mila recited a Celtic prayer:

> *"Deep peace of the running wave to you.*
> *Deep peace of the flowing air to you.*
> *Deep peace of the quiet earth to you.*
> *Deep peace of the shining stars to you.*
> *Deep peace of the gentle night to you."*

Wherever Charlie's soul was, I felt sure he was at peace.

The next evening, I was once again performing a ritual by the light of the setting sun, but this time I was alone. A broad tree stump served as a makeshift altar. In the back of the round surface were a grouping of ten candles. In front were my Book of Shadows and a beautiful bronze bell. It was the bell Mila had used in the cleansing ritual at Moonstone Treasures. She had given it to me as a thank-you gift.

I opened the book to the page where I had recorded my Candlemas spell a couple weeks earlier. Candlemas was all about hope and new beginnings. Now that the recent danger had passed, I could move on with my life. But I wasn't returning to the same old life as before. I was entering a new phase, one in which I could be completely honest with both my best friend and my boyfriend.

Given all these changes, I felt inspired to perform another Candlemas ritual—this time outdoors. I cast a circle, sounding the bell at each of the four quarters. Then I proceeded to light the candles. After lighting each one, I took a clear glass cloche from a box at my feet and covered the candles. I read from my book as I went.

> *"One flame to purify*
> *One to transform,*
> *One flame to beautify*
> *One to keep warm.*
>
> *One flame for innocence*
> *One for desire,*
> *One flame for benevolence*
> *One to inspire."*

As before, I saved the two largest candles for last: one to honor the young god, just beginning his journey around the wheel of the year, and one to honor the patron goddess of Candlemas. I chanted:

> *"A flame for the god, born anew*
> *A flame for Brigid, goddess true."*

Finally, to close the ritual, I rang the bell three more times and said:

"Once . . . to keep evil at bay.
Twice . . . to thank the woodland fey.
Thrice . . . for peace, come what may."

I wiped the snow off my boots before kicking them off on the doormat. After hanging my white hooded cloak on a hook, I made a beeline for the fireplace and held my hands close to the screen. Then I turned to warm my backside and survey the cozy scene before me.

Farrah and Jake were preparing dinner in the small kitchen, filling the cabin with the heavenly aroma of homemade vegan chili. Jake took a small taste, then stirred in more chili powder. Farrah sliced avocados and fresh cilantro for garnish.

"Perfect timing!" she called. "We'll be ready to eat in a few minutes."

"Smells wonderful," I said. "This is such a treat."

Wes looked up from his laptop. "It sure is. They've refused my offers to help, so you and I can take cleanup duty after dinner."

"That's fine by me." I walked over to join Wes on the sofa, and he moved over to make room. "How did your pictures turn out?"

He shifted the laptop so I could see. "You tell me."

"Beautiful." Wes scrolled through the photos he had taken during our hike earlier in the day. Among my favorites were images of a frozen waterfall, a snow-speckled forest path, and ice-covered branches glittering like diamonds in the sunlight. I especially liked how he had captured the frost-covered trees surrounding the hidden cove.

In spite of the cold, it had turned out to be a gorgeous Valentine's Day weekend. And I couldn't imagine a better way to spend it. A few weeks earlier, Jake had reserved a Briar Creek cabin as a surprise for Farrah. When they found out they had been assigned one of the larger cabins, they decided to invite Wes and me along.

"Okay, everybody," said Jake, placing the lid on the counter with a clatter. "I'm calling it done. Let's eat."

Wes set his laptop on the coffee table, then stood up and extended his hand to help me up. We joined Farrah and Jake in the kitchen, filled our bowls, and gathered around the table. After one spoonful, I nudged Jake. "This chili is delicious. I need to get the recipe."

"Glad you like it," he said.

Farrah grinned. "I keep telling him he should have been a chef instead of a personal trainer."

"Oh, that reminds me," I said. "I finally heard from Yvette this morning."

"'Bout time," Farrah said. "She was probably embarrassed, huh? Were the Thomisons the nameless clients she was protecting?"

"Well, they may have thought Yvette would help them purchase Mila's shop. But it turns out Yvette was not pestering Mila on their behalf."

"Oh?" said Farrah. "Who was her client?"

"Herself," I said. "She wanted to open her own small business in that space."

"A real estate agency?" Farrah asked.

I shook my head. "No. Actually, she confessed to me that she's tired of the real estate game. She's been wanting to switch careers for a while now. She wants to open an artisanal cheese and wine shop."

"Really?" said Wes. "But she's been so successful in real estate."

"I know," I said. "I guess that's why she felt pressured to keep it up and not reveal her true feelings. She ran herself ragged and got burnt out. She's been holding on to this other dream, trying to figure out a way to make it come true." I took a sip of water and thought about the aloof real estate agent. I could definitely sympathize with her inner struggle.

"Interesting," said Farrah. "Can't she find another location?"

"As a matter of fact, she does have another location in mind. The Cadwelle Mansion."

Everyone gave me questioning looks, and I continued. "Yvette told me that ever since she sold the mansion to the Thomisons, she's been wishing she had bought it instead."

"Did she want to run a B&B, too?" Farrah asked.

"Well, after watching Danielle and Marco, Yvette started to think she could do it. She was reading up on it. In fact, the book she hid when Marco showed Wes, Sheana, and me the library was all about how to operate a bed-and-breakfast."

"Why was that such a big secret?" asked Jake.

"Yvette didn't want the Thomisons to know. See, she knew about the state of Danielle and Marco's finances. She told me they were way overextended.

They were spending money right and left—on clothes, food, furniture, cleaning services. Of course, now we know they were expecting a big payoff from the illegal rhino horns. Yvette thought they were just being irresponsible. She predicted the home would be foreclosed, so she was preparing to jump in as soon as the opportunity presented itself."

"She is shrewd, isn't she?" said Farrah.

"She's a smart lady," I agreed. "As Marco continued to spend money extravagantly, Yvette began to suspect he was the burglar. She didn't know how he was doing it, but she started to keep her eye on him. Then one day she overheard Marco on his cell phone saying something about a tunnel. After that, she started poking around in the speakeasy and Danielle caught her. This must have been right around the same time I found the tunnels myself."

Wes put his arm around me and gave me a squeeze. Farrah got up to put on a kettle of water. "Keep talking," she said. "I want to hear everything."

"Based on Danielle's reaction, it dawned on Yvette that there was something more serious going on. She remembered the break-ins at Moonstone and was afraid Marco had killed Charlie. She realized she might be in danger. So she skipped out that night, right after I heard her arguing with Danielle."

"It sounds like Yvette will have her chance to purchase the B&B after all," Farrah said. "I hope it works out for her. It would be a shame for the mansion to sit empty again."

The kettle whistled, so I hopped up to retrieve it. Wes followed me and prepared a plate of cookies, while I placed four mugs and a basket of assorted teabags on a tray. We returned to the table and passed around the kettle.

"Yvette told me another interesting bit of gossip," I said, cupping my hands around my mug. I inhaled the mint-flavored steam.

"Well, don't hold out on us," said Farrah. "What is it?"

"It's about Tish. Evidently, she's been cleared of any smuggling charges. She was just after Marco for money, trying to get him to pay her off to keep quiet about the tunnels. She had learned about them from old city files. Then Marco actually needed her help to escape, and she agreed—for a price. Of course, she still faces charges for aiding and abetting a fugitive. Oh, and she's been officially terminated from city employment."

"She wasn't in her position for very long," Wes remarked.

"Apparently she did a lot of damage in the short time she was at city hall. Mayor Trumley implied as much when I went to see her the other day. If you thought Marco was spending money recklessly, you should see the debts Tish racked up."

"Ha!" said Farrah. "I knew that Groundhog Festival was over the top. I can only guess how much it cost to bring Rhett Shelby to Edindale."

"That was a big part of it," I said. "Apparently she also had a habit of wining and dining business owners, like the investors she entertained in the speakeasy." I bit into a chewy gingersnap and thought about the flamboyant tourism director. From what

I had seen, I wondered if part of her trouble had been a tendency to overly wine herself.

"Well, I won't miss her," said Farrah. "She seemed kind of snobby to me. I didn't like the way she talked about Mila and her business."

I smiled as I sipped my tea. Looking back, it was hard to imagine I ever wanted to keep my friendship with Mila a secret, even from Farrah. It made me happy to hear Farrah speak of her as a friend.

Around midnight, I padded into the living room to check on the fire. Everyone else was asleep. As cozy and safe as I felt in the cabin, surrounded by friends, I still had trouble drifting off. I blamed the unnerving fact that I had met and interacted with a murderer. It was even more troubling to remember how close I had come to being his next victim.

But I survived. I had to keep reminding myself. *In the end, I was protected.*

I sighed and added a piece of wood to the fire. Sitting on a floor pillow, I watched the dancing flames and reflected on how two-faced Marco and Danielle had turned out to be. Instead of the nice, honest people they pretended to be, they were actually criminals. *It just goes to show you, people are not always what they seem.*

On the other hand, sometimes people were exactly what they seemed. Reverend Natty was entirely transparent about his beliefs and views. He never hid his agenda. And, as far as I could tell, he worked within the confines of the law to spread his message.

Catrina was also exactly what she appeared to

be—a passionate and strongly opinionated young woman. She never hid her beliefs either. Whether or not she always obeyed the law, I wasn't quite sure. It was never proven, but I still suspected she was responsible for Reverend Natty's flat tires. I spoke with Mila about this and my conversation with Catrina's ex-girlfriend. I told her she might want to keep an eye on Catrina. Mila assured me that she would, but she also said Catrina had begun to mellow out. Apparently seeing Mila arrested served as a wake-up call for Catrina.

Mila also told me something I should have thought of in the first place. She said she wouldn't necessarily take Andi's word at face value, given the way things had ended between Catrina and Andi.

Why didn't I think of that? I had represented enough divorce clients to know that a person's ex was not the most reliable judge of his or her former lover's character.

I shook my head and picked up the fireplace poker. I stirred the embers, making the fire crackle and spark. In spite of all the failed marriages I had witnessed in my profession, I also saw plenty of strong relationships—like the bond between my parents. When I called my mom to tell her I had found the location of her sister's commune, she mentioned the fact that she and my dad's fiftieth wedding anniversary wasn't too far off. She even suggested that I bring Wes along to the as yet unplanned party in Nebraska.

I chuckled softly. A road trip with Wes sounded like a fun idea.

In the meantime, I had promised my mom I

would continue the search for Aunt Josephine. Maybe I could track down some of Josie's old friends, starting with the other people in the photo.

Fantasizing about this new quest, I began to yawn. I stood up from my seat in front of the fireplace and hugged my arms. My eyes fell upon the mantel, reminding me of the rhino horn I had originally seen in Beverly's lounge. She turned it over to the police as soon as she heard the news reports about wildlife smuggling, though it wasn't yet clear whether hers was illegal. It turned out Edgar had purchased the horn from an antique dealer who claimed it predated the ban.

I liked to think my legal memo would have inspired Beverly to remove it anyway.

Warming my hands over the fire, I took one last look at the glowing embers. I was reminded of my Candlemas ritual and all the symbolism associated with fire. I thought of the legendary phoenix rising from the ashes, reborn and renewed, and I felt a surge of hope.

I had a good feeling about the coming year.

With Thanks

Encouragement means so much. To all the people who have encouraged me to write, from teachers, family, and friends, to other writers near and far: THANK YOU. Your encouragement really does make a difference. Some of those super-awesome encouragers: Mom and Dad; my J-sibs: Jon, Jana, Jay, and Jill; Grandma Lucille; Alan and Cindy; and Krista Myer.

Special thanks to my "beta readers": Tom David, Cathy David, Jana Hortenstine, and Jill Grabiec. Your honest opinions, invaluable feedback, and keen eyes were immensely helpful.

To my fabulous agent, Rachel Brooks: Thank you for your vote of confidence, great advice, and excellent agenting.

To my fantastic editor, Martin Biro: Thank you for your enthusiasm for my work, your insightful ideas, and, of course, your supersmart editing. Thanks also to the entire Kensington team, including the artists, editors, publicists, and promoters, who have worked their magic to make my series come to life.

To my husband, Scott, and my daughter, Sage: Thank you for letting me kick you off the computer more times than I can count. I promise I'll get my own sometime soon. More importantly, thank you for being in my life. I thank my lucky stars for you every single day.

If you enjoyed Bell, Book & Candlemas
be sure not to miss the first mystery
in Jennifer David Hesse's Wiccan Wheel series

MIDSUMMER NIGHT'S MISCHIEF

Keep reading for a special excerpt.

A Kensington mass-market
and e-book on sale now!

PROLOGUE

The intruder knew it was wrong to be there. It was not only illegal; it was indecent. The old woman was dead, for God's sake. She had passed away not even two days ago, hadn't even been laid to rest. *Yet here I am,* the intruder thought. *Sneaking around her home in the dark, like some kind of common criminal.*

I am not a criminal.

Sure, the intruder might exceed the speed limit more often than not. Who didn't? And, okay, maybe there was a slight deception or two come tax time. But the intruder had never stolen anything.

Well, nothing of real value, anyway.

Until now.

But this was different. These were extraordinary circumstances. Chances like this didn't come along every day.

One by one, the intruder searched all the rooms in the house, quickly but carefully. It wouldn't be tucked away in some obscure location. It had to be wherever the old woman had left it before she died. Still, the intruder took a cursory look in the bathroom, the bedrooms, and every closet along the way to the front of the house.

Creeping through the tidy living room, the intruder made sure the curtains were closed, then peeked under the coffee table, peered behind the potted ficus, opened the oversize sewing basket in the corner—all the while trying to avoid looking at the framed family photos lining the walls and standing watch on the mantel.

I am really not a bad person.

Opposite the living room was an old-fashioned home library. Standing on the threshold to this room, the intruder's heart started thudding uncontrollably. Maybe it was nerves. Time was running out. The longer this took, the bigger the risk of getting caught. Or maybe it was the intruder's conscience finally kicking in.

Or maybe it was the fact that the intruder had finally found it.

There it was, not ten feet away. A real, genuine four-hundred-year-old treasure. There for the taking.

The intruder's hands started sweating inside brown leather gloves. It was now or never. Noticing that the curtains were open in this room, the intruder dropped to the carpeted floor and crawled quickly over to the canvas messenger bag that lay open on a floral-print love seat. The bag was next to a stack of week-old newspapers and a crossword puzzle book, from which a pen stuck out to mark the last puzzle the old woman had been working on.

But thoughts of the old woman soon skittered to the dusty corners. The intruder was fixated on the prize now, which was poking out of the casually placed bag like in a game of peekaboo, just daring someone to grab it. Kneeling before the love seat, the intruder used both hands to remove the treasure.

For a moment, the intruder just stared at it, hardly believing it was real. Bound in faded leather, it was fragile yet whole. The stitching faded and delicate, yet intact. It was surprising how light it felt, especially for a nine-hundred-page work. Gingerly, the intruder opened the cover and read the amazing words *Mr. William Shakespeares Comedies, Histories, & Tragedies. Published according to the True Originall Copies.*

Beneath these words was a copper-engraved portrait of the immortal man himself. *What an odd-looking dude.* The "Bard." Looking positively Mona Lisa–ish, with that steady gaze and indecipherable expression. Did he know he was a genius? Did he realize the impact he would have on the world in the centuries to come?

Did he know this collection would fetch a cool million or two? Or three?

Exhaling softly, the intruder closed the book, then carefully wrapped it in a sweatshirt, placed it in a duffel bag, and surrounded it with another sweatshirt, sweatpants, shorts, and socks. Clean, of course. The canvas messenger bag was left behind, a little flatter but still in the same spot.

How could the old woman be so careless? She hadn't deserved to own this book, anyway. Maybe no one person should own it. But somebody would want it badly enough to pay big, big money. No doubt about it. And someone else would reap the mighty profit.

Someone like me.

At any rate, the intruder had as much claim to the treasure as the old woman had had. More importantly, she was gone, and the intruder was here.

But not for long.

After a quick look around to make sure no evidence was left behind, the intruder hurried to the kitchen and slipped out, quietly pulling the door shut.

Shielded by two overgrown lilac bushes on either side of the back stoop, the intruder paused for a moment to remove the gloves and stick them in the pockets of a hoodie. Glancing at the overcast sky and feeling grateful for the gloom that darkened the yard, the intruder breathed in the heavy, charged air.

I did it.

All that remained was to cash it in.

From somewhere in the shadows, an owl cried a single lonely call. And then it was quiet once more.

CHAPTER 1

Four days earlier

The soft breeze caressed my shoulders like a lover, and I slowed my steps to enjoy it. I had shed my blazer the minute I left the office, had tucked it over my purse strap, and had traded my heels for flat sandals. I was cutting through Fieldstone Park. The air was fresher there under the trees. The breeze carried the scent of roses mingled with the spicy-earth aroma of mature pines and flowering shrubs. I inhaled deeply. Summer had come early this year.

Just above the horizon, a vivid crescent moon, larger than life, began its nightly ascent. All around me, the first fireflies flickered in the dusky shadows, while hidden crickets chirped a timeless serenade.

As a matter of fact, the evening was so damn romantic, I couldn't take it anymore. I stopped in my tracks.

"Come on!" I said out loud. "What are you trying to do to me?"

A startled skateboarder skidded to a stop next to me, stamping one foot on the ground.

"Not you," I said. "Her! This!" I flicked my wrist, waving a hand at the trees, the sky, the beauty. "Oh, never mind," I muttered.

The skateboarder rolled his eyes and sped off. I sighed and continued down the path. I strolled past Memory Gardens and around Wedding Cake Fountain, breathing in the sultry fresh air. It was peaceful, for sure, but I felt restless. As I gazed around the park, I couldn't help feeling it was a setup. The Goddess was putting on a spectacular show tonight, and it was all for me.

My bag suddenly felt heavier, and I shifted it to my other shoulder. Why did I feel so irritated all of a sudden? The slender headband that earlier had reined my long locks into a sleek retro bouffant now felt like a vise on my temples. The flower-scented air, now humid and dense, was suddenly cloying. The whole world pressed in.

Despite this momentary unease, I still loved it here. Honestly, I loved it all: the big park, the small town, the perfect evening. After all, Edindale wasn't called the Eden of Southern Illinois for nothing. Yet, it was times like these that made me feel the most alone. That was it, I realized. The lovelier the night, the more deeply I felt my heart ache.

When I rounded a bend and caught sight of a dreamy-eyed couple heading my way, hand in hand, I decided I'd had about enough. I veered to my left, cut across a grassy stretch, stopped for a quick second to break off a purple stem from a riotously abundant bush clover, and then stepped onto the sidewalk toward home.

A few minutes later I climbed the steps to my cozy brick row house. Luckily, there was no sign of my neighbors, a happy older couple on my right and newlyweds on my left. Normally, I didn't mind chatting with them, but I wasn't in the mood just then. Even before my atmospheric walk home from work, I had been too painfully aware of my decided *singleness* today.

It had all started with the new client who walked into my office that morning. And it had ended when I flipped the page of my wall calendar and saw what I knew to be true but wanted to forget: My birthday was coming up in two weeks. I would be thirty.

Sigh.

I entered the row house and headed to the master bedroom. After shedding the suit and the headband, I pulled on yoga shorts and a soft old T-shirt and set about my usual evening chores. I seemed to have fallen into quite the domestic routine lately. First, I watered all my plants—the potted flowers on the front stoop, the hanging ferns in my front window, the herbs in my kitchen window boxes, the potted vegetables and palms and flowers on my back deck, and the houseplants throughout. Then I made myself a quick but tasty dinner consisting of granola cereal topped with fresh strawberries and organic almond milk—my go-to meal on nights I didn't feel like cooking—and sat down in front of the computer in the den to browse online dating profiles.

"Cute . . . nah. Nice . . . or not. Hot, but . . . nah." I found a reason to reject each one. The whole process seemed so shallow and hokey. These dating services might be helpful for some people, but they didn't feel right for me. They seemed to lack that almost magical element of serendipity in meeting people the old-fashioned way. This way felt too contrived.

Speaking of old-fashioned, I found my mind wandering back to the new client I had counseled today. Her name was Eleanor, and she was about the sweetest old lady I'd ever met. With her short gray hair, polyester slacks, and embroidered top, she was the picture of grandmotherly. In fact, what with her twinkly blue eyes and soft plumpness, I had had to resist the urge to hug her as we said good-bye.

Eleanor was my favorite kind of client. I loved helping nervous people navigate the legal intricacies that went along with so many momentous life events. Some such events were happy, like adoptions and real estate closings. Others, like divorces, could be contentious or sad—or joyous, depending on the client. My firm handled all sorts of family law issues, but I'd come to specialize in trusts and estates. Oftentimes, people put off preparing a will, not liking to face the idea of their own mortality. And sometimes they were distrustful of lawyers. Eleanor was like that at first, but it didn't take me long to put her at ease.

Plus, she was nearly bursting with excitement about her secret. Besides her daughter, Darlene, and the expert who had appraised her find, I was the only one to know that comfortably middle-class Eleanor was about to become a very wealthy woman.

I had learned this morning that Eleanor's husband, Frank, had died four years earlier, with a simple will that left everything to his wife. She had avoided having a will herself, thinking, like a lot of people, that however her assets were distributed by law when she was gone would be just fine. Besides, she'd thought she didn't have much—certainly nothing worth fighting over. But that had all changed last week. Going through some of her late husband's things in the attic with her daughter, Eleanor had made an astonishing discovery: a rare book in excellent condition. And not just any book. She had found one of the most valuable books in all the world: a 1623 compendium of Shakespeare's plays. It was the first ever Shakespeare publication, called the First Folio.

Eleanor knew what it was. Still, she was stunned to find it in the attic. Frank had inherited the prize from his great-uncle, an antiques collector, decades ago. Family lore had it that the book had been lost under somewhat mysterious circumstances. Some said it had been destroyed in a fire; others claimed the book had been stolen or maybe lost in a bet. Nevertheless, here it was, tucked in the bottom of an army trunk, under some olive-drab wool blankets.

Eleanor didn't know if Frank had even known the book was there, and she'd probably never know. Regardless, she realized that her estate would be significantly bigger now than she had ever dreamed. It was her daughter who had got her thinking about bequests and had encouraged her to see a lawyer.

I smiled to myself as I remembered how excited Eleanor was at the prospect of leaving substantial gifts to causes near to her heart—her alma mater, her favorite museum, the local animal rescue shelter— not to mention individual gifts to her family members.

Eleanor had two children and five grandchildren, plus an adorable new great-grandbaby, whose photo Eleanor had proudly showed me. She also had a brother who was still living and several nieces, nephews, and cousins. It was quite a big family.

A big, loving, supportive family.

I came from a pretty big family, too. I had a mom and dad, two older sisters, and an older brother. But they were all miles away and not really a part of my daily life anymore.

My house seemed exceptionally quiet.

I got up and took my bowl to the kitchen, washed it, and put it away. Then I threw in a load of laundry and generally puttered around, all the while feeling lower and lower. At one point I flipped on the radio and promptly shut it off. "What's the deal with the mood tonight? Is there something in the air?" Sometimes I spoke to the Goddess, like *Bewitched*'s Samantha Stephens called out to her mother in an empty room. Of course, on the TV show that was usually because Endora was up to some new high jinks to trouble Samantha's boringly mortal husband.

I laughed in spite of myself and shook off the gloom. There *was* something I could do, I knew. I didn't have to pine around, a victim of unalterable circumstances. I could take matters into my own hands. I had the means; I had the power.

But should I do it?

I felt a little sheepish, even though no one was around to know.

I went back to the kitchen and poured a glass of Merlot. Then I walked around the house, drawing the shades.

What I needed was a man. Strike that. I didn't

need a man. Still, I longed for a partner. And not just any partner. I stopped, with my wineglass raised halfway to my lips, as the realization sank in. I was yearning for my soul mate.

I went back to the kitchen and pulled out containers of herbs and spices from the corner cabinet. Then I got out my mortar and pestle and started mixing in a bit of this and a dash of that: patchouli, rose hips, cinnamon and basil, rosemary, jasmine, and a touch of hot chili pepper. I wasn't following any particular recipe, but experience and intuition told me what to add.

Grinding the dried leaves and powders was like a meditation. As I breathed in the heady aroma, I thought about the idea of having a soul mate. Was there one person out there meant for each of us? Was I truly incomplete without my missing other half? The thought of *needing* another person, especially a man, made my fiercely independent self bristle. I could take care of myself, thank you very much.

Still, people needed people . . . obviously. Community and cooperation were pretty much the last, best hope for this calamitous world. Or so I'd heard.

Besides, even if there was not one *particular* person destined for another, I did believe in balance. Like work and play, yin and yang, and the two broken parts of a heart-shaped locket, one without the other just wasn't right. Plus, you needed two to tango. I was looking for my perfect dance partner.

I spooned my herbal concoction onto a piece of cheesecloth, brought up the four corners, and tied it with a red thread. Then I poured another glass of wine and took it to my bedroom upstairs.

There's nothing wrong with what I'm doing, I told myself. Why was I so nervous?

I set the herb pouch on my antique console table, next to the sprig of bush clover I'd picked at Fieldstone Park. Then I gathered some candles and arranged them in a circle on the Persian rug before the console. I placed a large vanilla-scented pillar candle in the center, and on that candle I carved my name within the outline of a heart. I lit the candles.

Then I took off my clothes.

It was time for a serious love spell.

Afterward, I sat quietly on my deck, listening to the crickets and katydids and breathing in the night air. The slender moon was now completely overhead, and I basked in the soft glow while I came down from my psychic high. Spell casting could be a pretty intense experience. Even after sending the energy I raised back to the earth, I felt as if my cells were vibrating.

Not for the first time, I pondered what my friends and family would say if they could see me. What would they think if they knew I was a Wiccan?

Actually, I could imagine what they would think, which was why I couldn't tell them. Not that I was ashamed or anything. In fact, I was quite comfortable with who I was. I was secure in my identity and confident in my spiritual path. This particular pursuit of mine was probably the one area of my life where I harbored no dissatisfaction or misgivings whatsoever.

That is, as long as no one found out.

My Irish Catholic grandmother would blame my father and his whole side, and my Italian Catholic grandmother would blame my mother and her side. At worst, they'd all think I was mixed up in a cult of devil-worshipping crazies, worse even than my aunt Josephine, who ran off and joined a hippie commune back in the day. At best, they'd worry for my immortal soul. Or, more likely, they'd fear this would damage my chances of marrying a nice young Christian man.

As for my friends, they might just think I was a bit flaky, even weirder than they already knew. My current friends, anyway, already called me a hippie chick—not even knowing about Aunt Josephine— given my dietary leanings and other earth-friendly tendencies. But my old friends, from high school and earlier, would likely be surprised to learn I'd never actually grown up. It was with them, all those years ago, that I had first learned about Wicca and the exciting world of Goddess worship.

That was back when witchcraft was über-trendy. We watched *The Craft* and *Charmed* and read books like *Teen Witch*. We wore lots of black, painted our fingernails black, drew tattoos on our hands and ankles with permanent marker.

I smiled as I recalled our secret "coven meetings." We collected crystals and stones, wore pentagram jewelry, and read each other's palms. There were spells, of course, incantations read from books to curse our enemies and attract our crushes. Then again, there was also a good amount of high-minded antiestablishment, feminist rebellion. In spite of my affection for *Bewitched*, we were *not* the daughters of housewife Samantha Stephens.

But before long, hot-blooded vampire romance

edged out witchy girl power, and my friends pretty much lost interest. Not me. The Goddess had taken hold and wasn't letting go. My teenage experiment had morphed into a real-life spiritual journey. And it was a spiritual path that suited me perfectly: there was no dogma, no fearmongering, no judgment. There were no authoritarian gatekeepers standing between me and the Divine—the Divine was already in me. And in the trees and the trails, the rivers and streams, the birds and the bees. It was a beautiful religion.

Unfortunately, Wicca was not exactly an accepted, let alone mainstream, religion.

Which was another reason I had to keep this part of me under wraps. If anyone at work were to find out—or anyone in the community—it could cost us clients. And that would cost me my job.

I started to feel chilly sitting on the deck, and my stomach began to growl, chastising me for the too-light dinner. I had just gotten up and gone into the kitchen to scrounge up a bedtime snack when my cell phone buzzed from the counter where I'd left it. I glanced at the caller ID and picked up at once.

"Hey, groovy chick!" I said brightly.

"Hey, chickie mama. What's shaking?"

"Not a whole lot. You back?"

"Not till tomorrow, but save your evening. There's a band we gotta see and men we gotta meet."

I grinned. Evidently, my fun-loving friend Farrah was "off" again in her longtime on-again, off-again romance. That suited me fine. I had a spell to test out. And meeting men with Farrah was the best test method I could think of.

Somewhere out there was the answer to my prayer.